THE SHEPHERD'S CHASE

Also by Cap Daniels

THE SHEPHERD'S CHASE

CHASE FULTON NOVEL #27

CAP DANIELS

ANCHOR WATCH
PUBLISHING
** USA **

The Shepherd's Chase
Chase Fulton Novel #27
Cap Daniels

This is a work of fiction. Names, characters, places, historical events, and incidents are the product of the author's imagination or have been used fictitiously. Although many locations such as marinas, airports, hotels, restaurants, etc. used in this work actually exist, they are used fictitiously and may have been relocated, exaggerated, or otherwise modified by creative license for the purpose of this work. Although many characters are based on personalities, physical attributes, skills, or intellect of actual individuals, all the characters in this work are products of the author's imagination.

Published by:

** USA **

13 Digit ISBN: 978-1-951021-59-7
Library of Congress Control Number: 2024937742

Cover Design: German Creative

Printed in the United States of America

The Shepherd's Chase

CAP DANIELS

Chapter 1

The Warrior Class

Spring 2012

I stood behind Singer, the finest sniper I've ever known, and listened to his every word as he taught Sniping 101 to Gator, our newest teammate.

The sniper spoke in a soft, confident tone that gave his words authority without adding stress to the intensity Gator must've been feeling already. "What's the primary purpose of a sniper?"

Gator raised his head from the rifle and looked up at his mentor. "To eliminate targets as efficiently as possible and save the lives of those he's charged with protecting."

The new guy had walked right into the same trap that snared me when Singer put me through the same course so many years before.

Singer looked up and gave me a wink. "That's certainly one of the purposes of a sniper, but I want to know our primary purpose."

Gator closed his eyes, apparently digging deep in search of the right answer, and Singer threw him a bone. "It's three little words."

Finally, Gator said, "Kill the enemy."

"You already tried that answer," Singer said. "Let's back up and see if we can walk our way into a good answer. When we selected a position where we could achieve good cover and concealment, what was the third consideration in choosing this spot as our hide?"

Gator's confidence returned. "Battlefield visibility."

"Well done, Grasshopper. Why is battlefield visibility so important?"

"A sniper needs to see and understand everything in his environment because he's the eyes of the strike team on the ground."

Singer plucked a small, smooth stone from the ground, got his student's attention, and tossed a stone at me. "You're already better at this than our illustrious leader, the Great Chase Fulton, back there."

I snatched the stone from the air and landed it perfectly on the bill of Singer's cap.

Singer said, "Nice shot . . . for once." He returned to his student. "So, tell me the primary purpose of the sniper."

Gator proudly said, "To gather intelligence."

Singer grinned from ear to ear. "Will somebody ring a bell? We have ourselves a winner. We are, first and foremost, gatherers of information. We can see the battlefield, or at least our sector of the battlefield, better than anyone else in the fight. Unless, of course, there's an enemy sniper. He may have a better position than we do, but that's counter-sniper operations, and we'll learn that later. For now, let's focus on gathering and relaying information to the leaders, like Chase, who are making battlefield decisions."

Gator nodded but didn't interrupt.

Singer continued. "We're starting small and working up. Pick the left side of some prominent object within a thousand yards, point it out to me, and estimate the range."

Gator scanned the open field and St. Marys' North River. "There's a grove of palm trees at eleven o'clock and eight hundred yards."

Singer said, "Now, raise your left hand with your palm out at arm's length, and align the left side of your hand with the left side of that grove of palms."

He followed the instructions to the letter, and I was instantly intrigued. Singer hadn't conducted that exercise with me when he took me through his one-on-one sniper course.

"Good," the sniper said. "Now, place your right hand beside your left so both palms are facing away, and tell me what you see just to the right of your right hand."

Gator situated his hands and said, "I see a tall, metal power line tower."

"Good. You can put your hands down. Holding your hands like that represents approximately twenty degrees. For this exercise, those twenty degrees are your entire world. I want you to pretend nothing else exists. That is your sector of the battlefield, and I want you to note everything that changes in your sector."

"For how long?" Gator asked.

Singer's smile returned. "Until I come get you or I give you a target to engage, but do not chamber a round until I've given the command to lock and load. Understood?"

"Yes, sir."

Singer pressed himself up to his knees. "Oh, I almost forgot. Are you still confident with your range estimation on the palms?"

Gator looked back at the trees. "On second thought, they look more like seven-fifty."

"How about the power line tower?"

"That's well over a thousand. Probably close to thirteen hundred. What's your guess?"

Singer laughed. "I don't make guesses. I know exactly how far everything is from this point. The palms are seven-ninety, and the tower is twelve twenty-five. Range them from the edge of our hide when I'm gone, and I'll pay you one thousand dollars for every yard I'm off."

"Seriously?"

Singer laid a hand on his student's shoulder. "Seriously. Just make sure you've got the environmentals set correctly in your range finder."

"Wait a minute," Gator said. "This is a trap of some kind."

Singer pointed downrange. "Go ahead. Range them."

Gator pulled his laser rangefinder from a pouch, set the environmentals, and lased the trees. "You've got to be kidding me."

Singer said, "Let me guess. Seven-ninety?"

"Dead on. That's amazing."

Singer said, "Point to your feet."

Gator frowned and pointed toward his boots. "What's that about?"

"That's amazing," Singer said. "How did you know?"

"They're my feet. I always know where they are."

"That's exactly how I want you to approach every single battlefield. Commit everything to memory, and when you have time, write it down."

"Yes, sir."

Singer turned to walk away. "One last thing. If you're tired, hungry, or need to go to the bathroom, go take care of that now."

Gator shook his head. "I'm good."

"Okay, but don't say I didn't offer. Don't chamber a round until ordered to do so. Don't let anything happen in your twenty-degree sector that you don't notice, memorize, and write down. And for goodness' sake, don't miss when I tell you to shoot."

"I've got it."

Inside the truck cab, Singer tapped on the seat. "Let's have some fun."

I pulled away from his favorite training location. "How long do you plan to leave him in there?"

"Long enough to get hungry and generally uncomfortable, but the cruelty starts now."

We drove back to Bonaventure, my family's ancestral home on the banks of the North River, and across the back lawn to the boathouse, where I warmed up the rigid hull inflatable boat.

Singer made a call with the phone on speaker. "Good morning, Hunter. Are you ready for your big solo?"

Stone W. Hunter was an invaluable spoke in the wheel that was tactical Team Twenty-One, my merry band of misfits and ne'er-do-wells. He'd been an Air Force combat controller prior to sustaining a career-ending injury, but during his service he earned the respect of the special operators around him, from SEALs to Green Berets, and the insignia on his uniform melted away as he was absorbed into the world of covert operations. On our team, he was the waterborne operations officer and chief conditioning coach. If I were ever in a life-and-death struggle beneath the water, Stone W. Hunter is the man I'd pray to see. During a fight at depth, he had no equal, and I was exceptionally glad he was on the good guys' team. I wouldn't want him as an enemy.

Hunter said, "Just give me the word, and I'll make it happen."

"Excellent," Singer said. "We're headed up the river now, so stand by."

As soon as Gator's hide came into view to the west, I shoved the throttles forward and cut the wheel hard over. The overpowered RHIB sent a rooster tail of water rising into the air behind us as we drilled holes in the black surface of the water.

At the completion of our first high-speed three-sixty, Singer held the phone close to his mouth and said, "Hit it, Hunter."

I let us slowly progress upstream while still circling until we were directly between the electric tower and Gator's position. That's when the RHIB and I put on a show.

I raised the engines until the propellers were barely in the water and ran hard for the marsh grass to the east. With the bow high in the air, I plowed into the high grass and cut the engines. We settled into the vegetation and jumped to our feet, pretending to fight. Singer finally shoved me out of the boat, and I landed softly in the marsh. Every time I made a move toward the RHIB, Singer slapped the water in front of me with the blade of a paddle, sending black water spraying into my face. I struggled for several minutes before catching the paddle the instant it hit the water for the hundredth time. Just as we'd planned, Singer gripped the paddle, and I yanked him from the boat and into the water beside me.

He surfaced and caught his breath. "I wonder what our boy thinks about all of this."

I glanced toward the sniper's position. "I don't think he'll fall for it. It's too over the top."

Singer patted my shoulder. "Oh, please tell me more, Dr. Civilian. I've done this a hundred times, and it worked every one of those times."

"Yeah, but how many times have you done it to kids as bright as Gator?"

"It's not about being bright," he said. "It's about forcing yourself to continue observing, even when your mind insists on singular focus."

I peered across his shoulder and around the RHIB. "It looks like Hunter's done."

Singer said, "Let's have a little more fun, just in case he needs another minute or two." He drew his pistol, tilted it end over end to empty the water from the barrel, and pulled the trigger four times in rapid succession.

I said, "Thanks for the warning, gunfighter. That sounded like thunder inside my skull."

He grimaced. "Sorry. I forgot about the new hearing aids. How are they working out?"

"Obviously, the waterproof part is working fine. Dr. Mankiller is still working on the noise-cancelling function. That little feature clearly has a long way to go."

He reached for the boat. "Let's get out of the water. I'm getting cold."

"Cold? We've been in the water for three minutes and you're already cold?"

He pulled himself over the starboard tube and into the RHIB. "If you wanted a SEAL for a sniper, you should've gone shopping elsewhere. I'm a shooter and a choir director who just happens to have the bankroll to retire if I'm not living up to your expectations, civilian."

I slapped both hands onto the surface, splashing him with a wall of cold river water. "I guess we'll keep you around until you get Gator trained up, but I'll have Skipper begin the search for a nursing home for you."

He offered a hand and pulled me into the boat. Suddenly, his expression turned serious. "I want you to know that's not what I'm doing."

I shook the water from my hair like a duck dog after a retrieval. "What are you talking about?"

"I'm not training my replacement. I just saw some interest and potential in the kid to become a pretty good sniper, and I'm adding skills to the team. I'm not planning my departure. I was just messing around."

"I know. I didn't take it that way. You and I are in this for the long haul, but it's nice knowing there are young guys out there who feel the same fire that we do to devoting their lives to service."

"They call us the warrior class. We've always existed, even before humans were formed out of the dust of the earth."

He had my attention.

"The Archangel Michael wasn't afraid of a fight, and King David was no slouch on the battlefield. Just ask Goliath. Joshua and Samson handed out more than their share of good old-fashioned butt-kickings. Their blood flows in us and in the men who'll follow us. Don't worry, my friend. As long as there's something worth defending, good men will step up and fight for it."

That's when the explosion happened.

Chapter 2
The Real Thing

Explosions surprise everybody—even those who are expecting them. Singer and I knew that one was coming, but that didn't dissolve our incessant need to turn toward the thunderous report. As the plume of smoke rose from between two of the largest palms in the grove, I wondered what Gator was thinking while tucked away in his hidey-hole. I hoped he saw Hunter hang the satchel charge between the trees on the left side of his sector of the battlefield. Hoping didn't change the outcome, but I wanted the kid to do well. I saw a lot of me in him in those days, and I didn't want to watch him commit the same unforgivable transgressions I made in the early days of my career.

Singer peered up the slope to the position where he left Gator. "I can't see him from this angle, but I can't wait to hear his after-action report."

As if the movie's director had ordered the perfect timing, Clark, our handler, roared northward in our amphibious Cessna 208 Caravan and touched down just north of the power line tower. What Gator couldn't see was Hunter swimming toward the starboard pontoon of the plane. When he reached the float and climbed toward the cabin, that was our cue to fire a pair of flares into the air above our heads in hopes of forcing Gator's eyes skyward instead of focusing on the Caravan. Learning to divide one's attention and filter out distractions is a crucial skill set for a competent sniper, and we didn't want a competent sniper. We wanted a superior warrior with the eyes of a hawk. If anybody could turn Gator into that superstar, it was Singer and the team around me. We were some of the finest warriors to ever step onto the battlefield, and our experience made us some of the most highly qualified civilian operators on Earth. Gator was in good hands, and he had a bottomless well of knowledge, wisdom, and battle scars from which to drink on his way to becoming the gladiator I knew he could be.

If the ruse worked, Gator wouldn't see Hunter slip back into the water instead of into the Caravan.

With the overt portion of our training scenario behind us, we motored back down the river and locked the RHIB back in her pen. We grilled burgers and dogs on the dock and ate in one of my favorite spots: the gazebo overlooking the river on the back lawn of Bonaventure. The ring of Adirondack chairs lining the interior of the gazebo surrounded an ancient cannon from an eighteenth-century warship. There'd never be a better conversation piece than a battle-weary cannon from the Revolutionary War and War of 1812. Clark and I had pulled the cannon from the mud and muck of Cumberland Sound, just a few miles from Bonaventure. The ship that housed the gun was burned to the waterline and sunk on a fateful night two hundred years ago by workers and my ancestors during the latter of those wars.

Singer washed down a mouthful with a long swig of his sweet tea. "I wonder if our student wishes he'd taken me up on the opportunity to go to the bathroom."

I looked over my shoulder in the direction where Gator still lay, waiting for something else to happen in his sector. "I just hope he's still awake."

"Oh, he's awake," Singer said. "There's no chance he'd let himself fall asleep."

We ate, conversed, and enjoyed the company until the witching hour was upon us.

Singer said, "Let's go have a pop quiz and see how observant our little wizard has been this evening."

We drove back to the hide, where we'd left Gator thirteen hours before. Our headlights cast him in silhouette as we pulled to a stop, and he flipped up his night-vision devices to protect his low-light visibility.

Without the slightest of pleasantries, Singer said, "Sniper, report."

Gator pushed his helmet to the back of his head and peered over the front of his hide. "First, I'd like to shoot Mr. Hunter, who's been low-crawling for six hours and trying to sneak up on me. He's eighty yards down the slope to the northeast and armed with a sidearm and a pair of satchel charges."

Singer yelled, "Come on out, Hunter. You're busted."

He stood and shook off the debris he'd collected on the long, arduous crawl. "No way! There's no way he saw me."

Gator said, "I saw you slink back into the water when I was supposed to believe you climbed into the plane. Nice job with the flares, by the way, but the distraction didn't work."

"What else did you see?" Singer probed.

"While you and Chase were pretending to fight in the marsh, I saw Hunter hang the charge between the third and fourth tree from the left. To be honest, I thought the satchel charge was going to be the target until it blew up."

"Not bad," Singer said. "Keep talking."

"When the charge went off, that's when I noticed the object that looks like a bale of hay by the seventh palm tree from the left. That definitely wasn't there when we began this morning."

Singer nodded. "Lock and load and kill the hay bale."

"Yes, sir." The grin on Gator's face said those were the words he'd been waiting to hear.

He withdrew a round from his kit, laid it inside the breach of the rifle, and slid the bolt forward. As he nestled into the weapon and slowed his breathing, Hunter pulled the pin on a flashbang grenade and dropped it beside the hide.

The grenade exploded an instant before Gator pulled the trigger, and his round impacted the ground a foot to the right of the target.

"What was that about?" Gator demanded.

Singer leaned toward him. "Kill the target!"

Gator loaded a second round, focused through the scope, and pressed the trigger. The shock-sensitive explosive inside the bale of hay absorbed the impact of the round and set off a few ounces of C-4, sending hay in every direction.

Gator looked over his shoulder as if expecting a standing ovation, but none was forthcoming.

Instead, Singer asked, "Why did you miss the first shot?"

"The flashbang going off five feet away spooked me."

The master sniper said, "Everything on the battlefield will spook you if you let it. You have to learn to control your reactions—especially your reflex reactions. You gave away your position the instant you made the first shot. In real battle, that one miss could mean your life, and more importantly, it could mean the lives of your operators on the ground. Sometimes you're all they've got between themselves and their next heartbeat. That's a solemn responsibility."

"Yes, sir. I understand."

"Another thing," Singer continued. "I shouldn't have had to tell you to kill the target a second time. Missing is part of the reality of long-distance shooting, but a miss doesn't absolve us of the responsibility to eliminate the target. It's still a threat, and it still has to die, no matter how many times we miss."

"That makes sense," Gator said.

Singer peered into the hide. "Are your pants still dry?"

Gator sighed. "No. I should've taken you up on the offer to use the bathroom before we started."

"Yes, you should have. Did you see anything else change in your sector?"

"Yeah, and I have to tell you, it looked crazy real. I don't know how you pulled it off, but the man and woman in the upstairs window of the house was impressive."

Singer glanced at me, then back at Gator. "What are you talking about?"

Gator's eyes turned to saucers. "You mean you didn't set that up?"

"Set what up?" I asked.

He gasped. "Uh, some guy shot a woman in the head in that house ninety minutes after sunset." He jabbed an outstretched finger into the air.

I followed his finger across the river and marsh to the palatial homes east of the river, but Singer wasted no time lying behind Gator's rifle.

"Which house?" he asked.

"It was the second house from the right, just to the right of the marina. It was in the upstairs window, all the way to the right. The light's still on."

Singer repositioned the rifle until the scope was perfectly focused on the window. "And you're sure that's what you saw?"

"Absolutely sure, but I thought it was something you guys set up."

"No, it wasn't us," I said. "But it's ours now. It's time to wake up the St. Marys PD."

The first call was 911, and the second was to Skipper, our hotshot analyst. "Skipper, it's Chase. What do you know about a shooting on the east side of the river about ninety minutes after dark?"

"Tonight?" she asked.

"Yes, tonight. What do you know?"

The clicking through the phone told me she was typing furiously, but it didn't appear she was coming up with any answers.

"There's nothing on the police blotter or the local news. I don't know what you're talking about."

I said, "Gator witnessed a murder while we were doing some sniper training. We called nine-one-one less than two minutes ago. I need you in the op center to run this thing if it turns out to be the real thing."

"You got it," she said. "I'll keep scanning, and I'll be right here."

Gator, Hunter, Singer, and I leapt into the Suburban and headed for bridge. Blue lights flashed in front of us, and I prayed the first officer on the scene would be someone we knew.

My prayer worked.

Sergeant Andy McCall was at the front door of the house when we pulled into the drive. He held his pistol in one hand and knocked on the heavy door with his left. "St. Marys PD! Open up!"

The door didn't open, but Andy turned to watch us dismount our Suburban. "Are you the ones who called this in?"

I trotted toward the front porch of the house. "Yes, that was us. We were conducting some sniper training, and we saw it about an hour and a half after sunset."

Andy checked his watch. "And you waited until midnight to call it in? What's wrong with you?"

Gator stepped up. "I'm the one who saw it. I thought it was part of the training scenario."

Andy plucked his flashlight from his belt and pounded on the door with it. "St. Marys PD! Open the door!"

He rang the doorbell several times, with no signs of life coming from inside the house. Andy grabbed the knob and twisted, but it didn't budge.

Another cruiser and a pickup truck pulled into the driveway.

"What do you have, McCall?" a second officer asked as he stepped from the cruiser.

Chief Bobby Roberts slid from the pickup truck and stepped around the second officer. "How long have you been knocking, McCall?"

"Maybe two minutes."

The chief said, "Kick it in. We're going inside. If we're wrong, we'll buy them a new door."

He grabbed my arm on his way to the porch. "Are you armed, Chase?"

"Yes, sir. We're all armed."

"Good. Give me a perimeter in case we flush anybody out."

"You got it, Chief."

The four of us fanned out around the beautiful two-story home with our pistols drawn. The sound of a door giving way to a boot filled the air, and the officers pressed into the house in a three-man column.

By the time the chief and two officers stepped from the house, two more police cruisers had joined the party.

Chief Roberts propped himself against the railing at the top of the stairs. "We've got ourselves a homicide. One adult female, two shots to the head from close range. There's not enough face to ID her, but if it's who I think it is, our little town is about to get turned upside down."

Chapter 3
Not My Circus

Other than one of us being an eyewitness to the crime, my team and I had nothing to do with the murder on the edge of the marsh that musty spring evening. One of the monkeys may have been mine, but the circus certainly belonged to Chief Bobby Roberts.

I rounded up my team and said, "Let's give the crime busters some space, guys."

Chief Roberts grabbed my arm, "Hang on a minute, Chase. Bring that sniper of yours, and let's have a little talk."

"Which one, Chief? The new guy who saw it happen or Singer?"

"Bring 'em both."

Instead of just the snipers and me making the walk, Hunter joined us, and we leaned ourselves against the chief's tailgate.

The local top cop pulled off his cap. "You guys do know whose house this is, right?"

The four of us exchanged glances and shook our heads.

The chief said, "You've got to be kidding me. With that Hollywood wife of yours, you seriously don't know who lives here?"

"No, Chief. I have no idea. Penny's not really the Hollywood type. She just writes the stories. Are you going to let us in on the big secret?"

"It's no secret. This place belongs to Carmen Van Pelt, the actress."

We old guys shrugged, but Gator perked up. "Are you serious?"

The chief twisted his hat between his hands. "Yeah, unfortunately."

Apparently, I wasn't adequately impressed, so Gator thumb-typed something into his phone and stuck it in my hand. The young woman in the picture resembled a modern-day Marilyn Monroe.

I held the phone so the chief could see. "Is that her?"

"Yep, that's her when she's all dolled up, but she doesn't much look like that when she's down here. She's not even blonde."

I turned back toward the house. "Is that her up there?"

The chief shrugged. "Could be. Whoever she is, nobody's going to recognize her except the folks at the DNA lab."

I said, "You'll run her fingerprints, right?"

"Yeah, and that's why I called you over here. Plus, I need to interview him." He pointed toward Gator.

I nodded. "You called us over here so you could interview Gator?"

He finally planted his cap back on his head. "No, we can do the interview later. This is about the fingerprints. If I run them, there's no way to keep this thing under wraps. It'll blow up within minutes of the results coming in."

He paused and dug the toe of his boot into the sand, so I let him off the hook and said, "I can have Skipper run the prints for you. It'll still make the news sooner or later, but we might be able to keep it quiet for a day or two."

Off came the hat again. "Would you?"

"Sure. Do you want Hunter to lift the prints?"

The chief turned his attention to my partner. "It's a mess up there."

Hunter said, "No problem. I'm confident I've seen worse. I've probably created worse. I will need your kit, though."

The cop handed over a small leather bag and pulled out a pair of gloves and booties to keep Hunter from leaving evidence behind.

Gator leaned close to me. "Does this happen a lot?"

"What?"

"Us doing fingerprints for the local cops."

I said, "No, this is a first. But Tony and Hunter are both sworn officers with the St. Marys PD. That's a long story, but the badges come in handy sometimes. In return, we occasionally do unexpected stuff for the chief. It's one of those you-scratch-my-back things."

Gator chuckled. "I guess some people scratch harder than others."

Singer pulled the release and lowered the tailgate of the chief's truck. "Climb up here with me, Gator."

He followed the sniper into the bed of the truck, and I was intrigued, so I considered it a mutual invitation.

Singer pointed across the river. "Estimate the range to the dock at Bonaventure."

Gator cupped his hands around the bill of his cap and stared into the darkness. "Sixteen hundred yards."

Singer said, "Not bad. I'd agree with that. How fast can you cover that distance?"

"Five minutes on a hard surface."

Singer huffed. "Does any of that look like a hard surface to you?"

"No, sir."

"So, how fast could you cover that distance to save my life?"

Gator pulled a pair of nods from his pack and studied the terrain under the glow of the night-vision device. "The current is running out pretty strong, so I'd have to hit the river as far upstream as possible to keep from getting blown south of the dock. I think I could do it in half an hour."

Singer hopped down from the bed of the truck. "Do you have any more of those rubber gloves, Chief?"

The chief produced the box, and Singer pulled three from inside. He tossed one toward Gator and laid two on the tailgate. The new kid studied the glove as if it were something from outer space, but Singer pretended not to see his protégé's confusion. He pulled his phone from a pocket, dropped it into the glove, and tied it at the wrist. With the phone secure in its new waterproof environment, Singer slid it back into his pocket and said, "If I beat you home, your life is going to suck for a long time."

Singer was in the marsh and sloshing westward before Gator exfiltrated the police chief's truck. Instead of gloving his phone, he threw the device toward me and hit the marsh at a sprint. I gloved his phone, along with mine, and followed them into the muck. My longer legs gave me a slight advantage in the reeds and marsh grass, but Gator's youth and flexibility were impossible to overcome. He promptly caught Singer, and I closed the gap in relatively short order.

Interested in watching the two of them, I remained a few strides behind and took in every move the senior sniper made. He'd endured training in places I'd never see and learned skills I'd never know, so I rarely missed a chance to watch him work. I learned something every time I paid attention to Singer, both on and off the battlefield, and that night would be no different. Instead of angling northward to hit the river as far north as possible, he trod directly toward the Bonaventure dock, through the slicing blades of the marsh grass and ever-deepening mud.

At regular intervals, Gator shot glances over his shoulder at me until he finally asked Singer, "Why is Chase doing this?"

That's when I received the greatest compliment of my life. Nothing anyone else ever says about me could come close. Singer didn't look back. Instead, he said, "Because he's a leader and not a boss."

I'll never know if the weight of that statement was wasted on Gator, but it was a credo I'd carry with me for the rest of my life, and suddenly, that filthy mud and frigid water didn't feel so daunting.

I didn't understand why Singer wasn't angling upstream to beat the current of the North River like Gator said he'd do. If we hit the water in the three- or four-knot current of the outgoing tide, we'd be lucky to make landfall on the other side and still be north of Florida. As it turned out, there were a great many lessons to learn that night, and most of them were for me.

Singer, although a devout man of God, wasn't above sabotaging a competitor, so he took full advantage of his knowledge of the mucky terrain to guide Gator into holes that sent him into pools well over his head, but the kid soldiered on, undaunted. My position a few strides behind the pair gave me the advantage of following directly behind the teacher.

Finally, the ankle-deep mud gave way to much softer muck, and ultimately, into water several feet deep that was screaming southward far more quickly than any of us could swim. Gator's strength and endurance made him the faster swimmer, but Singer and I had higher percentages of body fat, giving us the advantage of buoyancy. Pure muscle sinks like a rock and requires kicking and stroking to stay afloat. Those particular activities aren't exactly easy after twenty minutes spent forcing one's feet out of the suction of the marsh. All of us, including the young guy, were spent when we hit the water.

Singer still had a slight advantage over me because of the negatively buoyant hunk of titanium and electronics attached to what was left of my right leg. Although the prosthetic had finally achieved waterproof status, it was still a bit of an anchor in the water. Blaming fake body parts for my failure wasn't in my DNA, so, like Gator, I soldiered on. The youngster outpaced us in the swim, but the wisdom of the ages gave us the confidence to roll onto our backs and backstroke our way across the surface while catching our breath. The old adage is true: old age and treachery will overcome youthful exuberance at every turn.

Halfway across the river, Singer and I were adequately rested to roll over and power for the shore. Our revival happened simultaneously with Gator's exhaustion. He drifted by us on his way to the Atlantic just as Singer and I poured on the coals and beat the water into submission. We made the western bank a few minutes later—cold, spent, and well south of the Bonaventure dock.

We lay on the bank on our backs, and Singer said, "Where do you think Boy Wonder ended up?"

"Maybe down by the gas docks downtown if he's lucky."

After catching our breath, digging mud from our ears, and climbing to our feet, we walked the walk of confident winners. But our arrogance was misguided. A hundred yards from the Bonaventure dock, Gator thundered past us in a full sprint, his breath coming hard and his boots pounding the earth like sledgehammers.

I said, "Are we just going to let him beat us?"

Singer gave me the smile that meant he knew something no one else knew, and I trusted my sniper. We continued our leisurely walk along the riverbank and found Gator on his back, on the back lawn of Bonaventure, with his chest heaving as his body demanded the oxygen it required to recover. Singer hooked a finger beneath my elbow and encouraged me to follow him. I obeyed, and we deposited ourselves on the bench at the edge of the floating dock.

Singer picked a lead fishing weight from the tray beside the bench and bounced it off Gator's belly. "How does it feel to get beaten by a couple of old guys?"

He propped himself up on his elbows. "What are you talking about? I was here a good five minutes before you two."

"Yes, you were," Singer said, "but our destination was the Bonaventure dock, not the Bonaventure backyard. Regardless of how well we run the race, if we don't arrive at the correct objective, the people who are depending on us to save their lives become victims instead of survivors. Never take your eyes off the objective . . . The correct objective."

Gator shook his head. "Everything's a lesson with you, isn't it?"

"Such is life," Singer said. "Why didn't you hit the river upstream? Before we started, you said that was the only way to make the dock and not succumb to the current."

"I was following you," he said.

Singer smiled again. "When you know the right answer, don't let anybody lead you into the wrong one. Your plan was perfect, but you let me talk you into a terrible plan without saying a word. That should sting even more than us beating you."

Gator threw his hands in the air and fell back onto the grass. "Can I go to bed now?"

I stood from the bench and tossed Gator's phone to him. "Nope, but you can get a shower and go find the police chief for your interview. Tell him the truth, but if he asks if you had anything to do with the shooting, shut your mouth immediately and call me."

Chapter 4
Our Cow

The shower felt like a gift from Heaven, and the pillow was even better. When I finally woke up, I opened my eyes to see Penny sitting on the edge of the bed and staring at me. I wiped the sleep from my eyes. "What?"

She said, "I like watching you sleep. You look like an innocent little boy with your hands curled beneath your chin like that. It's so sweet."

I reached for her hand and pulled her beside me. "I'm afraid I left my innocence on a battlefield somewhere years ago, but I like that you can still see it."

She traced my eyebrows with the tip of her finger. "I don't know how you do it. You put your body and mind through so much. If they only knew . . ."

"If who only knew?"

"Everybody. If everybody in the country knew how hard you and the guys work to keep them safe . . ."

I pressed a finger to her lips. "That's not how it works, sweetheart. We're supposed to be invisible. There's a million or so folks in uniform who get to take the credit for what we do. It's important that the American people believe their military is an impenetrable barrier between them and everybody who'd harm them if they could. It's the way of things, and I'm okay with it."

She smiled and kissed the tip of my finger. "And that's why you're so good at what you do. Speaking of what you do, where were you all night?"

I pulled her against me. "We were conducting some sniper training with Gator, and he saw something through his scope he wasn't supposed to see."

She perked up, and I continued.

"Have you ever heard of an actress named Carmen Van Pelt?"

"Sure. She's an A-lister. I'm working with a casting director to lure her onto a project I've got in the works. Why do you ask?"

My phone chirped on the nightstand, and I stuck it to my ear. "Hello, this is Chase."

"Hey, boss. It's Hunter. I hope I didn't wake you up, but we got a hit on the prints. They belong to Kimberly Marie Southerland."

I said, "I guess that's a relief for the cops, but I wonder what she was doing in that house."

"I called you first, so I haven't talked to anybody at the station this morning. Gator was giving his statement when I left the police department around two."

"Did Skipper pass the ID to the chief?"

"Not yet. We wanted you to know first."

"Thanks for keeping me in the loop. Go ahead and call Chief Roberts. I'm sure they've got a lot on their plates."

Hunter said, "Wilco. Wanna get some breakfast?"

"Sure. Come by in about an hour, and we'll either do something here or go grab a bite."

"See ya then."

I laid the phone back on the nightstand, and Penny said, "Are you going to tell me about Carmen Van Pelt?"

"It wasn't her, after all, but she's got a house across the river. Did you know that?"

"What wasn't her?"

"Gator saw somebody get shot through the window of the Van Pelt woman's house last night. It's a whole big thing."

Penny grabbed my forearms. "Slow down. What are you talking about?"

I held up a finger. "Hang on. I'll be right back."

I made the necessary visit to the head and threw on some shorts. "Let's go down and have some coffee. I'll tell you the whole story."

In the kitchen, she poured two cups and slid onto a chair at the table. "Tell me everything."

I took my first sip and ran my fingers through my hair. "This Van Pelt woman has a house on the other side of the river—"

Penny stopped me. "Wait. Are you saying Carmen Van Pelt lives across the river from us?"

"I don't know if she lives there or if it's just a vacation house. That doesn't matter. Gator saw some guy shoot a woman while we were conducting some training last night. We went over and helped the cops for a while, and Skipper ran the victim's prints this morning. It wasn't Van Pelt. It was somebody named Kimberly Marie Southerland."

Penny's eyes exploded. "That's her real name!"

"That's whose real name?"

She leapt to her feet. "Kimberly Marie Southerland *is* Carmen Van Pelt."

My heart hit my stomach, and I pawed for my missing phone. "Give me your cell."

Penny tossed it to me, and Hunter answered in seconds. "We know."

"Did you tell the chief yet?"

He said, "Not yet. I was trying to call you back. Where's your phone?"

"Upstairs, I guess. Come get me and bring the report. We'll go see the chief together."

I returned Penny's phone. "This thing is going to get ugly."

My wife stared down at her phone. "I don't understand. Who would do that? Why would anybody want to kill her?"

I gave her a hug. "We're not cops, baby. Chief Roberts just asked if we could run the prints to keep this out of the media for a few hours."

She squeezed me. "But you're going to help them find who did this, right?"

"That's not really our thing. We're not investigators. We're door-kickers. I've got to get dressed. Hunter's on his way."

"Should I call anybody in LA?"

I stopped at the bottom of the stairs. "I don't know. Was she married?"

Penny waggled a hand. "Well, sort of. Rumor has it they were on the rocks, but you never know what's true in Hollywood."

"Do you know who her agent is?"

"No, but I can find out."

I started up the stairs. "I wouldn't cold-call her if I were you, but if you know the agent, you might want to give her a little heads-up."

Hunter showed up at the same instant I hit the door, and we caught the chief at his favorite breakfast spot.

When he saw us coming, he shook his head and pushed his plate away. "Sit down, guys. And don't talk too loudly."

We slid into the booth across from him, and Hunter passed the folded sheet of paper containing the fingerprint results.

The chief unfolded it and read the report. "Who's Kimberly Marie Southerland?"

I checked across my shoulder before whispering, "That's Carman Van Pelt's real name."

The chief let out a long sigh. "Why didn't you have your sniper shoot the guy?"

"It wasn't a live-fire training event," I said. "And the kid thought it was part of the scenario. He was supposed to observe and take notes. That's all."

Chief Roberts pulled out a cigarette and stuck it in his mouth.

Hunter said, "I don't think you're supposed to smoke in here, Chief."

He yanked the cigarette from his mouth and threw it onto the table. "Do either of you want to be police chief for a couple of weeks?"

I threw up both hands. "No, thank you, but if we can do anything to help, don't hesitate to ask."

He refolded the fingerprint report and pushed his way out of the booth. "Thanks for this. I owe you one. Are you guys going out of town anytime soon?"

"Not that I know of," I said.

He situated his cap over what remained of his hair. "Then I hope your offer to help was sincere."

I moved to the opposite side of the booth, and Margaret showed up beside the table. "Hey, guys. Did the chief con you two into paying for his breakfast again?"

"It looks like it," I said. "Just add his to our ticket."

We had breakfast and very little conversation. Small-town ears can hear through walls, and especially through the backs of booths in the local diner.

Back in Hunter's truck, I said, "What do you think he'll want us to do?"

Hunter shrugged. "Probably stuff the department isn't allowed to do. I guess we should've let Gator shoot the guy, huh?"

"I guess so. Speaking of Gator, have you heard from him this morning?"

"Yeah, I talked to him for a second early this morning. He and Singer were going to see some sheep, whatever that means."

"What's that about?"

Hunter rolled his eyes. "It's Singer. There's probably some kind of life lesson Gator's supposed to learn from the herd."

"I'm pretty sure it's called a flock, but we could ask Clark."

He chuckled. "Oh, yeah. He's exactly who we need to ask. Speaking of Clark, do you think we should let him in on what's going on?"

I thumbed the number to our handler and pressed the speaker button. When he answered, I asked, "Why is Singer taking Gator to see a flock of sheep?"

Silence filled the line for a long moment before Clark said, "How should I know? And are you sure it's not a herd of sheep?"

"I'm confident it's a flock," I said. "Have you heard any news out of St. Marys this morning?"

He said, "If it's a flock, why are they called sheepherders and not sheep-flockers?"

I groaned. "You're a sheep-flocker. Now, answer my question. Have you heard any news out of St. Marys this morning?"

"Nope, not a word. That's part of the beauty of living in South Beach. If it isn't local to Miami, nobody really cares what happens on the news."

I briefed him on everything we knew, and his question was identical to mine. "What does Chief Roberts want you to do?"

"Hunter's got a theory. He thinks the chief may ask us to do some sketchy stuff the department can't do."

"He's probably right. Just don't get yourself involved too deep. We don't need you testifying in open court about holding sniper school at Bonaventure."

"Good thinking," I said. "Do you have anything for us?"

"Now that you bring it up, I, in fact, do. Have you ever heard of a place called Culver Cove in Oregon?"

I let the name ricochet inside my head for a few seconds. "I think I have, but nothing specific is coming to me. Why? What's happening in Culver Cove?"

He cleared his throat as if he weren't particularly comfortable having the conversation. "Am I on speaker?"

"Yes."

"Do me a favor," he said. "Head back to the op center and give me a call on a secure line."

Hunter gave me an eye, and I said, "Okay, we'll be back there in ten minutes or so, but before we go, do you want us to bow out of the murder investigation up here?"

He clicked his tongue against his teeth. "Let's talk about Oregon first, and then we'll see how many assets we can allocate to the cops. They're good guys, and they do a good job, but we have some skill sets they don't have."

"Maybe that's something we could work on," I said. "Maybe we could offer to train some of their officers like a SWAT team or something like that."

Clark said, "We're getting off in the weeds. There will be time for that discussion later. Right now, let's keep our eye on the assignment, then we'll see if there's any milk left in our cow."

"Our cow?"

He grumbled. "Yeah, I was trying it out. I'm working on my metaphors . . . or whatever they're called. I thought I liked the cow thing, but it didn't go right."

"Keep working on it," I said. "It's a lot better than looking a gift bird in the bush."

Chapter 5
All About That Bait

The main house at Bonaventure Plantation is a three-story antebellum-style brick structure that appears, from all exterior angles, to hold only two floors. In fact, from the outside, the house is a nearly identical recreation of the original structure built on the property by my mother's family in the nineteenth century. The differences begin behind the walls. The third floor houses a state-of-the-art operation center and supercomputer designed and constructed by Skipper, our intelligence analyst and practically my little sister. From the op center, Skipper could communicate with intelligence assets, law enforcement agencies, and my team anywhere in the world. The Pentagon may have a superior war room, but they don't have a Skipper.

Hunter and I climbed the stairs to the op center, entered our passcode, and scanned our thumbprints. Once verified and authenticated, the definitive click of the locking bolts signaled their withdrawal from their seats, and we were admitted into the inner sanctum. To my surprise, we were greeted by the inside of Clark Johnson's nose.

Skipper sat at her console, shaking her head. "Clark, get away from the camera and sit down. I'll take care of it from here."

The largest of the six monitors in the room showed our handler backing away from his camera in South Beach and relieving us of the tour of his sinuses. Skipper programmed the camera from her perch and pointed toward the conference table. Hunter and I obeyed like well-trained dogs told to sit.

I kicked off the meeting. "This is a surprise. I thought we were just going to have a nice little phone conversation, but lucky for us, we get to see your shining face . . . among other things."

Clark said, "Nice to see you two, too. I'm having some camera issues."

"We noticed. So, tell us about Culver Cove."

He repositioned himself in his oversized chair. "First, tell me what you know about it."

I turned to Hunter, and he wore the same look as me. "Okay, that pretty much covers what we know about it. Your turn."

"Look at it this way," Clark said. "At its core, it's a billionaire boys' club out in the woods in Oregon. No girls allowed. It started in the late eighteen hundreds with some artistic types and morphed into the elitist enclave it is today. Nobody seems to know exactly how anybody becomes a full member of the club, but guests are usually allowed as long as they're invited by a full member."

I slid a notepad from beneath the table and clicked my pen. "So, is it something like Skull and Bones?"

Clark said, "Not exactly. I think it's a little looser than that, but it's still pretty mysterious. The club's motto is something like, 'Don't bring your work in here.' It's supposed to mean members shouldn't bring their outside business to the club. In theory, it's a retreat from the world, but men of the stature of those who belong to such places rarely check their schemes and deals at the door."

"What kind of people are we talking about?" Hunter asked.

Clark said, "If the list of members is written down somewhere, we'll never see it, but from what we know, it's made up of elite celebrities, former presidents and other world leaders, high-net-worth folks from all over the place, and, for some reason, high-ranking military retirees. Think two-stars and up."

I asked, "Do we know anybody on the non-existent membership roster?"

"I'm sure we do, but I haven't had time to chase any of them down.

This assignment isn't even an assignment yet. It's just a blip on the radar at this point."

I tapped my pen against my notepad. "I'm still in the dark. What will the assignment be if the blip turns into a target?"

Clark bit his lip, and I called him on it. "That's the face you make when you know something you don't want to tell me, so spit it out."

He closed his eyes and took a long, deep breath. "All right, College Boy. Here's the meat in the stew. A crypto team in Bulgaria picked up some signal traffic about a mass hostage event of significant persons in June of this year."

"Significant persons?" I asked. "What does that mean?"

"Great question. We don't know, either, but the first things that came to mind were things like the G-Eight summit, some gathering of UN ambassadors, a dignitary's funeral, or something like that."

I scratched my head. "A dignitary's funeral? Are you telling me that somebody knows a dignitary is going to die and be buried in June?"

"We were just spitballing. There is one way to create a dignitary's funeral on demand, though."

I dropped my pen. "So, are you saying we could be looking at an assassination for the purpose of gathering high-value targets at a funeral?"

Clark said, "Stranger things have happened."

"Every day," I said. "But tell me more about this crypto team in Bulgaria."

"What do you want to know?"

"I'd like to know what color their uniforms are."

"That's an excellent question. I'll add that to my list of questions and get back with you. What else do you want to know?"

"My big question is, who?"

"Who what?" Clark asked.

"This is starting to sound like an Abbott and Costello bit. I want to know who the crypto guys were listening to when they picked up this particular piece of chatter."

"We're working on that one, too. From what I know so far, they were listening to everything they could find, but this particular signal is believed to have originated in Turkey."

"What kind of relationship do we have with the Bulgarians?"

He said, "We don't have any close friends in the crypto branch, but we could foster a relationship with them if we had the right bait."

"What kind of bait?"

Clark looked away. "Everybody likes pretty girls. Especially cryptographers."

I slid my notepad away. "Who are you talking about? Skipper's not trained for anything like that, and besides, we need her in the op center to run anything we put on the street."

Clark sat in silence, staring directly into his camera, and I stared back. Neither of us was going to say the name Anya out loud, so I offered a side road. "How about Dr. Mankiller?"

Celeste Mankiller, PhD. was the second newest citizen of our island of misfit toys. We plucked her from the Justice Department, where she'd been relegated to a basement lair designing and building high-tech gadgets for the country's top law enforcement agents. After growing bored of tech services at the DOJ, she found a home in a laboratory of her own, in a hangar at our airport, where she had free rein to design, build, test, and fall in love with everything her brilliant mind could dream up. We had the bankroll to finance almost anything she wanted to try, and the benefit for my team was a continual flow of clandestine gadgets to make us the most technologically advanced tactical team in the American inventory.

Clark groaned. "No, she's no good. If things get hairy, we need somebody who can fight her way out. Celeste may be a genius, but she's not a field agent by any stretch of the imagination."

The red light above the door came on, and Skipper tapped a switch, activating the entrance cameras. A second later, she buzzed in a collection of some of the finest tactical operators on the planet.

Gator led the entourage with Singer close in trail. I was suddenly reminded of the sheep, but no matter how anxious I was to hear that story, it would have to wait. Behind the sniper element was Disco, our chief pilot and retired Air Force A-10 driver. Bringing up the rear were Kodiak and Mongo, making the team complete.

"Would you look at that?" I said. "The gang's all here. Come on in. It's just starting to get juicy."

With the team in their seats around the conference table, I couldn't quash the feeling that we were practically modern-day Knights of the Round Table. The skill sets represented by the men in front of me were nearly limitless when it came to small-unit and individual tactics. If I were a hostage, those were precisely the men I'd ask God to send for me.

It took ten minutes to bring everyone up to speed, and Mongo, our resident giant, took copious notes. The only thing about him that was bigger than his physical stature was the grey matter inside his skull. Between him and Dr. Mankiller, nobody on the planet was going to out-think us.

After scanning through his notes for a third time, the big man said, "Irina can do it."

Irina Volkovna was Mongo's wife and a former Russian GRU officer. She was well-trained, strong, deadly, and beautiful enough to turn the head of almost any man on the planet, especially a crypto geek in Bulgaria.

"*Would* she do it, though?" I asked.

Mongo shrugged. "I don't know, but I can't see why she wouldn't. Let's ask her."

Twenty minutes later, Irina was fully briefed and full of questions. She said, "When?"

I turned to the monitor where Clark sat taking it all in.

He said, "Soon."

Irina laid a hand across Mongo's arm. "We have Tatiana's gala in May."

Irina's daughter, Tatiana, was the brightest new star on the worldwide ballet scene. A recent graduate of Juilliard, Tatiana was courted by every major ballet company with a bank account sufficient to attract such talent.

"When in May?" I asked.

Irina opened her calendar. "From eighth through sixteen."

"A weeklong gala?" I asked.

"That is full festival. I would like for us to be there for whole thing. Is pretty big deal."

I met Mongo's gaze, and he said, "Not that the operation isn't a big deal."

I waved a hand across the table. "Look around, big man. Unless we absolutely need somebody to carry a Volkswagen around on his shoulder, we can run an op without you. You're not missing Tatiana's gala for any reason."

His eyes fell to the table, and Irina squeezed his arm. She looked up at me. "I can do this after gala. I love being for Marvin, wife, and for Tatiana, mother, but sometimes I miss action of being intelligence officer in field."

I said, "We don't have a solid timeline yet, but if we can make it work, the job's all yours."

Her eyes lit up. "Thank you, Chase. This for me is wonderful gift, but if timetable is not favorable for this, what will you do?"

I said, "We'll cross that bridge when we come to it."

But the real answer wouldn't stop flashing inside my head.

I glanced at the monitor, and Clark gave me a barely perceptible shake of the head. He wouldn't say her name, either, but there was no question that Anya Burinkova was both the solution to our problem and the worst possible decision we could make.

Clark pulled me from my Anya-charged dread. "We're putting the oranges before the applecart here, and it's not time for that. I'll dig a little deeper into the Bulgarian crypto team, and maybe we'll get lucky. That's all I have for now, but let's reconvene tomorrow morning at nine."

Anya's face floated away from my brain, and I said, "Good. We'll chat then."

Clark said, "Oh, I almost forgot. For now, play nice with the local cops and give them the help they need, but don't get bogged down in it. And don't get your faces on the news."

Chapter 6
The Soul of a Sniper

Skipper disconnected the video conference call and spun in her seat. Her glare felt like red-hot daggers piercing my face. She held up a finger. "I've got just one word for what you're thinking, and it's *no*!"

"How do you know what I'm thinking?" I asked.

She narrowed her gaze. "No!"

I looked away. "We'll deal with that later. Right now, I want to hear about this field trip to the sheep farm. Are you guys signing up for Four-H and FFA?"

Gator perked up and turned immediately to his teacher. "Can I tell him?"

Singer shrugged, offered half of a smile, and said, "Sure. Go ahead."

Gator claimed the floor. "So, everybody knows Singer is always teaching, right? I've got to admit that it gets on my nerves sometimes, but I'm constantly learning."

Hunter said, "It gets on all of our nerves, but let's hear today's lesson from the schoolmaster."

Gator continued. "We were talking about the responsibilities of a sniper and all that, and he started talking about shepherds and their flocks."

I threw my pen at Hunter. "See, I told you they were called *flocks* and not *herds*."

He batted the pen away. "Would you shut up and let the man talk?"

Gator was undaunted. "It was all a bunch of metaphors and stuff about how I'm supposed to look out for the guys on the ground and make sure none of them go astray. You know, stuff like that. That's when he asked me if I'd ever seen a sheepdog work, and I told him I didn't know sheepdogs were real. I thought they were just on cartoons."

He paused to down a bottle of water before continuing. "Anyway, he said I had to see a sheepdog work with a flock to understand what he was trying to teach me about taking care of everybody on the battle-field. Singer knew about a sheep farm about half an hour from here. Who knew there were sheep farms in Georgia? Anyway, he dragged me out of bed after two hours of sleep and threw me in the truck to go see the sheepdog bring the flock out of the night pen and back into the pasture for the day."

Everyone was leaning in, completely captivated by Gator's story.

"When we got there, though, something wasn't right. Instead of pushing the sheep out of the night pen, the dog was guarding the gate and not letting any of the sheep out. This went on for five min-utes or so until the farmer closed the gate with the sheep still inside the pen."

Gator looked around the room and seemed pleased to see us hang-ing on his every word. "It turns out that the dog apparently knew something the farmer didn't, but the guy trusted the dog enough to close the gate and see what he'd do. What he did was amazing, man. That dog took off like he was shot out of a cannon. I've never seen a dog run that fast. He followed a creek into a grove of trees at full speed and disappeared."

Even Skipper was mesmerized as Gator kept talking.

"He was gone for maybe four or five minutes in the trees, and when he came back, he was a mess. His front leg was torn up, and his head and shoulders were covered in blood. The poor thing limped all the way back to the gate and barked at the farmer."

He took another drink and said, "I know it sounds crazy, but it's like he was talking to the farmer and he understood. The guy opened the gate, and the dog hobbled inside the pen and made his way to the back of the flock. He ran back and forth the best he could and pushed the flock out of the night pen and into the pasture. I expected him to lie down and die right there, but he didn't. This dog was hard-core. He limped behind the flock, all the way to the pasture, before carefully stepping into the stream for a drink."

Gator sat back as if exhausted, but his story obviously wasn't over. He said, "I asked Singer why the farmer wasn't taking the dog to the vet. He was clearly wounded and needed help. That's when my teacher asked what I thought happened to the dog when he ran into the woods. I told him I had no idea, but I bet that dog wouldn't go back in those trees again."

Singer laid a hand on Gator's shoulder. "I'll take it from here if you don't mind."

Gator threw up his hands. "Absolutely. You guys are going to love this part."

Singer spoke in his soft baritone that oozed confidence and humility, somehow simultaneously. "I took Gator to watch the sheepdog take care of the flock. I had no way of knowing it would turn into the best possible day for a young sniper to learn what his life would soon become. Instead of seeing the dog simply watching over the sheep, we got to watch a noble, loyal animal trap his flock inside the overnight pen until the farmer finally closed the gate. Once the dog knew his sheep were safe in the pen, he focused every ounce of strength and determination he had toward the threat only he knew existed. Whatever he fought in those woods—most likely a wolf or a pack of coyotes—he sacrificed himself to destroy that threat and protect his flock."

I fell back into my chair, utterly astonished at Singer's ability to turn a common situation into such a learning experience.

But he wasn't finished. "When the initial threat was gone, the wounded dog never considered walking away from his responsibility. He moved the sheep to the meadow, where they could graze and he could watch over them while he licked his wounds. The farmer didn't take him to the vet because removing that dog from that field where those sheep were grazing would've been the cruelest thing anyone could do to him. Until that flock was safely home in the overnight pen tonight, there's no way that dog would leave their side . . . And that's the soul of a sniper."

Chapter 7
The Unknowns

Some performances are impossible to follow, and Singer's was unquestionably one of those. I was left speechless in the moments following the story of the sheepdog, so I sat in silence, contemplating the self-sacrifice represented around the table in front of me. We were on the verge of an operation to liberate an unknown group of an unknown size, being held by an unknown entity at an unknown location for unknown reasons. Despite those unknowns, every man and woman before me was poised, ready, and anxious to strap on their armor, mount their trusty steed, and charge into battle in the name of freedom. And I was prepared to lead that charge.

Before dismissing the party, I said, "Skipper, I need you to know everything that can be known about everybody who's collecting crypto in Bulgaria—especially anybody listening to Turkey."

She said, "No problem. Is that priority one?"

"It is."

She spun back to her console and disappeared into an electronic world of ones and zeroes I'll never understand, and I turned to Hunter. "Let's talk about the murder last night."

He said, "Here's what I gleaned from the cops. Keep in mind, all of this info is pre-ID. They didn't know who the victim was when I put this together. I'm sure they've got a better working theory now, but as of midnight, suspect number one was the husband or boyfriend, whatever the case may be. It was two pistol shots at close range. There were powder burns on what was left of her face, and a pair of nine-millimeter shell casings were found at the scene. They were working on prints from the brass when I left the station, so I don't know if that generated anything useful."

"How about an exit route?" I asked.

"The only road out of there is the North River Causeway. Other than that, the only options are through the Navy base—which isn't going to happen—a boat into the Cumberland Sound, or a chopper." Hunter turned to Gator. "Did you see anybody fleeing the scene?"

I threw up a hand. "Wait, Gator. Don't think about that. We'll go through what you saw later."

He shrugged and leaned back, and Hunter grinned. "You're going to do some of that hocus-pocus stuff on him, aren't you?"

"I sure am," I said. "I don't know why I'm invested in this thing, but it's eating at me. I want to know who shot that woman a mile from our house."

Hunter nodded. "I get it. It's clawing at me, too. If you don't need me, I think I'll see if I can stick myself into the investigation. I may play the Navy angle and offer to liaise with the military."

"I like it," I said. "We'll call you if we need you back."

Skipper spun in her chair. "Sorry to stick my nose into this, but I'm sure Tony would love to tag along. He just finished a painting, and he's bored out of his mind."

Hunter glanced at me, apparently looking for permission, and I gave it.

Skipper's husband, Tony Johnson, was Clark's little brother and had been a crucial member of our team before a battlefield injury put him on the disabled list.

"What did he paint?" I asked before Skipper dived back into her research.

She said, "It was a commission from some high-ranking British naval officer. He wanted a painting of the Battle of Cape St. Vincent from seventeen-ninety-seven. Apparently, it was an early fight between the British and the Spaniards during the French Revolutionary Wars. If I remember correctly, it was Admiral Sir John Jervis who handed out a pretty good whipping to a Spanish admiral named José de Córdoba y Ramos off the coast of Portugal."

"That's pretty specific," I said. "How did it turn out?"

She rolled her eyes. "It was a masterpiece, just like all of them, but you know how Tony gets after he finishes a painting. He really needs a hobby."

Hunter collected his things and headed for the door. "I'll grab him on my way to the station."

Skipper said, "Thanks. He'll love that."

I tapped the edge of the table. "All right, Mongo. Let's hear it. What's cooking in that noggin of yours?"

He slid a finger down his page of notes. "About the murder or Clark's non-assignment assignment?"

"Both."

He said, "Let's start with the murder. I'm looking forward to hearing what you vacuum out of Gator's head, but my initial theory is that it's the husband or boyfriend. That's almost always the case. As far as the potential hostage situation goes, I'm not smart enough to deal with that many variables. We have no idea if anything will come of it. All we can do is analyze the signal intelligence, construct likely outcomes, and watch it build. When and if we reach an actionable set of data, we can begin looking at preventive measures. Until then, though, all we can do is listen and watch."

I laughed. "If you're not smart enough to put it together, I'm certainly not capable or qualified. Let me know if you come up with any ideas."

"Oh, I will."

I asked, "Does anyone else have anything to discuss?" No one spoke up, so I said, "Gator, you're with me. Everybody else, enjoy the day off, but keep your phones handy."

Gator and I made our way to my study, the only room in the house over which I had creative control. In fact, I'm not certain Penny had ever stepped foot in there. It was solely and uniquely mine. Gator was the only person I'd ever invited into the private space.

The room was spacious with a high ceiling, a small fireplace, and a few elegant paintings on the walls, including one of Tony's masterpieces entitled *Powderman*, a late eighteenth-century English warship in the fight of her life. The carpet was soft and inviting, but it was the furniture that made the space unique. A pair of reclining wingbacks faced the fireplace, with an antique walnut candle stand situated between them for cocktails or coffee. An overstuffed leather recliner sat stoically near one of the triple-pane windows overlooking the North River. Beside the recliner was my Herman Miller leather swivel chair in the softest leather I'd ever felt. Behind the sheetrock walls lay four inches of the best soundproofing insulation available, making the room the very definition of peaceful.

Gator took in the surroundings, and I motioned toward the plush recliner. "Have a seat and make yourself comfortable."

He hesitantly nestled into the chair. "What's about to happen to me? Are you going to stick me with a truth serum or something?"

"Nothing like that," I said in my smoothest therapist voice. "I'm merely going to ask you to relax, and we're going to talk about what you saw last night."

He squirmed in the chair. "I told you and the cops everything I saw. I'm not holding anything back, I promise."

I smiled and continued in the tone I'd learned from my mentor, Dr. Robert Richter, psychologist extraordinaire. "Actually, you only told us everything you can recall. Memory and recall are completely independent processes in the brain. Our senses take in and store far more information than we can ever recall under any circumstances. The area of your brain that stores those details is the very spot we're going to explore."

He furrowed his brow. "I'm not about to be abducted, weighed, measured, and probed, am I?"

Laughing in that setting was inappropriate but unavoidable. "No, there will be very little, if any, probing. Just put your feet up and relax. When it's all over, you'll feel the most rested you've ever felt."

"Are you going to hypnotize me?"

"Not exactly. I'm going to help you achieve a restful state from which we can tap into details even you don't realize you know."

He pressed the button on the side of the chair, allowing the footrest to extend and the back to recline.

I closed my eyes and let the elegance of my chair—designed and once owned by Charles Eames himself—absorb me. If a more comfortable chair existed, I'd never planted myself in it.

"Are you comfortable?" I asked.

"Yeah. I mean, yes, sir."

"Forget about formality. We're just two guys chilling out and having a conversation."

He sighed. "All right. I'll try."

I softened my tone even more. "I'd like for you to follow the line where the two walls meet in the corner of the room. Follow it only with your eyes until it meets the ceiling."

I watched his face move slowly upward until his neck was relaxed and the crown of his head lay solidly against the recliner. "Good. Now, imagine those three lines coming together, but instead of touching each other, imagine them stopping a millimeter before meeting."

His eyelids fluttered, and his grip on the arms of the chair softened.

"Now, I want you to think about that tiny, empty space where those three lines would meet if they could. Imagine that space and let yourself slowly drift toward it."

His eyelids continued to flutter, and the muscles of his face and neck relaxed even more.

"Now, imagine that tiny, empty space surrounding you and separating you from everything else until you're floating perfectly inside of it. Just float and feel the warmth and softness of the space around you . . .

Your space . . . Your perfect, personal space. Just let it absorb you and protect you."

His head fell ever so slightly to the right, and the toes of his boots fell inward until they rested against each other. His breathing grew slow and perfectly regular, and I sat in silence as his unconscious mind slowly caught up with his body's restful state.

"Let's talk about last night," I said, barely above a whisper. "Tell me about the reticle inside your scope."

"It's a perfect cross . . . fine . . . and crisp . . . graduated in minutes of angle. It's perfect."

"Now, I want you to think about that perfect reticle inside your scope and about that window across the river. Tell me what you saw through that window."

"They killed her. They killed her."

"Slow down," I said. "Let the scene play like a movie in slow motion. There's no sound, only video. Tell me what you see."

"They killed my mother."

I licked my lips and leaned forward. "Now, I want you to think about New York City. I want you to see the lights and the crowds. Let your mind paint that picture for you. Think about Times Square."

I leaned back and refocused while Gator's brain pulled itself away from the worst thing anyone could ever see. The loss of his parents at the hands of home invaders would forever linger near the surface, where new memories are formed. Pushing it away wasn't possible. God knows I'd tried for twenty years.

"Now, tell me about New York City."

"It's chaos in every direction . . . and it smells like pizza."

"Yes, it does," I said. "Now, think about that smell, and let's bring it into the sniper hide last night. Remember that smell."

His stomach growled, and he returned to the long, slow breaths.

"Put those crosshairs over the window in the house across the river —the house where the shooting happened last night in St. Marys. Stay with me here at Bonaventure and tell me what you see."

"They're fighting."

"Yelling at each other?"

"No, fighting. It's just a flash . . . just an instant. But she has the pistol. It's in her hand . . . Only one hand."

I glanced at the glowing light that meant everything was being recorded. "Did she pull the trigger?"

"Maybe," he whispered. "Maybe . . . but it's his now. Two shots."

"Pause there," I said. "Tell me about the man."

"Long hair. Not like a woman's hair, but long . . . Eight inches taller than the woman . . . Crossed . . . yeah, crossed. I don't . . ."

"It's okay," I said. "What's crossed?"

"His hands. They're wrong. Crossed."

"Okay, forget about his hands. Crossed hands are okay. Does he—"

Before I could finish the prompt, he jerked his head. "Two! Two shots. Low muzzle rise . . . great control . . . he knows how to shoot. Someone taught him to shoot, but they're crossed. Why?"

"Don't worry about the cross. What happened right after the two shots?"

"He's walking, not running. Just walking away."

"Good," I said. "Did you see a car leave the house?"

"I don't know. There were lights . . . bright lights . . . big lights. But only for a few seconds. It's . . . but the hands . . . crossed hands."

"The hands are okay. Tell me about the lights. Where did they go?"

He sighed. "I don't know. I thought it was part of the training. I looked away. I was missing the real action . . . I looked away."

I ran through the checklist of everything I wanted to cover in the session and placed a mark beside every item. "Okay, that's very good. Now, think about that space where the lines almost touch, and let them drift away."

I paused and let his mind slowly return inside the study. "Good. Now you can see the lines. Follow only one of them and watch it closely. Watch it form and let it grow. Think about that line and open your eyes."

His head lowered slowly as if he were tracing the vertical line where the walls met, and he yawned.

I pressed the switch, stopping the recording. "How do you feel?"

He widened his eyes. "Good. I feel good, but I still can't remember anything more than I told you last night."

I stood and placed a hand on his shoulder. "Things are rarely as they appear to be, and if they are, then we probably perceived them incorrectly in the first place."

Chapter 8
Crisscross

I left Gator alone in the study and wandered to the kitchen, where I found Penny doing the last thing I could've expected.

I said, "Is that a wedding cake?"

She glanced over her shoulder with a smear of icing on her cheek. "No, it's a mess, but it was *supposed* to be a wedding cake."

"Why?"

"It's a stupid long story that I'm sure you don't have time to hear."

I closed the distance between us and kissed away the icing from her beautiful face. "I don't care how stupid or how long the story is, but now I *have* to hear it."

The look in her eyes at that moment was something I'll never forget. It was something between elation and disbelief.

Perhaps I should make more time to listen to Penny's stories.

She laid down the pastry bag and wiped her hands on her apron. "Are you sure you want to hear it?"

"Absolutely."

"Okay, here goes. I'm writing a story about a pastry chef, and it occurred to me that I know absolutely nothing about what pastry chefs do, so I called the bakery on Osborne. You know, the one with the big oak tree that always looks like it's falling."

"I know the one. They have killer chocolate chip cookies on Fridays."

"That's the one," she said. "Anyway, I called over there and asked if

I could come watch for a day. The person I was talking to thought I was crazy at first, then she thought I was lying when I told her I'm a screenwriter. Do you know how hard it is to convince somebody you write screenplays for a living?"

"Nope. I've used a lot of cover stories, but never that one. Have you ever tried to convince anyone you're not a spy when you really are a spy?"

"Touché. Anyway, I finally told her I was your wife, and that did the trick. Apparently, you spend a lot of time in there when she's baking cookies."

"Only on Fridays."

"Whatever. So, she said I could come in, but I'd have to stay out of the way. That's not so easy in a kitchen that small. I don't know how they work in that place. We should buy them a new building or something."

"We? *We* should do that? You're the famous millionairess screenwriter."

"Oh, yeah, that's me," she said. "Anyway, I watched her make two wedding cakes and about a billion cookies."

"Did you get the recipe for the chocolate chip ones?"

She lifted a spatula from the counter and slapped the back of my hand as if I were an errant pupil at a Catholic school. "Stop it and listen. It looked so easy when she did it, so I had to try it. I cheated on the cake, though. I used a cake mix from Publix, but I made the icing myself."

I licked a dollop from the back of my hand. "And it's quite tasty."

"Thank you, but it's ugly. It's a lot harder than I thought."

I stood, slipped my arms around her, and pressed my lips to hers. You may not be a pastry chef, but you're a better kisser than she is."

Almost before I could react, she smacked me twice with the spatula. "Chase Fulton, I will whip you all the way out of this house if you ever say anything like that again."

I threw up my hands in self-defense. "Okay, okay! I'll start paying for the cookies like everybody else."

More spatula-whipping ensued, and I made a hasty retreat . . . but not hasty enough. She caught me in the library, shoved me onto a chair, and planted herself on my lap. She kissed me, and I disarmed her of the spatula. She playfully bit my ear and whispered, "Mine better be the only cookies you're nibbling on." I enjoyed the moment until she leaned back and asked, "Is it true?"

"Is what true?"

She said, "I heard a rumor that you were bringing Anya in for an operation in Bulgaria."

"How did you hear that?"

"Does that mean it's true?"

"No. Well, maybe, but . . ."

"When were you going to tell me?"

"Apparently, I don't have to tell you. It would appear you have a few spies of your own who've infiltrated my operation."

She flipped the tip of my nose. "Your little Russian girlfriend isn't the only one who can play the spy game."

"Which one?"

She grabbed the spatula again, and I panicked. "I was kidding! Don't hit me with that thing again."

She waggled it in front of my face in what was obviously meant to be a menacing gesture. "I'm not afraid of her, you know."

She tapped my forehead with her index finger. "She may dance around in there occasionally, but"—she planted her palm on my chest—"I'm in there."

"Yes, you are, and there's no room for anybody else."

She stood and stared down at me. "That's not a bad answer, but the correct answer was denying that she dances around in your head."

"That, too!" I almost shouted.

Gator stuck his head into the library. "Uh, sorry to break up whatever this is, but Hunter needs you . . . and you've got icing all over you."

I looked around Penny. "It's a long story, but trust me, icing is much better than blood."

I grabbed the bottom of Penny's apron and wiped my face. "Okay, I'm coming. I'll meet you out front."

When I reached the Suburban, Gator was already behind the wheel and ready to go somewhere. "What's up with Hunter?"

"He didn't tell me. He just said he needed you."

"Why didn't he call me?"

Gator tossed my phone onto my lap. "You left that in the study with me. Are you going to tell me what happened up there?"

"In the study?"

He said, "Yeah. You hypnotized me, didn't you?"

I sighed. "Hypnotism is a terribly misunderstood word. I helped you relax and get past your conscious memory and into your subconscious. Short-term memory is stored in the temporal lobe in a part of the brain called the hippocampus. Memories stay there until the brain decides whether the information is worthy of being stored long term. Think about tying your shoes. You learned that skill when you were six, and your brain recognized it as a memory worthy of hanging onto, so it stuck it in a region of the brain called the cerebral cortex."

His eyes glazed over. "You're losing me, Doc."

"It's not important that you remember what the parts of the brain are called. It just matters that we have short-term and long-term filing cabinets. Sometimes they overlap, and pieces of memories will get screwed up with other memories, and we get a little confused."

"All right. I can buy that."

I continued. "Your brain is young, sharp, and extremely active. Wait twenty years. That'll change. Your young, healthy brain grabs information far more quickly than mine, and especially Clark and Disco's. I'm not picking on them, but their brains are a little slower than mine and a lot slower than yours. Ultimately, what you and I did together in the study was getting your conscious memory out of the way so we could take a peek at everything your brain saw in the few seconds you watched through that window."

"So, you hypnotized me."

"Yes, I hypnotized you, and we learned a lot of details we didn't know."

I thumbed through my phone, brought up the recording, and pressed the play button.

We listened intently to every word, and when it was over, Gator asked, "What was that about my mother?"

I bit my bottom lip. "I considered not letting you hear that part, but if there's one rule we live by on this team, it is full and complete honesty. We don't hide things from each other."

"Okay, so what was it about? Why did my brain bring it up, even though it happened over two years ago?"

"That's the most fascinating part of the human brain, in my opinion. Your brain knows it should store that memory in long-term storage in the cerebral cortex, but because of the raw emotion of the memory, your hippocampus won't let go of it. Subsequently, your brain doesn't differentiate that memory as being old or fresh. That's part of the reason you still have nightmares about that night. It's perfectly normal, and there's nothing wrong with you."

"That's fascinating. Can you hypnotize me again and force that memory into the cortex part?"

I pointed down the driveway. "Let's go. Hunter's waiting, and even if I could do that, I wouldn't. Our brain knows what we need when we need it. You'll deal with the emotions over time, and I'm here to help you do that if you want. Ultimately, you have nothing to worry about. Your brain is very good at what it does, even though we keep filling it full of new stuff."

He pulled the truck into gear, and we pulled from the driveway. We found Hunter sitting on the tailgate of his truck outside of the crime scene on the other side of the river.

I said, "I hear you're looking for me."

"Yeah, what's the deal with you losing your phone lately?"

"I don't know. Don't make this about me. What do you need, you grumpy old man?"

He scratched at the paint on his tailgate. "I'll take the grumpy part, but I'm not old. I need you to see something. A lot more happened in that bedroom than just a murder."

I glanced up at the house that dwarfed Bonaventure. "I'm starting to get that impression, too. What did you see up there?"

He pulled a pair of boxes from his truck and tossed them onto the tailgate. "Put on those booties and gloves and come with me."

I followed his command and turned for the house.

Hunter paused, looked back at Gator, and said, "You too, Junior. Let's go."

Gator grabbed a pair of each and trotted behind us. At the top of the stairs, before we entered the house, we slipped the booties over our shoes and stretched the gloves onto our hands.

Stepping through the front door, Hunter said, "Don't step any-where near any of the little yellow flags. The forensic techs are already gone, but they may need more pictures before it's all over."

He led us into a massive living room, down a pair of steps, and into a sunken section surrounding a circular fireplace. "Check it out."

"It's a pair of wine glasses," I said.

"That's right. A pair. What's missing?"

"The wine bottle?"

"Nice work, inspector. Now come with me."

Our next stop was a wet bar near the hallway.

He said, "There's the empty bottle, and there's an unopened one. Same grape. Same vintage."

I said, "Somebody was opening a second bottle of wine to enjoy by the fire, but they decided to head upstairs instead."

Hunter studied the bottle for a moment. "They lifted prints from the bottles, so we'll know whose they are later today, but my money is on the mystery man. The prints are too big to be hers."

"Where's the corkscrew?" Gator asked.

Hunter turned. "What?"

"The corkscrew. If he was opening a bottle, where's the corkscrew?"

Hunter yanked his phone from his pocket. A few seconds later, he said, "Hey, Carter. This is Hunter. Is there a corkscrew on the inventory list?" We waited in silence, then he said, "How about the bedroom?" A few more seconds passed. "Okay, thanks." He tucked away the phone. "There's no corkscrew on the inventory sheets."

He carefully opened each drawer of the wet bar and peered inside, then he pulled his penlight and shone it down the drain of the sink. "Nothing. Good eye, Gator."

He said, "When I drink wine, it comes from a box because I don't have a corkscrew."

I shook my head. "We'll get you a corkscrew. You've got to stop drinking wine out of a box."

"Let's take a look at the bedroom," Hunter said. "That's what I really want you to see."

We carefully followed him up a set of stairs that were far too industrial for a luxury house.

"What's with the warehouse stairs?" I asked.

He said, "I guess this is the stairwell for the staff."

I asked, "If there's a staff, where were they last night?"

He shrugged and continued the climb.

Inside the bedroom, there was far more blood than I expected. The wall behind the bed was crimson and pink, and the bedding was practically dripping.

"That's a lot of blood for a pair of head shots," I said.

Hunter stared at the scene. "It's the right amount. You're just used to shooting people in the head when they're outside. It makes a lot bigger mess inside."

"Is all of it hers?" I asked.

"We don't know yet, but we're assuming so since there's no blood trail leading out of the room or anywhere else in the house. The techs will test about a hundred samples looking for other blood types, but there's no real reason to think it's anyone's except hers."

I glanced at Gator. "Well, we've got something to tell you, but it has to be off the record."

Hunter froze. "What is it?"

I pulled up the audio file on my phone. "Listen to this."

He played the recording twice and listened with the ears of a seasoned investigator. Finally, he said, "So, they fought, and the gun was originally hers, but what's the cross-handed thing about?"

Gator looked at me, and I said, "Nobody knows, but it means something."

Hunter stared back at the bed. "Whatever it is, something tells me it's going to tell us a lot about our shooter."

Chapter 9
Bigfoot

Hunter crossed the causeway behind us but didn't turn toward Bonaventure. He was undoubtedly bound for the police department to figure out what to do with his newfound collection of information and unanswered questions.

Gator said, "Do you mind if we drive by the cemetery?"

Something in his tone told me he had no interest in the cemetery, but it made for a handy excuse to stay in the truck a few minutes longer. His hesitance to say what he was thinking led me to breaking the ice.

I said, "Nice job back there at the crime scene. Sometimes, seeing what's *not* there is more important than seeing what is."

He kept staring straight ahead as we drove ten miles per hour below the posted speed limit. "Thanks. It's interesting that you put it that way. Singer asked me a question. Well, I guess it wasn't really a question. It's more like something he said that was supposed to lead me down 'a path of discovery,' as he calls it, but I'm stumped."

"Let's hear it. Maybe I can help."

He grimaced. "I don't know if I should. He didn't say I couldn't ask for help, but it feels a little like cheating."

"In that case, I have an idea. Tell me what he said that was supposed to start you on this path of enlightenment, and I'll decide if it's okay for me to nudge you in the right direction."

"That's fair," he said. "But he calls them paths of discovery, not enlightenment. You know how he is. Enlightenment only comes from one place."

I smiled. "He's right about that."

"Oh, I know. I wasn't questioning that. I think his faith is cool. I've just never been around anybody who lives like him."

"What do you mean?"

"You know. He never cusses. I've never seen him get mad. He prays a lot, which is cool. To tell you the truth, I kind of envy the peace he's got."

"Talk to him about that," I said. "And you'll be surprised how enlightening that path can be."

He tapped out a short rhythm on the steering wheel. "Yeah, I'll do that."

"Now, let's hear this mysterious quest he sent you on."

He pulled to the side of the road and parked the Suburban. "It was after the whole night in the hide when I was watching my sector. Man, what a night that was. I learned that I suck at lying still for twelve hours."

"Then sniping might not be for you."

"Maybe not, but I'm not telling Singer that. He sees something in me that I don't even see. Maybe whatever it is that makes a man a sniper is in there somewhere. I know this is going to sound corny, but it's kind of noble, you know?"

I said, "Yes, I know. That's the yardstick I use to measure everything we do. I don't always live up to the full thirty-six inches, but I want everything we do as a team to solidly fall into the category of noble."

He stared down through the steering wheel. "Before . . . Well, you know. Before all of that, I never really thought about nobility other than like knights in books and stuff. I never really thought I'd be one of those guys one day, but maybe Singer's right about callings. Maybe we end up doing what we're supposed to do in life."

"Maybe so," I said. "You're certainly living up to the standard. Everybody on the team trusts you and likes you. Those are things we don't hand out easily. You've earned them. Now, tell me what Singer said. I've got a wedding cake to eat."

He scowled. "Is that what that thing in the kitchen was supposed to be?"

"Dear, God. Please don't let Penny hear you call it 'that thing.'"

"So, that's what the icing was about. Who's getting married?"

I laughed. "I don't know, but I hope they're drunk by the time they bring out that monstrosity of a cake."

He laughed until tears rolled from his eyes. "Penny would kill you for that one."

"She almost killed me with a spatula twice already, but I deserved both of those. Now, stop stalling and tell me what he said."

Gator got his laughter under control. "He told me I needed to understand the difference between *looking for* and *looking at*."

I couldn't stop the smile. "Trade seats with me." We swapped places, and I said, "Look at the houses on this street, but only the ones on your side."

He said, "Okay, whatever you say."

I drove three blocks and turned around. "Now, look at the houses on that side."

We drove the same three blocks, and I made another U-turn. "Now, look for houses with sections of glass in the front door." We drove the same route, and I asked, "How many houses did you see?"

He froze. "Uh, I don't know. I didn't count."

"How many of them had windows in the doors?"

"Eighteen," he said with enormous confidence.

"How many of those eighteen had American flags flying?"

He slumped in the seat. "I don't know."

"That's the difference between *looking at* and *looking for*. You looked *at* every house, but you weren't looking *for* American flags. You can bet your next lesson will be about looking *for* everything in an environment. Just staring at the same piece of ground for hours at a time doesn't qualify as overwatch. You have to constantly scan the environment for everything. When I'm on the ground kicking in doors, I want to know you're somewhere on a rooftop, seeing absolutely everything that could be a threat to me, and I expect you to kill it when you see it."

He looked away. "I'm ashamed I couldn't put that together on my own. You shouldn't have had to explain that. It seems elementary now that you've talked me through it."

"Those aren't things we instinctually know," I said. "We all had to learn them. I'm not a sniper, and I never will be, but I know what I expect from one, and if you're going to step into Singer's boots when he finally packs it in, you'll need to grow some mighty big feet."

He perked up. "He's not quitting, is he?"

"Not any time soon, but he's doing what his instincts tell him to do. He's protecting his team by training you to a standard higher than any sniper school in the world. He could teach a monkey to shoot, but he sees something inside you that makes you a sheepdog puppy. If you want to be a sniper, listen to everything he says, but don't forget to listen for what he's not saying. Sometimes, that's where the true lesson is hiding."

He tapped lightly on his kneecap. "It never ends, does it?"

"What?"

"The learning."

"It better not," I said. "The moment you stop learning is likely the same instant your heart stops beating in this business."

"I guess I thought once I got out of The Ranch, I'd use what I learned there and do whatever my assignments were."

I said, "You've already learned more since you've been in the field than you ever learned at The Ranch. What you learned up there was a foundation, an undergraduate degree, if you will. What you learn in the field when real bullets are flying will be a master's degree, and when you're in charge, you'll earn your PhD."

He huffed. "I don't ever want to be in charge."

I pulled the Suburban into gear. "Nobody asks if you want to be in command. Trust me. It just happens."

He cocked his head. "Do you mean you didn't get any official training about being a team leader?"

"That's funny. I didn't even know we were building a team. It just happened. That's a long story, but it all started when Clark was dispatched to kill me after my first official mission."

"Kill you? What's that about?"

I pulled back onto the road. "He was only supposed to kill me if I'd been flipped."

"By Anya, the Russian?"

"I told you, it's a long story. We'll get Clark to tell you about it sometime. Needless to say, he didn't kill me . . . yet."

"So, you and Anya were—"

I held up a hand. "Let's put it this way. I'd much rather you talk to Penny about her god-awful cake than about my history with Anya."

"Was it worth it?"

"Don't ever ask me that question again."

He said, "I'm sorry. I didn't mean to . . ."

"It's not you," I said. "But that's a question I'm not willing to let myself think about."

I don't know what he was thinking, but whatever it was, he made the excellent decision to keep it to himself.

"Let's get back to the house. We've got a lot of work to do."

The five-minute drive back to Bonaventure was silent, and when we pulled into the drive, I spotted Penny sitting alone in the gazebo without her apron.

"Have you got something to do?" I asked.

Gator said, "Oh, yeah. There's no shortage of stuff for me to do. I'm supposed to meet Singer for some ballistics academics."

"I know it sounds boring, but learn it inside out. The better you understand the science of shooting, the better you'll be at putting lead on target a mile away."

"Yes, sir."

Instead of following Gator inside, I strolled to the gazebo. "How'd the cake turn out?"

She giggled. "It kept getting worse until I finally gave up."

"That's not like you. I've never seen you give up on anything."

"I accomplished what I needed. I don't have to be able to do the job a pastry chef can do to understand the process. I learned that it's hard, and that's what I needed for my story."

"In that case, congratulations."

She glanced toward the house. "Yeah, but now somebody has to eat that mess."

"Too bad Clark isn't here. He'd gobble it down like the Cookie Monster."

She said, "How's the murder investigation going?"

"I don't know, but Hunter's all over it. You would've been proud of Gator. He picked up on a missing piece nobody else noticed. We were walking through the crime scene, and there should've been a corkscrew somewhere near the bottle of wine that was obviously next on the consumption list, but it was nowhere to be found. That got Hunter's juices flowing."

"A missing corkscrew?"

I told her the story, and she seemed more fascinated by the minute. When it was over, I asked, "Did you call Carmen Van Pelt's agent?"

She bounced her phone on her thigh. "I have her number, but I can't decide if I should call. What's the official notification process like with the police department?"

"I don't know, but I doubt the agent is on the notification list. I suspect it's just next of kin, and next of kin is likely the murderer. It's going to be a mess, no matter how it plays out."

She got the look she gets when I'm not going to approve of whatever she's thinking, and I said, "What's going on in that head of yours?"

"You're not going to like it."

"Probably not, but let's hear it anyway."

She said, "I want to write it."

"You want to write what?"

"The story of Carmen Van Pelt's murder and the subsequent investigation."

"You're not a journalist."

She slid to the edge of her chair. "I don't want to write a news story. I want to write the documentary film. Can I?"

"Why are you asking me? You don't need my permission to do anything. I think the police chief is the person you need to ask."

"Will you ask him for me?"

I pulled up the chief's contact and stuck the phone to my ear.

He said, "Chief Roberts."

"Sorry to bother you, Chief. I know you're busy, but I have a favor to ask."

"Name it. I owe you about six hundred favors, so the answer's probably going to be yes."

"I don't know," I said. "This is a big one. In fact, if you say yes, we'll wipe the slate clean of those six hundred."

"Please tell me the favor is for me to retire and you to become police chief."

"No such luck. There's not enough money in Georgia to get me to do your job, but here's the favor. Penny wants to write a documentary piece on the investigation into Carmen Van Pelt's murder."

He said, "I can't stop her from writing whatever she wants."

"No, I wasn't clear. She wants insider access."

"Into an active, high-profile murder investigation?"

"Yep. It would give you the opportunity to control the spin. I'm sure she'd give you editorial review before release."

I glanced at my wife to make sure I hadn't overstepped my bounds, and she nodded with great enthusiasm. "Yes, she's saying you'd have full editorial review prior to anything going public. She's not going to make your department look like a bunch of jackasses, I assure you."

"Don't be so quick with promises like that, Chase. There are jackasses everywhere, and some of them have badges. Let me give it some thought, and I'll have an answer for you shortly. In the meantime, do you think she could dig up some Bigfoot footage or something to get absolutely anything on TV other than this case?"

"We could put Mongo in a gorilla suit and shoot some film. Will that do?"

Instead of an answer, I got a click and silence. By the time I had my phone back in my pocket, Penny was already on the phone with Hollywood. At least I assumed that's who she was calling.

She said, "Get me Anton Blaire."

A few seconds passed, and she said, "Anton, it's Penny Fulton. I need a cameraman and a producer in St. Marys, Georgia, right now. I've just been given exclusive access into the investigation of Carmen Van Pelt's murder . . ."

Another few seconds passed, and she said, "Yes, last night. She was shot twice in her house on the Georgia coast, less than a mile from my house. Jacksonville, Florida, is the closest airport. I'll pick them up as soon as they land."

I scowled. "What about the chief's answer sounded like approval to you?"

She ran a hand up my thigh and planted my favorite lips on Earth on mine. "Nobody can tell you no, Chase Fulton. You know that."

Chapter 10
A Few of My Favorite Things

When my phone rang, it wasn't the police chief, but it was a number from City Hall. "Hello, this is Chase."

"Chase, Gerrard Pimberton, city attorney. Do you have a minute?"

"Hang on just a second, Mr. Pimberton. Let me put you on speaker with my wife, Penny."

I pressed the button and laid the phone on the arm of Penny's chair. "Okay, Mr. Pimberton, we're both here."

He said, "Tell me exactly what you want to do."

Penny laid it out for him. "I want to film the investigation, write the story, and release the documentary film after the case is closed."

Pimberton said, "That's not how crime documentaries are done, Mrs. Fulton. The film footage for those shows are almost always recreations using actors and trial footage in the public domain."

Penny gave me a wink. "You obviously understand the industry. I'm impressed. I've built my career on breaking boundaries and blazing new trails. You sound exactly like the kind of man who's a trailblazer. You draw up the temporary nondisclosure agreement prior to publication, and I'll sign it, giving your office one hundred percent editorial review. Make sure you word the NDA strongly enough so the studio can't bully you into releasing the footage. I'm on your side in this thing. We want to see justice done. Just picture the publicity and goodwill an honest, thorough, behind-the-scenes documentary featuring the professionals of St. Marys—like you—solving the highest-profile crime Camden County has ever seen. I'm sure you're happy here in small-town Georgia, but if you have ambitions for something grander, imagine what this kind of positive publicity could do for your career."

The line was silent for several seconds before Pimberton said, "Okay, Mrs. Fulton. Come down to my office tomorrow morning, and we'll get the ball rolling."

"I'll be there in two hours. There's no reason to wait until tomorrow. You're a man of action, aren't you?"

"Well, I try to be."

"I knew it. I can hear it in your voice. I'll see you in an hour."

She ended the call and smiled up at me. "She may not be able to make a wedding cake, but your wife can wrap any man she wants around her little finger."

"Oh, I know. I've been wrapped since the first time I saw you."

She stood from her chair and kissed my cheek. "Thank you for calling in the favor. I'll make you a cake . . . or maybe some chocolate chip cookies."

In that moment, I had no idea what sort of Pandora's box I'd opened, but it was obvious that I'd never get it closed.

I found myself suddenly in possession of one of life's rarest gifts: solitude. I was completely alone in my favorite place on Earth: my gazebo overlooking the North River. I wondered how many generations of my bloodline had sat or stood on this piece of ground and felt the same sense of home I felt in that moment. My life had been shredded by the murder of my parents and sister in Panama when I was barely a teenager, and since that moment, I could count the hours I'd spent completely alone on my fingers.

Instead of questioning the forces that put me in that coveted position, I simply closed my eyes, leaned back, and listened to the river drift softly by until a yearning overtook me and I left the tranquility of the gazebo for the placidity of *Aegis*, our 50-foot custom sailing catamaran.

Motoring down the winding river toward Cumberland Sound, the wind in my hair felt like a siren's song calling me to open water where the boat could soar. I hoisted the genoa and sailed downwind through the St. Marys Pass and into the great North Atlantic, that mass of open water three thousand miles wide that beckoned sailors onto her waves since the dawn of creation.

The ocean won't kill a man, but she will gladly let him kill himself without regret or remorse. No matter how deeply we want that boundless ocean to care for us, she never will. Instead, she'll cry out for our attention and affection without giving anything in return. It's been said that a man will only find what he takes with him on the bounding main, but in my experience, exactly the opposite is true. There are answers on the wind and waves that exist nowhere else.

With nothing on the limitless horizon, I felt as if I could accomplish anything. My ship was strong, and the wind was pure. I could've touched the English Channel in a few days if I possessed the freedom to do so, but too many demands weighed on my shoulders. Too many faces I'd never see relied on me to do what men like me were created to do, and I lacked the fortitude to shun those faces. I'd answer their call. I'd pull them from the engulfing flames, and I'd disappear into the deepest night when it was done, for such was my lot, for such was my purpose.

Aegis rose and fell like a stabled horse freed from her confines, and I squeezed every knot of speed from deep within her. The rush of the wind and the slice of the water brushing against the hull were the only sounds in my world. No one was shooting at me. No one was telling me where'd I'd be in twenty-four hours and who I'd have to kill. It was only wind, water, the boat, and me, and that was a glorious moment.

I never looked down to check the speed. *Aegis* was giving her all, and I had the sails perfectly trimmed. Nothing could be done to gain even a quarter of a knot. We were alive, free, and absent from everything that wasn't sublime.

After running far enough to lose sight of coastal America, I hove-to and let *Aegis* relax on the twenty-knot breeze. She held her position as beautifully as any boat could, and we drifted slowly downwind, anchored to nothing except the air. I took the moment to pretend I was a retired Major League baseball catcher. Oh, how different my life would've been. I would've never met Penny or Anya or any of the family I loved. I would've never known the freedom that comes from protecting and preserving it. I would've never known true brotherhood that only comes from fighting, bleeding, and dying together in miserable corners of the world. Dressing like the other players on the field doesn't make a team. A team is built in blood, sweat, and sacrifice, and I'd known more than my share of all of those, but I was far from finished. I yet had bonds to form, brotherhoods to nurture, and evil to vanquish. That wouldn't be done fifteen miles offshore, so *Aegis* and I came about and set a course for the fast-approaching tomorrow.

The homeward leg always felt longer than the outbound course. Although we never wish for war, riding into battle fills the soul with vigor and hope. The homebound trek is peppered with anticipation of holding the ones we love and marinated in the pain of what we endured. The concept of home for men like me is an abstract compared to those who leave every morning and return every evening with a briefcase and an umbrella instead of body armor and a rifle.

America held out her welcoming arms as I neared the coast and angled for the St. Marys Pass, but far more than my country was reaching out for me in those moments. A glance at my phone showed a series of missed calls, texts, and emails, and it was ringing again.

"Hey, Skipper."

"Where are you? Why haven't you been answering your phone?"

"Take it easy. I went for a sail."

"A sail? Seriously? We need you in the op center."

"What's going on?"

"Nothing we can talk about on the phone. How far away are you?"

"An hour or so," I said. "And there's nothing I can do to make it faster."

She groaned. "Please tell me you have your sat-phone."

"I do."

"Good. I'll call you back in two minutes, and I'll patch you into the op center. Everyone else is here."

"Everyone? Even Hunter?"

She sighed. "Okay, he's not here, but the rest of us are. I'm hanging up now. Answer your sat-phone."

I pocketed the cell and pulled out the satellite phone just as it vibrated in my hand. "Okay, I'm here."

Skipper said, "Stand by. We're going secure. You'll hear a series of clicks."

"Yes, I know. This isn't my first time."

While waiting for the clicks, I set the autopilot and surrendered *Aegis* to the electronics. Somehow, that turned off the magic, and I was no longer master of the vessel. I'd been reduced to little more than a passenger.

Skipper's voice played through the receiver attached beneath the flesh of my jawbone as if she were living inside my skull. "Are you there, Chase?"

"I'm with you. Whatever this is, it must be pretty important."

"Here's the roster," she said. "Mongo, Singer, Kodiak, Gator, and Disco. Clark is with us via sat-phone, like you. Hunter and Tony are playing rent-a-cop, but I'll bring them up to speed when they return."

"Sounds good," I said. "Let's hear it."

She wasted no time. "We know the identity of the two cryptologists in Bulgaria, and it's not good news. They're private contractors working for a company called Ontrack Global Resources. I did some digging, and OGR is an organization registered in The Hague that does all sorts of data mining and provides the spoils of their labor to the highest bidder."

I cut her off. "Who's their customer?"

"That's the slimy part," she said. "It appears they don't have a customer until the data is gathered."

"What? How does that work?"

"If you'll shut up and let me talk, I'll tell you. They gather massive amounts of information from all over the world, and then they shop that information around to potential buyers. From what I've been able to find, the Israelis routinely buy from them, but so do a lot of defense contractors."

"Do they have any loyalties?" I asked.

"Only to the dollar. Their client list isn't easy to find, but I've picked up a few names, and from all appearances, they'll sell to anyone with a big enough checkbook."

I pondered the situation and let my conspiratorial mind run wild. "How did we initially find out about the intercepted chatter?"

Skipper's fingers danced across the keyboard. Finally, she said, "It was picked up by a Defense Intel operative in the region."

"Do we have his name?"

"Try not to be so sexist. *Her* name is a code name. It's Dagger. I'm working on an identity, but she's several layers deep. I'll keep on it, but it'll be slow going."

Mongo asked, "Can we buy the information from OGR?"

Skipper said, "Maybe, but we'd have better luck working through an ally who's already a customer."

"Israel?" Mongo asked.

Skipper said, "I don't have any direct contacts inside Mossad, but I could start working on it."

"Did you have someone other than the Israelis in mind?" I asked.

"I was actually thinking about Interpol."

"They're a customer?" I asked.

"Yep."

I said, "If that's the case, the FBI and/or CIA probably have their tendrils laced through OGR as well."

Clark jumped in. "I'm already working that angle, and so far, I'm coming up dry."

I drummed my fingertips against the bill of my cap. "Is this an offi-cial assignment yet?"

Clark made a noise that sounded like a buffalo awakening. "Well, it's, um . . . practically."

"What does that mean?" I asked.

"Okay," he said. "It's not an official assignment, but once I brief the Board on this new information, it will be, so let's treat it as active."

"That's a much better answer," I said. "The Board may have some insight on how to buy information from Ontrack Global Resources. That's their name, right?"

Skipper said, "Yes, that's it. OGR for short."

Clark spoke up. "Good idea, College Boy. If anybody knows how to buy information, it'll be the Board. They've got their fingers in everything."

I asked, "Does anyone else have anything?"

Skipper cleared her throat. "Excuse me, but this is my meeting. You're playing on your boat. You can only be in charge of a meeting if you're physically at the meeting."

"I hadn't been briefed on that rule."

"Now you have," she said. "Since this is a confirmed assignment, I'd like to recall Hunter from his side hustle and brief him up."

"Make it happen," I said. "But leave Tony with the cops, if you can. Have you talked to Penny about the murder investigation?"

Skipper laughed. "Actually, she talked to me and was so excited, I couldn't get a word in. She may be an investigative journalist behind the façade of a screenwriter."

"If you're finished with me, I'd like to get back to sailing."

Skipper said, "I don't have anything else for you. How about anyone else?"

Clark said, "There's just one more thing you should know."

Chapter 11
Captain Jack

I stared down at my sat-phone and then back up at the sails perfectly trimmed in the 20-knot wind. For the moment, I was experiencing the epitome of smooth sailing, but Clark Johnson was about to conjure up a storm. "Let's hear it."

"There's a little unrest going on in Bulgaria at the moment."

He had my attention. "Unrest, you say?"

"Yeah, you might call it that. There are some grumblings about a coup d'état."

"Look at you with the big words."

He said, "I'm a lot smarter than I think I am . . . or whatever. Anyway, nobody's storming the castle yet, but there's enough political unrest for the State Department to be on high alert."

I considered the new information. "That means we need to find a way to deal with OGR as soon as possible. If the country is falling apart, they won't be there long."

Clark said, "I agree, but if that breaks down, we may end up plowing into a war zone to pluck one particular needle out of a whole stack of intelligence needles."

"Let's hope it doesn't come to that," I said. "Buying the info would be a much better option."

"I agree, but we all know there are forces at work we can't control, so we have to learn to roll with the crumbling cookie."

"Nailed it," I said. "I'll be there in less than an hour and we'll go to work."

With the demands of my world tugging at every limb, I stood, stuck my hair in the wind, and sailed my boat. The wind inside the St. Marys Pass and Cumberland Sound chose to behave like a spoiled child and ruin my perfect day on the water. I only had two options: founder in the doldrum or fire up the diesels. I made the poorer of the two choices and listened as the pair of finely tuned machines came to life. Motoring up the North River in a boat the size of *Aegis* is no picnic, but the exercise served to hone my boat-handling skills.

The breeze freshened as I approached the dock at Bonaventure. That's the way of the wind, especially the north wind, as it strives to battle the captain on a schedule. It took longer than it should to wrangle *Aegis* into her stall and tie her down, but she and the wind finally succumbed to my insistence.

Stepping into the op center felt like walking into a pressure cooker. Every eye was focused on the large monitor at the front of the room, where two men in open-collared shirts with neckties hanging loose stared back.

The older of the two said, "There you are, Mr. Fulton. Nice of you to join us."

"Thank you for not waiting," I said, unsure if his opening statement was an intentional jab. "What did I miss?"

"We were just about to begin the classified portion of the briefing. Ms. Woodley, please verify that our connection is secure."

Skipper said, "Connection is secure."

I held up a finger. "Forgive me, but have you two identified yourselves yet?"

The spokesman closed his eyes and sighed. "The formalities were established before your arrival, Mr. Fulton."

Yep, that's animosity.

I said, "That's *Doctor* Fulton, if you don't mind."

The other man on the screen said, "Oh, for God's sake. Grow up, both of you. Here's the situation. Ontrack Global Resources is believed to be based in Dubai, but we're not fully certain that's their actual headquarters."

Mongo interrupted. "What difference does it make where they're based?"

"You'll soon understand," the man said. "An unnamed U.S. intelligence agency discovered that OGR was working closely with less-than-scrupulous factions in the Middle East, who are, let's say, less than friendly to American interests."

I let the enigma machine in my head decipher the statement. "So, the CIA doesn't trust these guys. Is that what I'm hearing?"

The man ignored me. "After confirmation of the affiliation between Middle Eastern entities and OGR, the technical branch of an American intelligence agency targeted their databases with a cyberattack designed to create a back door so our intelligence agency and others would have unfettered access to the information stored inside those databases."

I couldn't resist. "So, the CIA hacked the OGR's computers, and let me guess, the geeks at Langley got caught."

Still ignoring me, he continued. "The efforts of the unnamed intelligence agency were consequently discovered by either automated or manual processes within the structure of the organization's storage system."

"So, the CIA got busted. Come on. You scolded me and your associate as being childish, and you're talking to us like we're a bunch of ignorant children. Let me remind you, sir, of the number of bullet holes, knife scars, and prosthetic limbs there are in this room because of the missions you dispatched us on. We're not children. We all have TS clearances, and we're all battle-proven warriors who deserve not only your respect but also the courtesy of briefing us as if we're on your team, because time after time, we've proven that to be the case. We'll fight the wars you start, including this one, but we won't do it without absolute and unadulterated honesty from you. So, in the words of

Captain Jackson Augustus, speak plainly, sir, so that I may know what level of hell to unleash on the Earth."

Mongo frowned and stared at me as if scouring the annals of history in search of the quote, but the man on the monitor broke before the big man could interrupt.

"Mr . . . Dr. Fulton, forgive me. You're exactly right. No team of operators under our direction has done more to prove their loyalty and capabilities in combat. You're owed more respect than I was giving, and I apologize."

I nodded. "Just give us the facts, the guesses, and the objective. That's all I'm asking."

"Then allow me to start again. The CIA screwed up and got caught when they broke into the OGR network after determining the company was selling information to Al Qaeda, Hezbollah, Islamic Jihad, and some others who enjoy seeing American dead bodies in the street. I think it's safe to say we burned that bridge, so we're not getting anything out of OGR, no matter how big the check is."

His no-nonsense approach was exactly what my blood pressure needed. I said, "Excuse me a moment, gentlemen."

They both nodded, and Skipper muted the audio and cut the outgoing video feed.

I said, "You told me we had the identity of the two crypto techs in Bulgaria, right?"

"Yes, I have a dossier on each of them."

"Do we know their whereabouts now that the country is falling apart?"

"We did as of an hour ago, and the country isn't exactly falling apart. There's some political stuff in the capital of Sofia, but out in the east, it's still relatively quiet."

"Is that good for us?"

She said, "Yes, the crypto operation is in Burgas on the Black Sea."

"Literally *on* the Black Sea?"

"Yep, on the Burgas Bay, to be exact."

The pieces may have been falling apart for the Bulgarians, but they were falling right in place for me. "Find out where the *Lori Danielle* is, and get her steaming for the Black Sea at full speed."

"No problem."

Her fingers moved across the keys too quickly to see, then she looked up. "Ready to go live again?"

"Let's do it."

The outbound video feed flickered into place, and the audio went live.

I said, "Sorry about that, gentlemen, but I had to manage a little logistical matter."

The man on the monitor almost smiled. "Did you point your ship to the east?"

I gave him a shrug. "Maybe, just as a precaution. You know how we Boy Scouts are . . . always prepared to punch somebody in the nose if they need it. That's still the Boy Scouts' motto, right?"

"If it's not, it should be. Do you have a plan, Dr. Fulton?"

"I'd like it better if you called me Chase, and I always have a plan. Can you authorize a little cash for some MGD?" Both men frowned, and I said, "That's 'boat fuel' for you landlubbers."

"Consider it a blank check, Chase. Let us know if you need anything else."

"Oh, I will. Hopefully, our next conversation will be an intel report from the Black Sea."

He gave me a salute. "Happy hunting."

The screen went dark, and all eyes turned to me.

Hunter said, "Let me guess. A cell phone in the pocket of the deadliest Russian we know is about to ring."

"Let's see if she answers. Hit it, Skipper."

Our analyst slowly shook her head. "This is a bad idea, Chase."

"Most of my ideas are, but somehow, things keep working out."

Seconds later, a voice I hadn't heard in months filled the room. "*Da, kto zvonit?*"

I took a long breath and let it slowly escape my lips. "Hello, Anya. It's Chase."

"Chase who?" she asked in her still-prominent Eastern European accent.

"That's cute," I said. "Something tells me I'm the only Chase you know."

"I have small memory of maybe person named Chase. He is player in baseball match, yes?"

"Something like that. "You're in quite the mood this morning."

"Is not mood. Is only sadness that you only call to me when I am needed to do something you cannot. This is reason you are calling, no?"

"It's not that we can't do it. It's just that you can do it better." I expected a comment about how she does everything better, but it didn't come, so I continued. "Have you ever been to Bulgaria?"

"Yes, many times. Is beautiful country and is now having problem with revolution."

I said, "I'm not sure it's a full-blown revolution, but there is some political stirring happening in the capital."

"What do you know about revolution?" she said.

Anya's cold tone was out of character, and I didn't like where it seemed to be going.

"Anyway, we've got a potential operation in Bulgaria, and we need to get the undivided attention of a couple cryptologists."

"And you are calling for me to be whore and trap these men for you, yes?"

"No, that's not what—"

She cut me off. "I am not this person any longer. I am true American girl now. I have real American job with government, and I have small business with many workers."

The conversation felt forced and cold.

"Is everything all right, Anya? You don't sound . . ."

"I am fine. Is not fair to me to call only when you need me for mission to do something terrible. I do not know if I am available."

Available, I thought. *This is getting stranger by the minute.*

"Look, Anya. I'm not asking you to do this for free. We'll pay you well, and all we need you to do is draw these men out and make them believe—"

"I know demands of Russian red sparrow. I am trained to be perfect bait and give to men great pleasure. You remember things I did to give to you pleasure, yes?"

I considered cutting the speaker and having the conversation one-on-one, but I had nothing to hide from my team. "Anya, whatever's going on with you, I'm sorry, but we have a mission requirement that falls outside our skill set."

"I do not know. Maybe I will do for you this thing. What is time?"

"Within the next ten days," I said. "If the unrest in Bulgaria becomes a revolution like you said, I want to be out of the country when it happens."

"Make telephone speak only to your ears."

Skipper raised an eyebrow, and I said, "Transfer the call to my cell."

I stood, walked through the door, and into the foyer of the op center. "Okay, Anya, it's just you and me now. What's going on?"

"I am sorry, my Chasechka. I do not mean to be angry with you. It is girl thing. I am sad I cannot be for you friend. Is okay I cannot be for you wife. This I understand, but you call to me only for mission. I would like for one time you to call and say to me, 'Anya, I do not have mission. I only wanted to say hello.' Why can you not do this?"

I swallowed hard. "I do think about you sometimes and hope you're safe and happy. I'm married to Penny, so she is my first priority. Intentionally doing something to hurt her is unthinkable for me, and calling you just to have a chat would crush her."

"She is afraid of me, no?"

"She's not afraid you're going to hurt her, but she knows how I felt about you, and she's afraid those feelings will come back if you and I spend time together, even if we're just talking on the phone."

"If you were for me husband, I would also be jealous. You are good person and good man, Chasechka. You were first man in all of my life who was kind to me. I can never forget this. You are beautiful, but this is never why I loved you. I love you for kindness inside heart, not strong body and beautiful face. You understand this, yes?"

"That's very sweet of you to say, and I appreciate it, but that doesn't change—"

She cut me off. "Yes, I will do for you mission. I am sorry for being mean to you. There are so many things I want you to know that I cannot tell to you on telephone."

"What things?"

She said, "I can tell to you only when I can see your face."

"It feels like you're dangling a carrot on a stick in front of me, trying to lead me down a road I don't want to take."

"Why would someone put carrot on stick? This makes no sense."

I tried not to laugh. "The point is this. No matter what you have to tell me, I'll still feel the same way about you after I hear it. You don't have to hide it from me, whatever it is."

"You do not understand, Chasechka. Is personal thing I am learning about what is inside of me. Maybe you will feel always same for me, but there was time in our lives when you loved me."

"Okay," I said. "You and I will have a face-to-face talk soon, but I won't do it without telling Penny. I won't keep it a secret."

"I know this," she said. "This might be conversation you do not tell all of details to Penny. Maybe is only for you and me."

"I'm not willing to go down that road with you right now. I have to focus on the mission. Will you help us?"

"Yes. I said already I will do this for you. Tell to me details of mission and when and where I should come."

"Thank you. I'll give the phone to Skipper, and she'll brief you in."

Back inside the op center, I handed the phone to our analyst and tried to flush thoughts of whatever Anya needed so desperately to tell me from my head.

Skipper pressed her lips into a thin line and narrowed her eyes as she took the phone from my hand. With obvious reluctance, she briefed Anya, and I sat in my chair—that had once been comfortable —and drew a long, deep breath that felt like swallowing razors.

Mongo saved me from the abuse that was, no doubt, headed my way from our overprotective analyst. "Who is this Captain Jackson Augustus character you quoted? I've never heard of him."

I stared back at him. "Who?"

"Captain Jackson Augustus. You quoted him when you were talking to the Board."

"Oh, that. I have no idea. I made him up. But it was a pretty good quote, wasn't it?"

"Yeah, it was solid. I'm impressed."

I laughed. "Typically, if I say something impressive, I made it up. I'm not smart enough to remember phrases like Clark does."

Chapter 12
PEW-PEWS

Anya Burinkova would forever be a part of my life, no matter how hard I pushed her away. There was some cosmic force binding the two of us together, and I'd never understand it. Everything about it was unfair to Penny, and perhaps to both Anya and me, but fairness rarely plays a role in reality, and in a relationship as complicated as mine and Anya's, fairness would never be a factor. I did wish her well, and I did think about her back then, but those weren't conscious decisions on my part. They were merely the way things were, and I was powerless to change them.

I asked, "Did you find Captain Sprayberry?"

Skipper said, "Yes, and we got really lucky. They were just finishing a mission to support an archaeological dig in Egypt at the north end of the Suez Canal."

"Well, isn't that handy?" I said. "He's right there in the neighborhood where we need him and the *Lori Danielle*."

Skipper said, "Sometimes, we get lucky. So, what's the plan, boss?"

"I'm meeting Anya in Burgas, and we're going to snare ourselves a couple of cryptologists."

"You're not going alone," she said.

It sounded a lot more like a command than a question.

"No, I'm not. I'm taking the whole team, including you. We're going to run this op from the ship."

Skipper cocked her head. "The whole team?"

"Yes, everybody. I'm not willing to risk losing these guys. They're our only source of information concerning the mass kidnapping. Although unlikely, it is possible that Anya could fail. One or both of these guys could be immune to her, well, charms. If that happens, we have no choice but to conduct a snatch-and-grab."

Skipper said, "Oh."

"Exactly," I said. "That's why we'll be operating from the *Lori Danielle*. In case we need to rattle these guys' cages a little, it'll be a lot easier to do it aboard the ship than anywhere in a country that's on the verge of a revolution."

Kodiak leaned forward. "I know I'm low on the totem pole, but how long has it been since any of you have done snatch-and-grab training?"

I said, "We definitely need a work-up period. Gator, did they do any snatch work at The Ranch?"

Gator nodded. "We had about a week of grabs. We worked on city streets, houses, vehicles, and open spaces. I can't imagine an environment we didn't cover."

"Good," I said. "Then you're in charge of our work-up. Put us through the same drills you did at The Ranch. We may modify some of the techniques, but you're the freshest on the procedures, so it's your show."

He tried not to react, but his pupils dilated. "I don't know if I'm . . ."

I lowered my chin. "I didn't ask if you were anything. I told you what class you're going to teach."

He ducked his head. "I'm sorry. I didn't mean any disrespect. It's just intimidating to think about me teaching you guys anything, except maybe football."

I chuckled. "Our gridiron skills are no doubt lacking, but we'll save that class for another day. Let's go work on our kidnapping game."

We began on a street-grab with the Suburbans, using the airport taxiways as city streets. Gator's nervousness soon vanished as he demonstrated the technique at full speed. Mongo was our victim, of course, since he was likely the hardest of us to kidnap. Wrestling with a three-hundred-pounder made of muscle isn't an easy task for anyone.

"It's about balance," Gator said. "If we keep ourselves on-balance and the victim off-balance, the scales are tipped in our favor, regardless of his size. Remember, nothing athletic is done on your heels. Stay on the balls of your feet and try to keep the victim leaning back."

Each of us practiced wrestling the big man out of his vehicle and into ours. When it was over, everyone was exhausted except for Mongo. He thought the whole experience was exhilarating.

We caught our breath and downed enough water to float the airport.

I asked, "All right, teacher. What's next?"

Gator said, "Let's work on grabs in the open. Those are the most difficult."

We moved to a grassy field at the southeast corner of the airport, and Gator described the procedures he'd been taught. "Grabs in an open environment are tricky because there are so many avenues of escape. It takes a team of well-trained operators to pull it off." He positioned Mongo in a prone shooting position and said, "Where do you approach this potential detainee?"

Kodiak said, "Any direction except the front one-eighty."

"Exactly," Gator said. "You don't want to catch a bullet by approaching where he can see you and get off a shot. The weapon opens another tactical issue. If the mission is to abduct and not kill, the weapon has to be neutralized immediately on contact."

Kodiak said, "Immediately on physical contact or visible and audible contact?"

Gator sent his eyes to the sky as he, no doubt, played the training through his memory. Finally, he said, "The weapon has to be neutralized immediately upon physical contact. The only two ways to neutralize it prior to physical contact is to either kill the target or talk him into laying it down."

Kodiak grinned. "The kid's got it together."

We conducted an hour of drills designed to get us into a position to not only neutralize the weapon but also provide us with the physical advantage to overpower the target. Unless our victim was more powerful than Mongo, any two of us could overcome him in a fistfight or wrestling match.

We moved on to abductions inside buildings, and the rules changed.

Gator said, "This has to be approached as a room-clearing exercise. Bad guys have a lot of places to hide once they go inside a building they know well. We're at the decided disadvantage because we don't know the layout of the building as well as our victim does. We may have some general idea where he is, but knowing who else is inside is almost impossible."

We'd beaten Mongo up so badly that I insisted we change crash test dummies, and I volunteered. Room-clearing or close-quarters battle was an art my team knew as well as anyone on Earth. All of us had spent thousands of hours training in CQB, and our skill was at an elite level. Once the structure had been adequately cleared to approach the target—me—the abduction became little more than cuffing and stuffing.

Our day of snatch-and-grab training honed our rusty skills and gave us an opportunity to remember how everyone else moved and communicated. In a real fight, movement and communication are key elements of success. Failure in either area is lethal.

* * *

Back in the op center, Skipper asked, "How'd Kidnapping One-Oh-One go?"

Mongo twisted and stretched his bruised back and arms. "You missed a good time. You should've been out there with us."

She huffed. "Not hardly. If the day ever comes when you need me —all hundred and twenty-five pounds of me—to help kidnap somebody, things have gone terribly wrong and you should be retreating at full speed."

Kodiak furrowed his brow. "Retreating? Could somebody tell me what that word means?"

I shrugged. "Beats me. I've never been taught to do that, whatever it is."

"Cute, guys," Skipper said, "but I just got off the phone with our resident mad scientist, and she's got something to show you that just might make the whole snatch-and-grab thing a lot easier."

"Does she want us to come to her, or is she coming to us?"

Skipper said, "She told me to ask you guys to come to the lab when you can."

I said, "Before we go, have you come up with anything new in Bulgaria?"

"Oh, yeah. I almost forgot. Captain Sprayberry wants to know when and where you want to rendezvous. He said the farther from the Black Sea, the better."

"How about Athens?" I asked.

She pulled up a map of the Aegean Sea.

All eyes went to the monitor, and heads nodded.

Skipper said, "Athens looks pretty good, but why not Istanbul?"

Mongo said, "Istanbul is too close to the Bulgarian border. You guys keep throwing the word *revolution* around, and I don't think we want to leave our Gulfstream that close to a country that's melting down."

I said, "There's another consideration, as well. The Greeks are a little friendlier to American interests than the Turks, so my vote is for Athens."

Gator's eyes darted back and forth, and I asked, "What's going on, Gator? You look like you're watching a ping-pong match."

He said, "I was trying to figure out if we were really going to vote. This thing's still not a democracy, right?"

I chuckled. "No, it's not, but I'm always up for suggestions, thoughts, and opinions."

Singer said, "Especially if they agree with yours."

That got a laugh, and I said, "Athens it is."

* * *

We took our gospel bus to the airport instead of driving two vehicles, and Singer said, "This thing is ridiculous at best and sacrilegious at worst."

"What's wrong with our short bus?" I asked.

"There's nothing wrong with it except for the paint job."

"What's more covert than a gospel quartet?"

He shook his head. "I'm the only one on the bus who can carry a tune."

I said, "It's not like we could paint 'Tactical Team Twenty-One' on it."

He said, "It's just wrong, and the whole lot of you need a lot more Jesus in your lives."

"You're right about that," I said. "But I can sing."

He laughed. "Is that what you call that noise you make?"

Dr. Celeste Mankiller, our technical services officer, met us at the door to her lab. "Oh, good. You're here. You're going to love this."

"Look at that," I said. "Did you ever get *that* excited when you were working in the basement at DOJ?"

She laughed. "I've never been this excited in my life. I probably don't tell you enough, but thank you, thank you, thank you for rescuing me from that dungeon. Getting to design, build, and test anything I want is my absolute dream job. You just don't know."

"Oh, we know," Disco said. "We're all living the dream, and it's all thanks to Chase."

I threw up both hands. "Don't blame this on me. You guys make all this work. I just sign the checks."

Mongo said, "We could stand out here and suck up to Chase all day, or we could go inside and see what you've come up with this time."

I said, "Maybe a little more sucking up would be nice before we go inside."

I'm not sure which one of the Neanderthals shoved me through the door, but I deserved it.

Dr. Mankiller's lair was a 5000-square-foot, climate-controlled laboratory housed inside of a 40,000-square-foot commercial aircraft hangar, and from the looks of things, she was already in need of an upgrade.

In the open space inside the hangar, she had constructed what appeared to be an indoor shooting range with targets from mannequins to vehicle-sized mockups, but the target that immediately caught my attention was a torso cast from ballistic gel with ribs, a spine, and organs visible through the transparent gelatin.

I said, "I'm impressed by what I see already, but it's what I don't see that has me concerned."

Celeste smiled. "Thanks for noticing. You were a catcher, right?"

"A long time ago."

"I guess that means you know a lot about backstops, huh?"

"You're quite the mind reader," I said. "Just what kind of weapon are you shooting in here that doesn't require an earthen berm to stop an errant round?"

Her smile widened. "The kind that doesn't shoot tangible projectiles. I call it PEW-PEWS."

"I just pray it works because I can't wait to say, 'Load up the PEW-PEWS. We're going to war.'"

"It's an acronym," she said. "It means Pulsed Energy Weapon Prism Enhanced Warfighter System."

Singer stepped around me. "Let's see this thing."

He couldn't have voiced my sentiment any better.

Celeste pulled a black veil from a device resembling an electric Super Soaker with a thick cable connecting the head to the base. "Gentlemen, meet PEW-PEWS. If you want to wear eye protection, I've got glasses, but I assure you they aren't necessary. Feast your eyes on the mannequin on the left."

She stepped behind the weapon, flipped a pair of switches, and plugged her phone into a thin cable attached to the butt of the rifle-like portion. The mechanism moved silently until a mark appeared on the mannequin's chest displayed on her phone, but not on the mannequin itself."

"It's an infrared laser," I said.

She looked up. "That's like saying your airplane is a cargo door. The IR laser is part of the overall system, but only a tiny part. Let me show you what it does, and then we'll talk about the individual components." She entered a short code on her phone, and the mannequin exploded as if it were packed with C-4.

Singer was first to speak up. "I'll take a thousand of them. How much are they?"

"They're not for sale," she said. "They're for you guys."

I had a hundred thousand questions, but I started with, "What was that?"

With the pride of a new mother all over her face, she said, "It's pulsed energy, mostly sound waves far outside the range of human hearing. There's a microwave pulse, as well, but that's not what causes the apparent damage. The microwave travels at almost the speed of light, so it gets there way ahead of the sonic pressure wave. The two waves can be used together, or you can just use the microwave portion."

"What's the difference?" I asked.

"I'm glad you asked. Watch the gel dummy. In fact, go downrange and watch the dummy from about three feet away. I promise not to shoot you."

Without hesitation, we relocated with haste and stared into the dummy's guts as if they were going to do a trick.

"Ready?" Celeste asked.

A chorus of "Send it" arose from the team, and the internal organs of the ballistic gel dummy turned to soup.

We instinctually closed in on the dummy, and several hands reached for flesh. It was cool and undisturbed, but the heart, liver, spleen, lungs, and kidneys were mush.

Singer turned with disbelief painted all over his face. "How . . ."

"It's extremely complex," she said. "But have you heard of GPR?"

"Ground-penetrating radar?" Mongo said.

"Exactly. Think of one of the components of this weapon system as body-penetrating radar. It's not exactly the same, but it's close enough. You don't need to understand the science to understand how deadly this thing is."

I said, "Why hasn't anybody else come up with this?"

"They have," she said. "But what they *haven't* come up with is the aiming and limiting system. That's where the second PEW comes from. The technology to melt your guts isn't new, but I'm the first person to perfect the Prism Enhanced Warfighter System. It's a CDAM, a computerized discriminatory aiming mechanism. Here, I'll show you." She rolled the gel dummy aside and replaced it with an identical copy. "Now, watch this."

The dummy appeared in the center of the screen on her phone, and the IR laser designation appeared just below the mannequin's heart.

She handed the phone to me and pointed to the screen. "When you're ready to fire, press and hold the silver button. It'll read your fingerprint, verify your body temperature, and if you pass the biometric verification, it'll activate the weapon. But don't do it yet."

She trotted toward the dummy and positioned herself directly between the weapon and the target. "Okay, press and hold the button."

"No!" I said. "I'm not interested in melting your guts."

"Just do it," she ordered.

"Are you sure?"

"Yes, I'm sure. Just do it."

With enormous hesitation, I pressed my finger against the silver button, but nothing happened. "What's going on?"

She said, "That's the computerized discriminatory aiming mechanism doing its job. Now, watch this."

She stepped aside, and an instant later, the guts of the second dummy turned to pudding."

Again, I stood with my mouth agape. "How?"

She giggled. "It would take ten years to explain it to you, but I'll keep it simple. When the CDAM identified the target, it set a bunch of parameters and lockouts for the weapon. If anything organic steps between the weapon and the target, the firing mechanism won't function, but the instant the CDAM recognizes a window for a clean shot, it pulls the trigger."

I threw my arms around the scientist. "I love you so much right now."

She pushed me away. "Yeah, yeah. I love you, too. But that whole wedding ring thing you've got going on is a real turn-off for me."

"It's not that kind of love," I said. "But you're definitely getting a raise."

The look on Singer's face said the sniper was still in awe, but he asked, "Is that as small as you can make it? If so, it's a vehicle-mounted weapon. That thing's too big to carry, even for Mongo."

"Oh, ye of little faith." She spun to a second black cover. With a flourish, she yanked the cloth away, revealing a miniaturized version that looked a lot like a heavy shotgun.

Singer reached for it immediately, and Celeste said, "It works exactly like its big brother except for the control. All of the electronic displays are inside the digital scope. The trigger is identical to the blade on your Lapua, with one exception. Just like the phone, it checks for your fingerprint and body temperature before activating the weapon."

Singer aimed downrange at a mannequin. "May I?"

"Sure, go ahead," she said, and the mannequin turned to splinters of plastic in an instant without a sound from the weapon.

Singer examined the weapon. "How's it powered?"

"That's the issue at the moment," Celeste said. "It's a power hog, and I tried to keep it as light as possible. The power supply is essentially the stock and butt of the weapon. In its current configuration, it'll make ten shots up to fifty meters or four shots up to two hundred meters. Every extra long-range shot adds one pound of battery weight to the stock. Every additional two and a half short-range shots add a pound, so I can give you all the shots you want, but they come with extra weight."

He hefted the weapon and then stuck it in Gator's hands. "What do you think?"

Gator shouldered the rifle and balanced it on his palms. "It feels like twice the weight of my M4, but not as heavy as the Lapua."

Singer said, "Would you consider the weight worth the firepower?"

I was intrigued at the pop quiz our seasoned sniper was administering.

Gator gave it some thought. "It depends on the environment. If I were clearing buildings, I wouldn't want it, but if we were advancing on a target where stealth was critical, I'd gladly carry it."

Singer lifted the weapon from Gator's hands. "Good answer." He handed the device back to its creator. "I was wrong. I want a thousand of these and a dozen of the big one."

"That's a pretty tall order, but I have two of each. I'd like to keep a pair in the lab for further development."

I stepped away from the team and stuck my phone to my ear. Skipper answered on the second ring, and I said, "Put a million dollars in Dr. Mankiller's R and D fund and a quarter million in her personal account. Code it as a bonus."

Chapter 13
That Thing I Like

While Singer and Gator were still admiring Celeste's handiwork, Disco stepped beside me. "We're leaving soon, right?"

I nodded. "Early tomorrow morning."

"I'll make sure the plane is ready. Do you want the typical loadout?"

"Pack heavy. I plan to stock the armory aboard the ship."

He said, "That'll add a fuel stop somewhere at the top of the world."

"Iceland?"

"Either there or Newfoundland."

"You choose," I said. "I've got a lot to do before we ship out, so take whoever you need to help with loadout."

I left the gospel short bus with the team and rode a bicycle from the hangar back to Bonaventure.

Skipper was hard at work when I pushed through the door into the op center.

Without looking up, she said, "It's getting worse. The military has been activated in Sofia to protect the capital, the president, and the prime minister."

"Don't they have protection forces like the Secret Service here in the States?"

She said, "They do, but they're small forces, and the military is a much more visible show of power."

"It sounds like they're circling the drain."

"Yep. If you're going, you'd better go now."

"We're going," I said. "The guys are loading the plane now."

"Should I get Anya on the phone?"

"No, I'll take care of that, but first, where's Penny?"

Skipper said, "She's still playing investigative reporter with Tony, as far as I know."

To my surprise, Penny answered her phone.

She said, "Hey, sweetie. How's it going?"

"Not bad. We're ramping up for deployment tomorrow morning. How's the investigation?"

"Do you need any help?"

"No, we've got it under control. Is there anything new on the murder case?"

"A few small things, but nothing major yet. It's going to hit the news tonight, and there's nothing we can do to stop it."

"I was afraid of that," I said. "Listen, I wanted to tell you before it happens, but I'm calling Anya in for this one. We need her help."

She said, "Chase, you don't need my permission to bring on contractors. Do your job and come home to me when it's over. Just don't do anything that wouldn't be okay for me to do. You know, no double standards."

"I promise. Thanks for understanding. I have to run."

"I'll see you before you leave, right?"

"Yes. I'll be here until around four tomorrow morning."

"Okay," she said. "I'll see you tonight. Love you."

"Love you, too."

I hung up the phone and dialed Anya's number. Even though Penny knew everything, it still felt wrong.

"Hello, my Chasechka. You are calling to me for mission, yes?"

"Actually," I said, "I'm calling to invite you to dinner tomorrow night."

"What?"

"How does Athens sound?"

She hesitated. "Georgia?"

I laughed. "No, not this time. I'm talking about the original Athens. Can you make it?"

"This is first time."

"You've never been to Athens? I find that hard to believe."

"No, I have been to Athens many times, but is first time you have asked me on date."

"We've been on dates."

"Yes, we have, but you have never asked me. Always before, we just did it and no one asked."

I paused. "Yeah, I remember, but . . . this isn't a date. We're meeting the ship in Athens, and we'll run the operation from on board."

"Oh, is perfect idea. Bulgaria is getting worse, but I suppose you know already this."

"Yes, we're monitoring it closely. Fortunately, we'll be at the other end of the country where the unrest is taking place."

She said, "I do not know this word, *unrest*, but it sounds too simple for revolution."

"Maybe I chose a poor word. Perhaps it's somewhere between unrest and revolution."

She said, "No, is revolution. You will see."

"I hope you're wrong, but either way, I'll see you in Athens tomorrow night."

She asked, "Do you know Platanos Taverna?"

"No, what's that?"

"Is wonderful restaurant and very old. I will make for us reservation at eight o'clock. Goodbye, my Chasechka."

"Wait. It's not—"

I was too late. The line was dead, and I was committed.

* * *

The hours leading up to deployment feel different than any other passage of time. I had both mental and physical checklists for everything that had to be accomplished before the *Grey Ghost* blasted off toward destinations unknown, but no matter how thorough they were, those lists never felt complete. There was always a lingering doubt that we'd left off a critical piece of gear that would prevent us from completing our mission. I was surrounded by one of the most competent tactical teams the world has ever known, so my concern was unwarranted, but that didn't stop it from pecking at my mind.

Instead of our traditional family-style meal before deployment, the team opted instead for an early night to pack as many hours of sleep as possible into the darkness.

I lay on my back with Penny's head resting on my shoulder and her hair cascading across my chest.

"When will you be back?"

I savored the feel and scent of the woman I adored. "Not soon enough."

"That's always the case, but do you have a real timetable for this one?"

"It'll be a compressed schedule," I said. "With the country devolving into chaos, we have to get in and back out before Ontrack Global Resources closes down their crypto station and recalls their technicians."

"How bad will it be over there?"

"I don't know. Our plan is to hop in, let Anya lure at least one of the cryptologists into her web, grab the intel we need, and fly away. But it's never that simple."

She huffed. "It's not like Anya will have any trouble getting their attention. It's not fair."

"What's not fair?"

"The fact that she doesn't age. She still looks exactly like she did the first time I ever saw her."

My mind drifted back to the last time I'd seen the Russian. The tiny crow's feet around her eyes were barely visible, and the flesh around her lips bore only the first hints of the weight of time, but I couldn't say that to Penny. She didn't need or want to hear that my eyes had paid so much attention to Anya's features. She needed reassurance that I wanted to come home to her every time.

"She's aging like the rest of us," I said. "But not you. I remember the excitement in your eyes the night I met you on Kip and Teri's boat in Charleston. It was like you couldn't wait to show me your screenplay. I'll always remember you with that glowing anticipation on your face. You were and still are the most beautiful woman I've ever seen."

"Nice redirection," she said. "Don't worry, Chase. I'm not concerned about you running away with Anya. If she were who and what you wanted, she'd be the one with you in this bed."

I pulled her close and kissed the top of her head. "You're exactly who I want. By the way, your wedding cake tastes a lot better than it looks."

She slapped a palm onto my chest. "That's mean."

"It was supposed to be a compliment."

She chuckled. "Well, I'm afraid you missed the bullseye on that shot, but I'm glad you like it."

"To answer your question, it shouldn't take more than a week to get everything we need in Bulgaria. Hopefully, it'll just be a few days."

We spent the next hour reminding each other that in our most intimate moments together, the rest of the world melts away, nothing beyond our bodies and minds holds any weight, and nothing happening in any dark corner of the world could wedge itself between the two of us.

* * *

Dawn broke over the endless blue horizon to the east as we climbed out of the darkness of St. Marys, Georgia, and into the welcoming sky. While the world behind us was still bathed in darkness, our cruising altitude provided us with a front-row seat to the coming of a new day.

Once in cruise flight, the *Grey Ghost* essentially flew herself, and the pilots became little more than system monitors. A glance into the dimly lit cabin reassured me that even though the loneliness of command would often engulf me, I had a team behind me that would fight until the final breath left their bodies so they could complete our mission and bring everyone home when it was over.

"How's Gator's flight training coming along?" Disco asked.

"He's doing really well," I said. "I plan to sign him off to solo next time we fly."

"Good. I was concerned when he initially didn't show much enthusiasm about flying."

I watched the wispy clouds between us and the eastern horizon disappear in the bright morning sun. "I think he had a bad experience with one of the instructors at The Ranch. He seems to love it now."

Disco said, "Good. I'm looking forward to having him in the right seat."

"Are you kicking me out already?"

He shrugged. "Variety is the spice of life, my friend. It'd be nice to look over there and see a mug that ain't yours every now and then."

I dabbed my fingertips against my face. "I'm hideous!"

"Yes, you are. Now, fly the airplane. I'm going to get a cup of coffee. Want one?"

"Please."

Despite my horrid appearance, according to our chief pilot, I greased the landing at Reykjavik, Iceland, and we topped off the tanks and our stomachs. There's something magical that happens when an Icelandic native cooks a piece of meat. It doesn't matter if it's fish, fowl, or beast, it tastes like morsels of Heaven. The chow aboard the *Lori Danielle* would be exceptional, but the cooks would have a tough time competing with our friends from the frozen north.

Athens International Airport is situated a few miles southeast of the city center and is a concrete scar on a bland background of sand and scrub brush. If the sea weren't just two miles off to the east, it would be easy to believe we were landing in West Texas. Skipper's masterful arrangement had the *Grey Ghost* being tugged into a private hangar only minutes after refueling. My body believed it was one p.m., but the clock on the hangar wall said I was almost late for my eight o'clock dinner date. I didn't want to leave Anya waiting alone, but duty called, and I dialed Captain Barry Sprayberry's sat-phone aboard the ship.

"Go for the captain."

"Good evening, Barry. We're safely on deck in Athens. How's your progress?"

"Good evening, Chase. It's good to hear your voice. We're lying a mile offshore and awaiting your arrival. Shall I dispatch the Huey?"

I checked my watch, which still believed both it and I were in the Eastern time zone of the U.S. "Yes, send her our way and we'll start shuttling. We've got about two thousand pounds of gear."

"Can you sling-load it?" he asked.

I covered the phone and turned to Kodiak. "Can we sling-load the two pallets of gear?"

He was only one of the Air Assault–qualified former soldiers on the team, but he was the closest. "Sure, why not? I'll get on it."

I uncovered the phone. "We'll have two pallets ready to fly outside hangar seven."

"The chopper's on the pad, and it'll be airborne in minutes."

"We'll see you soon. Thanks, Captain."

The next call was also to someone who once wore the rank of captain. The difference was that Barry earned his at sea, and Anya earned hers under the Russian flag.

"Chasechka, please tell to me you are not calling to stand me down."

I chuckled. "I think the phrase is 'standing you *up*.'"

"But I am sitting down."

"Then, I'm sure you're right, and yes, I'm standing you down, but I have a good excuse. I've flown over six thousand miles in the past ten hours, and I'm exhausted. What are the chances I could get you to take a cab to the airport?"

"I will bring for you bag of dogs. Which airport?"

"Bag of dogs?"

"Yes, this is phrase meaning 'food taken from restaurant inside bag.'"

"Oh! Yes, of course. A bag of dogs sounds fantastic. Meet us at hangar seven at International. We're shuttling gear and personnel to the ship."

"Okay," she said. "I will see you soon. I will be tall blonde wearing that thing you like. Goodbye, my Chasechka."

"You really have to stop calling me Chasechka," I said, but it didn't matter. The line was dead, and I was left wondering what "that thing I like" was.

By the time the team deposited the second pallet of gear on the ramp outside the hangar, our Huey landed only feet away with two of the most important women in our lives in the cockpit. Barbie, call sign Gun Bunny, shut down the engines, and the rotors slowed to a stop while Ronda No-H, CPA extraordinaire and the finest door gunner any flight crew ever had, climbed down from the cockpit. Ronda made short work of finding Disco and wrapping herself around him. The reunion made it look like one of them had just come home from war, but everyone knew exactly the opposite was happening.

Gun Bunny didn't run into Kodiak's arms, but she gave him a wink as she inspected the rigging of the pallets. "Are we taking them together or one at a time?"

Kodiak looked a little envious of Disco's welcome and said, "I've got them rigged as singles, but that's easy to fix if you can manage the weight. It's twenty-two eighty combined."

"No problem," she said. "Rig them to stack, and I'll get airborne."

He pulled a bag of rigging from the chopper and went to work on the first pallet. Minutes later, Gun Bunny hoisted the first pallet into the air a few feet while Kodiak connected the rigging to the second stack of gear. After a short hover to feel the weight, Gun Bunny soared away to the east with every piece of gear we could pack onto the two pallets.

She and the Huey returned simultaneously with Anya's arrival, and I instantly knew what the Russian was talking about. She was dressed in jeans, boots, a University of Georgia Bulldogs sweatshirt, and a baseball cap with her blonde ponytail protruding through the hole in the cap. She was right. She was definitely wearing "that thing I liked."

Chapter 14
'Tis Better

By the time we landed aboard the *Lori Danielle*, the deck crew had our gear pallets broken down and ready for transport into the ship's armory.

Skipper caught me by the arm. "So, where are we headed?"

"The Black Sea."

She rolled her eyes. "No, not ultimately. I mean, right now."

"Uh, I'm going to my cabin, but I wasn't expecting you to join me."

"Oh, you can expect a lot more of just me following you to your cabin. As long as Little Miss Russian Thang is hanging around, you can consider me part of your skin. I'm not letting you screw up what you've got with Penny."

I gave her a hug. "You're worried about nothing. Trust me. I'm not about to screw that up. I've got way too much to lose."

"Darn right, you do. So, let's go check out that cabin."

"Are you planning to sleep with me, too?"

"If you're going to sleep with anybody on this ship, it's going to be me or one of those guys out there."

"Seriously," I said. "You and Penny have nothing to worry about."

"You may believe that, and it might even be true from your perspective, but see that girl wearing your class ring?"

"She's not wearing my class ring."

"Then, whose sweatshirt and ball cap are those?"

"It was just a joke, Skipper."

She took me by my hands and stared into my eyes. "It may be a joke to you, but it's not one for her. Penny may be cool with all of this, but I've seen Anya pull too many underhanded tricks to ever trust her again."

I squeezed her hands. "She saved your life."

"Oh, I know. She saved my life twice, but that doesn't mean I trust her. If she sees one tiny little crack in your armor, she'll crawl her way through it so fast you'll think you've been struck by lightning."

"Thank you for worrying about me, but I'm a big boy, and I can handle Anya. I promised her we'd have a private conversation, and I'm a man of my word."

She lowered her chin. "Does Penny know about this *private* conversation?"

"Yes," I said. "Penny knows everything, and that's how it's going to stay."

She threw up her hands. "Okay, but don't say I didn't warn you, Big Boy."

My cabin was just as I'd left it but with fresh sheets and a fully stocked head. I took advantage of the moment alone to lie down and think. The upcoming mission was just phase one of what could turn into an international incident. If the cryptographers had real intelligence about a mass hostage situation, either Anya or I would get it out of them by any means necessary, then we'd find a way to stop the kidnapping before it grew into something no one wanted to manage.

The tap at my door was almost too soft to hear, but I said, "Come in."

The soft-knocking someone was Anya Burinkova. She stepped through the hatch and pulled off her cap. "Hello, my Chasechka."

"Hi, Anya. Thanks for returning my sweatshirt."

She tugged at the oversized shirt. "Is not yours, but you can borrow if you want. It maybe smells like me."

"What are you doing in my cabin, Anya?"

She planted herself on the edge of my bunk. "I came to have private talking time you promised."

I threw my legs over the edge of the bed and sat up. "I know your English is excellent, so you don't have to keep up the accent."

She smiled. "But this is how I talked when you fell in love with me so long ago. I thought maybe—"

"No, don't think maybe. Let's talk like grownups instead of swooning teenagers. We've come a long way since those days."

"I do not know this word, *swooning*, but I suppose you are right," she said.

I immediately missed the accent.

"So, what is it you want to talk about?" I asked.

She suddenly looked like the shy child I imagined she may have once been. "First, I will not do anything to try and take you away from Penny. She is choice you made, and I will respect choice."

Her accent would likely never fully diminish, and her natural predilection to avoid English articles amused me. Hearing the word *the* probably wasn't going to happen.

"Thank you for that," I said. "What you and I once were is gone forever, and I have a wonderful life now."

She smiled. "This makes me happy for you, Chase."

Hmm, no more Chasechka.

She spoke barely above a whisper. "This is what I have to tell you."

I listened intently as the drone of the ship's engines resonated inside my head.

"Is not really something to tell to you. Is really question. This is okay, yes?"

"English, Anya."

She ducked her head. "I am sorry, but here is question. If Penny did not survive automobile accident, would you think of me when you finished mourning?"

"What kind of question is that?"

"Is serious question, Chase. Please answer it for me."

"Look, Anya, what you did for Penny was amazing, and there's no way I can ever repay you for giving up part of your liver to save her life, but you can't use that as some warped way of getting us back together."

"No, Chasechka . . . Chase. That is not what I am doing. I am only asking question. Would you think of me after time of mourning if she did not survive?"

I closed my eyes and replayed the emotions I felt after Penny's accident when she lay dying in the hospital. "She didn't die . . . thanks to you."

She slid an inch closer to me and laid her palm against my chest. "She is your heart, and I know this. I once knew how that felt, and it was best feeling of my life. I believe I will never have this feeling again, and that is okay. It is so much better to have known that feeling and have it taken away than to live all of my life without knowing someone cared for me so deeply."

"There's an English phrase for what you're describing. It goes like this. "'Tis better to have loved and lost than to have never loved at all."

"Yes, this is exactly what I mean. Who said this thing?"

"Alfred, Lord Tennyson, an English poet."

She said, "Yes, I remember this now. So, I have one more thing to tell you. If you are ever alone and do not wish to be—"

I stopped her. "Don't say it, Anya, and I need to know that you'll never hurt my wife."

Her eyes bloomed into giant blue orbs. "Oh, Chasechka, I could never do that. Please do not even think such of me. I would never hurt you like that. I am not the cold, heartless killer I was when you first saw me. I have now friend. Her name is Gwynn, and from her, I am learning to be human and also American. It is wonderful gift she is giving to me."

I smiled at the stunning woman beside me. "If that's true, your friend Gwynn is giving the world something beautiful, and I'm envious of the man who wins your heart."

She tilted her head. "That man will always be you because I will forever give only to you my heart."

"That's sweet, but I don't—"

She pressed a finger to my lips. "You might be in charge of men on this ship, but you cannot tell to me who gets to have my heart. Is forever yours whenever you want it."

I stood. "Let's go bag a couple of cryptographers before the whole country of Bulgaria implodes."

She stood, slid a boot between mine, and wrapped her arms around me. I returned her embrace, and we shared a silent, private moment that may have been the last one we ever experienced together.

We left my cabin together and found Skipper standing in the passageway with her arms folded across her chest.

She said, "The captain wants to see you."

Anya frowned. "Why would captain want to see me?"

Skipper glared back. "Nobody wants to see you. The captain wants to see Chase."

As much as I feared leaving the two women alone in the passageway, when summoned by the captain, an appearance isn't optional.

I stopped short of the hatch and leaned through the opening. "Permission to come aboard the bridge."

Barry stood from his perch behind the console and stuck out a hand. "Come aboard, young man. How was the trip?"

"It just keeps getting weirder."

"That happens around you," he said. "Mongo tells me everyone is aboard and the gear is stowed. We're ready to make way for the Bosporus when you give the word."

"She's your ship, Captain. I'm just a passenger. Make way when ready."

He turned to the helmsman. "Mr. McCord, weigh anchor and make way for the Bosporus."

"Aye, sir. Weigh anchor and make way for the Bosporus Strait."

The captain turned back to me, and I said, "I love when you guys do that."

He chuckled. "We only do it for your amusement."

"I'm sure. I do have a question, though."

"Shoot."

"I thought we were finished with the research portion of the ship's mission. I was under the impression that the *Lori Danielle* was to be used exclusively for our tactical operations now."

"You're correct," he said. "The mission in Egypt had been on the books for almost two years. We were bound by contract to see that one through. That was the last official research mission we'll ever serve."

"I see. There is one more little wrinkle in that plan."

I clearly had his attention, and he said, "A wrinkle?"

"Yes, the granddaughter of a good friend of mine will finish her PhD in marine biology and conservation in a few months, and I thought it might be nice to make a place for her on the crew."

"Does she have any maritime credentials?"

"No, she's not a captain or anything. As far as I know, she doesn't have any licenses, but she has a scientific understanding of the ocean, so a technical position without operational responsibility would be nice."

He said, "I'm sure it would, but who's going to pay her salary?"

"If her salary comes out of the ship's budget, I'll make sure the budget is adequately increased to manage the additional expense."

"She's not going to lose her mind if we plow through a school of some mysterious, protected species on our way to put out a fire, is she?"

I laughed. "I don't know her that well, but I'll make sure she understands the order of priorities of the ship."

"In that case, it's fine with me. Does that mean we'll conduct research between tactical missions?"

"Maybe," I said. "But I'll make sure they aren't boring."

"In that case, I'm all for it. Just tell me where to pick her up."

"We'll plan a rendezvous after we survive this mission. How long before we make the Black Sea?"

He said, "We've got a hundred fifty miles of crowded water between us and the Dardanelles Strait into the Sea of Marmara. From there, it's another two hundred to the Bosporus. We have to make hull speed in the open water and maybe ten knots through the straits. We can't risk being seen on the foils, so we're looking at almost twenty-four hours until we taste the Black Sea."

"That's certainly better than walking. I'll leave you alone and go pester my crew."

He tipped his hat. "Just don't pester mine."

"Aye, sir."

I called a huddle in the compartment that used to be the combat information center before Skipper relocated the CIC to a higher deck and a much larger space.

With everyone in place, I said, "Okay, gang. Here's the scoop. We'll be in the Black Sea in a little less than twenty-four hours. That gives us just enough time for our bodies to adjust to the time zone change. Let's start with Singer. Do you have any training requirements prior to reaching our objective?"

The sniper said, "Nothing for the team, but I'd like to do some work with Gator if you can do without him."

"He's all yours," I said. "Just don't shoot any friendlies."

"We'll do our best," he said.

I turned to Hunter. "How about you?"

"I don't have anything unless there's something you guys want to work on."

Nobody spoke up, so I said, "How about you, Skipper?"

She wouldn't look at me, but she said, "I've got plenty to do. When are you going to brief Clark?"

I asked, "Does anyone else have anything?"

Disco stuck a finger into the air. "I'd like to get a few approaches and landings to the ship when the sun comes up tomorrow, if that's operationally possible."

"Good idea," I said. "I'd like to do the same. We don't want to be crippled if something happens to Barbie. I'll check with the captain and put that on the schedule for right after breakfast."

No one else had anything to add, so I said, "All right. Get some rest, and keep your radios and sat-phones with you. Gator, you're with Singer. Skipper, I need to see you, but everybody else is dismissed."

The small room emptied, leaving Skipper and me alone, and I floated the first balloon. "We can't do this. You and I have to work together even tighter than I work with anybody on the team. If there's a rift between us, everything breaks down."

She huffed. "There's no rift, Chase. I just don't trust her."

I leaned closer. "That's not how this looks. It looks like you don't trust me, and that's a problem."

"It's not that. I'm a woman, and I know how women are. We're devious, deceitful, and dangerous when we think somebody else has what we believe is ours, and that's exactly how Anya feels about you. To her, you'll always be hers, and Penny's just borrowing you for a while."

"That's not how it is."

She met my gaze for the first time in hours. "Okay, then. Tell me what she had to say to you all alone in your cabin."

I replayed the talk in my head and sighed. "She wanted to know if I would think about her if something ever happened to Penny."

Skipper flushed red. "If she does anything to hurt Penny—"

I held up a hand. "I already called her on that one. It's not in play."

"I'm just saying, she may be a Russian badass, but I'll put a bullet through her skull if she ever thinks about hurting Penny. That's out of bounds."

"Look at me," I said. "You'd have to beat me to the gun. Anya may be thinking the things you suspect, but it takes two to tango, and I don't dance. Your trust is paramount in my mind. I won't do anything to break that trust. You and I've been together longer than anybody on this team, and we've got something they'll never have."

She almost smiled. "You know, I had the biggest crush on you when you first started coming to our house."

"Stop it," I said.

"No, seriously. You were this hotshot freshman catcher at UGA that everybody was talking about, and I was nerdy little kid."

"You *were* pretty nerdy."

She gave me a slap. "You know you're the reason all my friends wanted to have sleepovers at my house. My dad was your coach and all, and you were always around. We'd giggle like little lovesick girls when you were there."

"That's ridiculous."

"It's true. All of it. But it all changed for me the day you broke Billy Carter's collarbone."

"How did you know about that?"

"I saw you do it through my bedroom window. Apparently, you heard about what he did to me, and you put his lights out. That was the day you turned from high-school crush to protective big brother, and you're a lot better at that role."

I gave her a hug. "Did Billy Carter really deserve what he got?"

"Oh, yeah. And more."

"I'm sorry that happened to you."

"Don't be sorry," she said. "He never so much as looked at me again after that. It was awesome. I should've known then that you'd be a serious sheepdog someday."

Chapter 15
Just One of the Boys

A phone call home, a nice hot meal, vaccinations, a pill from Dr. Shadrack, and nine hours of uninterrupted sleep made up the remainder of my first day back aboard the Research Vessel *Lori Danielle*.

Morning chow was eggs, bacon, biscuits, gravy, and gallons of coffee.

I swallowed a mouthful and said, "Skipper, are you ready to do the full mission brief?"

She nodded without swallowing, and we policed up our plates and cups on our way out of the mess deck. Inside the shiny new combat information center, our hotshot analyst already had the briefing maps displayed on the overhead monitors and wasted no time getting started.

Two faces appeared on a monitor that had been black. "Ladies and gentlemen, meet Andreas Berger and Gregor Klein, both German citizens in the employ of Ontrack Global Resources as cryptographers. They are our target."

Anya squinted and leaned toward the monitor. "They are both very handsome men. I think I will enjoy this assignment."

If that was intended to spark a flicker of jealousy inside my head, it may have worked . . . a little.

Skipper couldn't help herself. She grinned in spite of her distrust and perhaps dislike of Anya. "Yes, they're cute. Let me know if you need any backup."

It was Anya's turn to smirk. "You are married woman, Skipper. This will not do."

"I'm just kidding. Now, back to the boys." She used her mouse to point to a street west of Burgas. "They share a rented house here on Pirgos Street. The address and local maps are on your tablets." Everyone checked their tablets, and Skipper continued. "They work at a temporary location masquerading as an abandoned construction site, but there's a fiber-optic connection to the house, so they have similar listening capabilities at home as they have at work. It would appear that they record everything and filter through it during quiet times."

Mongo asked, "Just the two of them?"

"As far as we know," Skipper said.

"It seems odd that they only need two personnel to monitor twenty-four hours per day. Sorry to interrupt."

"Don't be sorry," she said. "I thought the same thing, but I haven't been able to spot anyone else coming or going from the construction site."

Mongo said, "That probably means there's another listening site we don't know about, or there's a third and maybe fourth guy who never leave the house."

"It's possible, but I've never spotted a third or fourth man."

"Just something to think about," Mongo said. "If we have to hit them, we have to keep that possibility in mind. We can easily deal with four guys, but nobody likes surprises like that."

"I'll keep looking for more," she said. "But let's continue with the briefing."

She zoomed in on a satellite photo of the house. "We don't have a floor plan for this particular house, but I got a peek inside one that has the identical footprint."

She brought up another satellite photo of a house under construction in the same neighborhood. "Here's one, like I said, with the identical exterior footprint before they put the roof on. We can see the interior framing. It's likely that our target house is identical or at least similar."

"Excellent work," I said. "Can you shoot that one to our tablets, too?"

"It's already done. Everything you see here today is in your electronic briefing packet."

She changed pictures. "This one is especially for Anya. This is the boys' favorite restaurant. It's about half a mile from the house, and they walk there a couple nights a week. If I were planning to accidentally bump into them, this is the spot I'd pick."

"I like it," Anya said. "Restaurants are always good places for meeting first time. Is easy to make target think it was only chance encounter and not plan."

"That's what I figured," Skipper said. "So, Anya, your briefing packet has a few extra pieces. I'd like for you to review them and let us know how you'd like to work the op."

The Russian said, "Is simple. I have done this many times. I will simply wait outside restaurant, where I cannot be seen, until they go inside. I will then watch them together inside before choosing one of them."

I cut in. "Forgive me for interrupting, but how do you choose?"

"There are many factors, but in any group of men, there is always one who feels superior to rest of them. I will always start with him because beautiful woman makes already big ego even bigger, and when a man believes he deserves a woman like me—or also like you, Skipper—he is open in his mind when I tell to him he is beautiful."

"What if it doesn't work?" Kodiak asked.

Anya laughed. "It always works. Men are clay inside fingers of beautiful woman. Ask Skipper. She knows this."

Skipper nodded. "I think the expression is putty in their hands, but yeah, you're right. There's not a guy in the world who'd turn you down."

Anya glared directly into my eyes. "There is one, but this is because he has more beautiful wife than me."

I re-situated myself in my seat. "Let's get back to the op."

Anya smiled. "Yes, the operation. I will first approach alpha male, and I will know in minutes if he is going to play ball, as you say. If no, I will flirt with other man. He will have even bigger excitement because his superior failed to keep my attention, and he will do everything I ask."

Skipper said, "How far are you going to take this? I mean, is it just flirting and talking or . . ."

Anya said, "Is okay. I know what you are thinking, and I will not do this unless there is no other way."

It may have been the jealousy lashing out, but I'd rather believe it was some sense of morality that drove me to say, "It won't come to that."

Every head in the room turned, and the spotlight I so detest nearly blinded me. "I mean, if it comes to that, we'll have you get the target on the street, and we'll snatch him up. You're not in that business anymore."

Anya's smile said a thousand things that morning, but the only one I heard was, *Thank you, Chasechka.*

Time seemed to stop in that moment, and I silently begged anyone to say anything.

It was Skipper who wound the clock. "Okay, well . . . anyway. Back to the briefing."

Heads turned back to face the monitors, and I wiped a bead of sweat from my brow. An involuntary glance at Anya showed that she had not, in fact, turned back to face the front. She was still wearing that rare and illusive smile of the Russian woman.

Skipper said, "So, how long do you think it will take for you to . . . captivate one of these guys?"

Anya finally looked away. "I believe maybe only one hour, so timing is matter of finding next time they will be inside restaurant."

Skipper flipped through a few pages of notes. "They've not been to the restaurant in three days, so it's time."

I asked, "Do they have a regular schedule for going to the listening site and returning home?"

Skipper shook her head. "No, it's random. I haven't been able to find any pattern at all."

Mongo said, "That's probably because they're being directed by the other team of listeners or some kind of chain of command."

"That's possible," Skipper said, "but there's no way for us to know for sure."

Kodiak asked, "Why can't we just bug the listening site? That seems a lot simpler than all of this cloak-and-dagger business."

Skipper said, "It *would* be simpler, but the problem is that the listening site is listening to so many different types of transmissions, and many of them are coded. Even if we intercepted them, we don't have the technology to decode them. We need what's inside the heads of those cryptographers, and there's no way to bug their brains."

Kodiak chuckled. "I'll bet Anya could come pretty close to doing it."

It didn't get the laugh he was expecting, but it made the Russian giggle.

Skipper said, "Focus, you bunch of twelve-year-olds. We'll be in position off the coast of Burgas in four hours. If our boys are out and about, will that give you enough time to be ready to pounce?"

Anya asked, "How will we go ashore, and how many of us are going?"

Skipper said, "I've arranged for two vehicles at the Burgas Airport. The plan is to chopper ashore, as long as the weather cooperates. The forecast calls for showers and low clouds. If it's too ugly to fly off the ship, we'll tender ashore using the RHIB."

Anya said, "And how many?"

Skipper turned to me, and I said, "We'll take you and four hitters. If we get lucky, you'll rope your target and have him eating out of the palm of your hand in no time, but if it comes down to a snatch-and-grab, we'll be ready."

Gator looked up. "Who's going?"

I said, "You, Singer, Kodiak, and me."

Singer cleared his throat. "Uh, Chase. Have you ever been to Bulgaria?"

I shook my head, and he said, "If you put me on the ground, I'm going to stick out like, well, a black guy in Bulgaria."

"Oh, I didn't . . ."

He laughed. "It's okay, but you might want to think about taking Hunter instead of me."

"Okay, then. Hunter, it is."

Anya said, "I have question. This device all of you have inside face for communication . . ."

Skipper said, "Yeah, the bone conduction device."

"Yes, this. I do not have one, but I would like one. We can do this, yes?"

I spun to see Dr. Mankiller in the back of the room, and she had that thinking look on her face. "Uh, yeah, I can do it, but it's about a one-centimeter incision, and are you sure you want me to cut a hole in *that* face?"

Suddenly the whole team was watching the exchange like a tennis match.

Anya said, "Is small incision. I can cover with makeup for mission."

Celeste said, "I wasn't really talking about the mission. I mean, you'll have a permanent scar."

It was Anya's turn to hit a strong backhand. "All of them have scar and is not problem."

Celeste sighed. "Yeah, but none of them look like you, and they have beards."

Anya moved in for the crushing overhead. "Gator, come to me for moment, please."

The new guy looked around as if he needed permission, and I said, "Go before she yanks you out of that chair."

He stood and slid between the rest of the team to approach Anya, who'd stood to meet him. She curled a finger, motioning him closer, and he didn't hesitate. He stepped to within a foot of the Russian, and she took each of his hands in hers and placed them on her hips. Then, she draped her hands around his neck and pulled him closer until their bodies were pressed together and she was staring into his eyes. I could almost see him sweating.

She said, "You like being here, yes?"

He stuttered. "Uh, I mean, who wouldn't?"

She pulled her left hand from around his neck and touched a spot on her jawline. "If I had small scar here, would you find me to be hideous, or would you still like being this close to me?"

He licked his lips. "I would . . . you know. I . . . no, I wouldn't find you hideous. Nobody would."

She kissed his cheek. "Thank you for making for me point. I will have bone conduction device like rest of boys."

The ship accelerated beneath us, and I assumed that meant we'd cleared the Bosporus Strait into the Black Sea. The memory of my last visit to that particular piece of water poured through my head. I'd intentionally sunk a nearly identical copy of my beloved *Aegis* with Clark and Anya on board to convince some Russians we were dead. It worked temporarily, and we air-locked onto a Navy submarine where Anya caused quite a stir among the crew. With any luck, we wouldn't get wet on this mission.

The briefing broke, and while Anya was having her implant installed, I took a walk to see the captain. "Permission to come aboard the bridge?"

Captain Sprayberry glanced over his shoulder. "It's your ship, Chase. If you keep asking, I'm going to start saying no."

"It just feels wrong to step in here without permission."

The captain plucked his pen from a pocket and scribbled on a slip of paper. He shoved it into my hand, and I read the note.

Perpetual permission to come aboard the bridge.

Love,

Cpt. B.S. Sprayberry

"Thank you. I'll treasure this forever."

He groaned. "What do you want now?"

I glanced through the glass and across the sea, where ships of every description lay scattered across the surface. "Never mind. I was going to ask for some time on the foils and sixty knots, but it looks like there are far too many prying eyes out there."

He checked his watch. "We're just four hours out. Even if we could run on the foils, that would only cut the time in half."

"You know me. I'm always in a hurry."

"I noticed you brought your girlfriend along for this one. Are you in a hurry so Penny won't think you're on some kind of—"

"No! Definitely not."

He chuckled. "Good. Now, get off my bridge. I've got ships to dodge."

Chapter 16
Smarter not Harder

As I stepped from the bridge, I heard the unmistakable sound of the Huey's rotors spinning on the helo deck. My timing worked out perfectly so I could hop aboard before Disco and Gun Bunny lifted off. I sat in the back seat and watched our chief pilot fly six flawless approaches and landings to the helipad. When he lowered the collective and brought the engines to flight idle, I said, "Show-off."

He gave me half a grin. "I just got lucky."

"Six times in a row?"

"Some of us are luckier than others. Your turn."

I traded seats with him, and my competitive nature took over. I brought the engines back to normal operating range and yanked us off the deck like a rocket. Despite the Huey's horsepower, I asked a little too much of the workhorse, and she faltered.

Gun Bunny said, "I have the controls," and I surrendered the chopper to her capable hands.

She put us back in a stable climb away from the ship, and I felt like a hapless flight student again. She winked from behind her aviators and surrendered the controls back to my much less capable hands.

I said, "I have the controls."

Everything I did from that moment forward was strictly by the book. I didn't push any limits of any performance envelope, and I managed to make six survivable landings aboard the ship. Each was a little better than the previous, but I had a long way to go before I'd be half the helo driver Disco and Gun Bunny were.

Right on time, the captain dropped the hook a mile offshore from the pink waters of the Burgas salt pans, where tourists coat themselves in some of the most mineral-rich soil on the planet. To me, the pink water looked like something out of the plagues of Egypt, and I had no interest in smearing that mud, or any other mud, all over my body for any reason.

The team and Anya were more than ready to go as soon as the ship came to rest. The weather forecast was just wrong enough to allow us to sneak out beneath the cloud layer and touch down at Burgas Airport without losing visibility. The trucks Skipper arranged weren't Suburbans, but they'd fit in nicely in town, and we had no problems with the pre-stamped passports Dr. Mankiller manufactured for the four Canadian businessmen and one Belarussian clerk.

"Well, that was easy," Gator said as we drove away from the airport.

"Too easy," I said. "That's usually an indicator that things are going downhill soon."

"Let's hope not," Gator said.

Hunter and I answered in unison. "Hope ain't a plan."

"Yeah, yeah, I know. Hey, why didn't Anya ride with us?"

Hunter raised his hand. "I'll take this one."

He turned to Gator. "If you were married to Penny, and you had the same history with her that Chase has, would you want Anya riding in your vehicle?"

He grimaced. "Ah, I get it now, but why does Kodiak get to be her driver and not me?"

I said, "Because he's old enough and wise enough to resist her. He's already learned those painful lessons."

Gator said, "You guys don't have to shelter me. I've got to learn sometime, and that woman looks like a lesson that would be a lot of fun to learn the hard way."

Hunter chuckled. "Just wait 'til you see her cut a man's heart out of his chest and play in his blood. She may be fun to look at, but don't let that exterior fool you. She could probably kill everybody on our team before we could react."

"Come on," Gator said. "Nobody's that good."

"She is," he said. "Part of the reason she's so deadly is because of the way she looks. Nobody would ever expect somebody who looks like her to be one of the world's deadliest assassins."

Gator shook his head. "Assassin?"

I said, "KGB- and SVR-trained assassin."

He looked up at me in the rear-view mirror. "The KGB doesn't exist anymore."

"It did when Anya was a four-year-old girl. That's when she became the property of the motherland, right after a KGB colonel killed her mother."

He swallowed hard, and the conversation was over.

The GPS guided us to the house where the two cryptographers lived, and we circled the block before stopping at a gas station just down the road from the house.

I asked, "What do you see, Gator?"

He scratched his beard. "I see way too many people and way too many houses way too close together. If we hit them in this neighborhood, everybody's going to see us."

"Good eyes," I said. "Let's go check out the listening site."

We drove the half mile to the site, and Gator said, "This is more like it. No streetlights, no sidewalks, no people."

"What else do you see?"

"Is my life always going to be a pop quiz?"

Hunter said, "If you want to stay alive it is. If no one else is asking you questions, you'd better start asking yourself some. That's how we keep our eyes and minds sharp. Never start thinking you're finished learning. Two days after you stop learning, we'll put what's left of you in a pine box six feet under."

He studied the environment. "I see a lot of avenues of escape. This area is pretty much the opposite of the area where the house is."

"Good," I said. "Now you're thinking like an operator. You taught us how to abduct a target in an open space. Do you think that technique would work here?"

"We approached a stationary target. Anybody with half a brain cell would take off running out here. It'd be a footrace."

I said, "Without saying the word *hope*, how should we approach a snatch-and-grab if we have to do it out here?"

Without hesitation, he said, "It would take both vehicles and careful coordination. I think it would be better to hit them closer to the housing area, where they have limited avenues of escape."

I patted his shoulder. "Good thinking, kid. You're going to be an operator pretty soon if somebody doesn't shoot you in the face."

"I'm already an operator," he said. "Just not on your level yet."

"Indeed, you are, my man. Indeed, you are."

With my sat-com bouncing invisible signals through space and back to the CIC aboard the *Lori Danielle*, I said, "Okay, Skipper. We've got the lay of the land. There's nothing here that disagrees with your aerials. We're ready to move. Where are our targets?"

She said, "It's nice to know the satellite cameras don't lie. The boys are at home, but something's crawling around in my head that you need to hear."

"Let's hear it."

"I've been reviewing some videos of the cryptographers' movements, and I think they might have security. It's not tight, but it looks like they may have shadows at fifty yards. I may be overreaching, but I think you should take a look before you move in on these guys."

I groaned. "I really wish you would've mentioned this before we left the ship."

"I know," she said. "And I should've picked up on it earlier, but it's subtle. If they're security, they're very good. But even if they're not security, they're something. It's too coincidental to be nothing."

"What do you think, Hunter?"

He puffed out his cheeks. "It doesn't make sense. Why would you put security on a pair of radio guys in Bulgaria?"

Skipper answered before I could. "Maybe to keep guys like us from rolling them up and throwing them in a van."

"It's hard to argue with that," I said. "Can you send the video to our tablets?"

"I can, but it'll take half an hour or more through the satellite link, and the clarity won't be great. It's a lot better on the monitor here in the CIC."

My watch and the position of the sun told me that a trip back to the ship would postpone our mission at least twelve to fifteen hours. As I wrestled with myself inside my head, Anya's voice came over the sat-com and into my bone conduction device. "Security does not change my mission. You can go watch video on ship while I meet boys and convince them pretty Russian woman wants to make them smile."

"I don't like putting you in that position without us standing by, in case you get in trouble."

She laughed. "Trouble? What kind of trouble do you think I cannot handle? I am trained for this with no one standing by within thousands of miles. Is what Soviet Union created me to do. Just because I am American girl now does not mean I do not still have skills."

I said, "Give me a minute to think about it."

She didn't give me the minute. "This requires no thinking. I will do mission for you because I said I would. You go to ship and watch movie. Do not worry about me."

"You're not calling the shots here, Anya. I'm responsible for the mission and the safety of everyone involved. Just give me a minute."

To my utter surprise, she said, "I am sorry. It has been too long since I worked with you. I know this. I was not thinking like team, only like one person. Remember, I have skill, training, and experience to do this alone, if you agree."

Perhaps Anya was playing me, but she wasn't wrong. She absolutely possessed the skill to pull off the mission without our involvement, but that didn't relieve me of the responsibility I felt for the entire team, including her.

"Okay, Skipper. Launch the chopper. Everybody except Anya is coming back to the ship."

She said, "That's not a good idea, Chase."

"Launch the chopper. We'll rendezvous at the airport."

We pulled to the side of the road, where I dismounted the vehicle and opened the passenger-side door of the other SUV. Before Anya could say a word, I said, "Watch for security. If you ID them, walk away. Do not get in a fight unless your life is at risk. Walk away! Do you understand me?"

She nodded, and I said, "Just dangle the bait. Don't set the hook."

Her frown said she didn't understand, so I said, "Don't try to flip either of them tonight. Just make contact, flirt, dance, whatever, but don't go beyond that. Got it?"

She smiled, leaned toward me, and whispered, "Thank you."

"Don't make me regret leaving you alone."

She laid a hand on my arm. "Does this mean only now, or in all of life?"

I pulled away. "Now's not the time, Anya. We've got work to do."

Kodiak left the vehicle with the Russian, and the rest of us arrived at the airport only minutes after the chopper touched down. Back aboard the ship, Skipper had the video queued up. She let it run without any introduction, and we all watched like hawks.

Mongo said, "That guy's definitely a shadow. He was almost jogging until he got them in sight, then he matched their pace exactly."

Skipper said, "That's exactly what I thought, too, but watch."

The video played, and the man in question turned away and walked down a cross street.

"That's odd," I said. "Was that a rolling exchange?"

"If it was," Skipper said, "it was the smoothest one I've ever seen, and whoever picked up the primary isn't visible in the shot."

"What else have you got?" I asked.

She played four more videos, and they all showed similar activity. When the cryptographers moved, people around them moved with them in short stints, but they were never the same people.

"That's too weird," I said. "It looks completely coincidental. There's no way they have a dozen shadows for these two guys."

Mongo groaned. "There's no such thing. There's a connection. We're just not seeing it." Then he snapped his fingers. "Turn on the timestamps."

Skipper recoiled. "Calm down, Simon Says."

He motioned toward the monitor. "Sorry. It just came to me. If you'll turn on the timestamps and bring up the satellite schedule to cross-reference."

I relaxed against the back of my seat. "No way."

Mongo said, "We'll know in a minute."

Gator's eyes flashed between the monitor, Mongo, and me. "Uh, what am I missing here?"

Mongo said, "Just watch. If I'm right, it'll come to you."

Skipper worked feverishly bringing up the timestamped video against the satellite passage logs, and the times matched to the minute.

I gasped. "Get Anya out of there, now!"

Skipper keyed up the sat-com. "Anya, CIC."

Nothing.

"Keep trying," I ordered.

"Anya, CIC. Come in, Anya!"

I withdrew my sat-phone and dialed her number. The line connected in seconds, but it wasn't her Eastern European accent that filled my ear. It was the German-accented voice of a man.

"We have your sparrow, and she is still alive . . . for now. How much is she worth to you?"

Chapter 17
Angry Russian

Skipper spun to her console and raced across the keyboard with un-equaled focus. The team were on their feet in an instant, and I dialed Clark's sat-phone on the secure line.

Gator said, "Would somebody please tell me what's going on?"

While waiting for Clark to pick up, I covered the microphone with my palm and said, "The cartographers know the satellite schedule better than the National Reconnaissance Office, so they knew exactly when we'd be watching."

"But how did they know we *would* be watching?" he asked.

"They didn't," I said, "but their company, OGR, is smart enough to play the game, just in case somebody like us was watching. During times of satellite passage, they put actors in play to look like security."

"But that doesn't explain how they captured the deadliest assassin on Earth, or whatever you said she was."

"No, it doesn't," I said. "We made the stupid mistake of thinking our comms were secure against one of the world's most high-tech cryptography firms. They've been listening to everything we said on the sat-com and sat-phones. They knew we were coming, and they knew—"

Clark said, "What's up, College Boy?"

"They've got Anya."

"Who's got Anya?"

"The cryptographers. They're better than we expected, and we walked right into a trap."

"Is anybody hurt?"

"The team is solid," I said, "but they claim to have Anya."

"They may claim to have her, but what proof did they offer?"

"They answered her sat-phone, and she's not answering any comm attempts."

"Proof of life?" he asked.

"Not yet, but we're in the first minutes."

"You're authorized whatever you need to get her back alive."

"Roger. We'll copy you on all comms and activity. I'm out."

I closed the circuit ".We're approved hot. We're getting her back, and we're keeping her alive."

Mongo stepped beside me and grabbed a handful of my shirt. In a whisper that could've cut steel, he said, "Calm down. Think clearly. Don't react emotionally. She's a captured asset, no different than one of us."

"She is one of us right now," I said.

He nodded slowly. "Just keep it together and make good decisions."

I lowered my head, took a long, deep breath, and gathered my thoughts. When I looked up, a team of the finest operators on the planet stood, patiently waiting for anything to come out of my mouth.

"We're going to approach this like a hostage negotiation while we're moving into position. Where's Dr. Mankiller?"

Gator yanked his phone from his pocket, but I stopped him.

"We have to work under the assumption that they hear everything we say over comms. Everything has to be face-to-face. Go see if you can find her."

"Yes, sir."

He disappeared, and I said, "Somebody get me two bottles of water, a notepad, and a phone line to these guys."

Singer grabbed the water and pad while Skipper set up the comms.

I turned to the team. "Mongo, it's your op on the ground. Have Gun Bunny put you and the team on the ground. I want you staged and ready to hit that house if I can't talk her out of there."

"What makes you think they're at the house?" he asked.

"It's just my first assumption. Skipper, can you get a fix on her cell, sat-phone, or bone conduction device?"

"I'm on it," Skipper said. "Comms are up when you're ready."

Gator came back through the door with Dr. Mankiller in tow.

She said, "Gator briefed me. What do you need from me?"

"I need a secure comm system the cryptos can't intercept, and I need it inside of ten minutes."

She closed her eyes as if she'd drifted into a mesmerized state of deep concentration. When she opened her eyes, she asked, "What range?"

"Two miles or less."

She said, "I need a few old-school walkie-talkies, an oscilloscope, a screwdriver, and twenty minutes."

Gator took off in a sprint, and Skipper almost yelled, "Got her!" I spun, and she said, "Her sat-phone and BCD are in the crypto shed at the listening site."

"What about her cell?" I asked.

"Still working on it."

I turned back to Mongo, but he beat me to the command. "We'll stage to hit the crypto shed."

Gator plowed back into the CIC with a plastic bag full of handheld radios and a pouch of tools. "There's a scope down in engineering, but it's too big to move. We can either go down there, or, I don't know what else, but here are the walkie-talkies."

Celeste snatched the bag from his hand and poured the radios onto a table. With a thin screwdriver from the pouch, she pried the back from one of the radios and studied the internal circuitry. "I don't need the scope, but I need you to help me open all the radios."

Gator didn't hesitate, and they had the radios open in seconds. The mad scientist stuck a pair of magnifying glasses on her face and dived into the back of the first radio.

I was mesmerized by what she was doing, but I yanked myself back into focus. "Okay, Skipper, ring the sat-phone."

I pulled on the headset for the comms station and slid the pad beneath my hand. While the phone was ringing, I jotted the time at the top of the sheet.

A voice filled my ears. "I thought you would call back. How much is she worth to you?"

His thick German accent told me he wasn't the same man I'd spoken with on the first call. I rolled the dice. It was likely one of the two crypto geeks, either Andreas Berger or Gregor Klein, so I asked, "Do you want me to call you Andreas or Mr. Berger?"

"You may call me Herr Schlauer als Sie, and I will call you Clark Johnson."

I took the last breath I remember taking during the conversation. "Okay, it's obvious that you're smarter than me. Tell me what you want so I can have my agent back."

He laughed. "Oh, Clark . . . This is your name, yes? Clark?"

"Fine," I said. "Just tell me what you want."

"I am more curious what it is you want, Clark. Your agent, as you called her, isn't interested in talking, no matter how aggressively we encourage her to have a friendly talk with us."

I wanted to explode, but I pretended to remain calm. "All we want is some information on a transmission you intercepted two weeks ago. If you'll just tell us the details of that conversation, we'll pick up our agent, and we'll be out of your hair forever."

"Come now, Mr. Johnson. Surely, you understand this has escalated beyond just picking up your agent. You have disrupted our operation, costing us time, money, and resources. We must be compensated for these things, so tell me, how much is she worth to you alive? If your offer is not sufficient, you will get her corpse back at no charge. So, think carefully before you make a silly opening offer. You see, Mr. Johnson, this isn't a negotiation. It is a game of what you Americans call 'chicken.' Who will flinch first?"

Keeping him talking was the only way I had to give Dr. Mankiller the time she needed to program the radios and my strike team the time they needed to get on the ground. "Tell me your demand, and I'll tell you if I can meet it."

"You clearly do not understand rules of this game. Perhaps you are a fighter and not a negotiator. Either way, it does not matter. If you want to play this way, our demands are simple. Get every American out of the Middle East in the next fifteen minutes or I kill your pretty little sparrow after we take turns doing whatever we wish to her."

I growled. "You know I don't have that kind of power."

"Then you must know that you are on a mission to recover a corpse."

"Wait! I have money."

He laughed. "Money? Really? This is what you think I want? Money? Clark . . . It is okay if I use your first name, Clark? I have vaults full of money and warehouses full of presses to print more. Would *you* like some?"

To my surprise, Dr. Mankiller shoved Skipper from her position at the console and sent her fingers across the keyboard almost as quickly as our analyst. A few seconds into her work, she slid a piece of paper toward me.

I read the note.

Go with your team. I grabbed enough audio to modulate my voice to sound like yours with the computer. I have the comms. You go kill those bastards. Gator knows the radios.

I suddenly wondered if I'd ever be able to pay Dr. Mankiller what she was worth.

She took the headset, and I led the team out of the CIC.

"Tell me about the radios," I said.

Gator stuck one in my hand. "See this button beneath the push-to-talk button?"

"Yeah, that's the Morse code button."

"Right. These radios worked on common VHF frequencies that are used in construction and all kinds of other applications. Dr. Mankiller retuned them to operate just between those frequencies.

They're no good for voice comms anymore, but the Morse code function will work fine. She recommends using RMC."

"Reverse Morse Code?" I asked. "Why?"

Gator said, "Just in case they're listening. They'll figure it out pretty fast, but not before we can hit them."

We were kitted up and in the helicopter before I had time to brief the team, so I gave the talk on the ride ashore. "Is everybody good with Morse code?"

Gator was the first to shake his head, but he wasn't the last. Mongo and Disco nodded, but everyone else was with Gator.

"Okay, so, that's out. Here's the comms code. One prolonged tone is danger. Two short blasts mean safe. Three prolonged blasts mean we're coming out. Got it?"

All heads nodded, and I said, "We're hitting that place fully dynamic. Hold nothing back. She's one of us, and we'll snatch her out of there just like you'd do if I were being held. Got it?"

"Got it," came the team reply.

I said, "Kodiak, you're the breacher. Get us inside double-quick, no matter what it takes."

"Roger."

"Hunter, you're leading the stack. Gator, you're number two, and Mongo and I will trail. Kodiak, you'll remain the breacher in case there are interior roadblocks. Everybody is hostile. There are no friendlies. Got it?"

"Got it!"

We soared across the coastline at 120 knots, and Singer lay on the floor with his rifle protruding out the door. As the listening site came into view, he yelled over his shoulder. "Two on the door. One on the fence. And one loitering thirty yards behind the building. Get down here, Gator."

Gator threw himself to the deck and stuck his rifle in the wind beside his mentor's.

"Kill 'em all," I said.

Singer said, "You take the two at the door. I've got the outliers."

Gator's rifle bellowed twice in rapid succession, followed by Singer's slightly slower pair of shots.

Singer elbowed Gator. "Report to your team leader, dummy."

The freshman sniper looked up. "Four down, sir."

I said, "What took you so long?"

Gun Bunny planted us in a cloud of dust and flying debris two hundred yards from the listening post, and the five-man strike team moved as one. We closed the distance on the structure in less than thirty seconds, and Kodiak pressed a shaped charge against the first exterior door.

While waiting the three seconds for the charge to blow the door open, I wondered if Celeste was making any progress pretending to be me pretending to be Clark, and I wondered why the cryptographer thought I was Clark.

The small explosive charge sliced through the heavy metal door, and Kodiak yanked it outward. Hunter was first through the smoke with his rifle at high ready. Gator was on his heels and turning left. I followed and broke right with Hunter while Mongo turned left behind me. The first interior room was empty, so there were no shots fired, but blowing the door announced our presence. It wasn't a surprise attack anymore.

Hunter twisted the knob on the first door inside, and it didn't budge, but the heel of his boot did the trick. The door bounced against the wall behind it, and we poured through like liquid hell, rifles shouldered and unstoppable. A man from the left corner raised a pistol, but two 300 blackout rounds pierced his chest, and a third burrowed through the cartilage of his nose before his trigger finger could react.

"Clear!" Hunter said as we pushed through the room and into a narrow corridor.

The fatal funnel of the hallway was the last place any of us wanted to be, so we cleared the space and split into two teams. Hunter and

THE SHEPHERD'S CHASE · 139

Gator charged through the first door on the right while Mongo, Kodiak, and I forced our way into the room on the left.

The *hiss-thud* of silenced rifle fire from the room behind us said Hunter and Gator pushed through more human obstacles, but the scene in front of me was something I could've never imagined.

Near the back wall, Anya was on bent knees with her ankles and wrists taped to a chair. The wooden chair attached to her back cut side to side through the air like something out of a cartoon. She had a man's forearm in her mouth like a ravenous dog, shaking and yanking with every ounce of strength she had. In the man's hand, a pistol shook violently, and with his other hand, he delivered blow after blow to the back of Anya's head and neck with a closed fist.

I put two in his left ear, and the concussion sent him crashing into the wall. Continuing to clear my sector of the room, I swung my muzzle to the left to see Mongo deliver a thunderous punch to a man's face, dropping him almost as efficiently as my rifle.

Kodiak called, "Clear," and I stepped toward Anya.

She spun, violently slamming the chair into the wall in a desperate attempt to free herself from her binding, but the seat was stronger than she anticipated.

I reached out to grab her but yanked my hand back before the wild animal inside her lashed out at me. Controlling the beast inside that killing machine wasn't possible, and calming her down after any engagement would be nearly as challenging.

"Anya, it's Chase. You're safe! Anya! Easy!"

She spun and looked up with the blood from her victim's arm staining her face. Her breath came hard, and her eyes were those of an enraged warrior deep in battle.

Finally, she slowed her breathing and leaned against the wall. "Cut me free, Chasechka."

I motioned for Kodiak to cut the tape binding her to the chair as Mongo and I continued clearing the building. We met Gator and Hunter in the next room, and we yanked our muzzles away from each other.

Hunter said, "Clear behind us, two bodies, but no Anya."

Mongo said, "Kodiak's got her in the room behind us. She's alive. We've got one unconscious bad guy and two bodies."

Hunter said, "We'll set security for the extraction."

I said, "When you get outside, send Disco and Singer in here to grab intel."

We backtracked to find Kodiak trying to get Anya to sit still long enough for him to triage her, but he was wasting his time.

Anya shoved him away when we walked in, then wiped her face with her sleeve. She pointed to the dead guy with extra ear holes. "He was in charge. His name was Berger. He was on telephone."

She pointed toward the man Mongo had sent to the ground. "He was Klein."

I said, "Not *was*. He still is Klein, and I've got a few questions for him."

"You are wrong, Chasechka. Marvin punches harder than rifle."

It had been years since I'd heard anyone call Mongo by his first name, "Marvin," and it caught me off guard.

"I guess so. Let's get this place packed up and get out of here before the *politsiya* show up. Grab everything that even looks like it has a hard drive."

We bagged equipment for three minutes before I realized no one in the CIC knew what was happening due to our radio silence.

I grabbed Anya's sat-phone from the floor and stuck it to my ear. "Is anybody there?"

"Is that you, Chase?"

I relaxed. "Yeah, Skipper, it's me. We're secure and collecting intel. We've got a pile of bodies, several sacks of hard drives, and one extremely angry Russian."

She said, "Get out of there! The police are seconds away."

We ran to the chopper as the wail of the local police sirens echoed through the air. We left them with a mess they'd never figure out and the vision of an American Huey's tail rotor.

Chapter 18
Stupid

My boots hit the deck before the skids of the Huey kissed the helipad, and I was on the bridge without asking permission before the rotors stopped turning. "Weigh the anchor and run!"

Most captains would've thrown me off the bridge and had me clasped in irons, but not Captain Sprayberry. He hit the intercom to the engine room. "Maximum continuous power, all engines, now!"

The ship hummed with energy as the junior officer of the deck weighed the anchor. "Off bottom, sir."

Fifteen seconds later, he said, "Anchor home, sir."

"Thank you, Mr. Adams. The captain has the helm. Recall the watch."

Mr. Adams pulled his radio from his belt. "Recall the watch. Aye, sir."

I initially lunged for the officer before he could push the radio button, but there was no one left ashore to listen or care what he had to say.

Soon, the bridge was full of officers and crew, and the captain surrendered the helm to a young seaman who'd spent far more time at the helm of the *Lori Danielle* than had the captain.

Once the full complement manned the bridge, Barry gave the order. "Fly the boat, Mr. Adams."

"Aye, Captain. Fly the boat." Adams turned and ordered, "Make ready to fly the boat."

The order was echoed by every crewman involved in the process of transforming the mild-mannered research vessel into a flying machine of unprecedented speed and capability.

The eyes of a seasoned warfighter and man of the sea met mine. "Guns, Mr. Fulton?"

"Aye, sir."

He didn't hesitate. His left hand flipped the hood from above the red switch, and seconds later, after the claxon sounded, he spoke into the mic. "All hands, this is the captain. Man battle stations. This is not a drill."

The ship rose from the water as the foils were deployed, and our speed doubled in less than a minute. Once established on the foils and all systems were running as designed, the captain pulled his radio. "Weps, Bridge."

"Go for Weps," came the prompt reply from the weapons officer.

The captain said, "Make ready all defensive capabilities for anti-missile, surface vessel, and air assets. This is not a drill."

Weps said, "Aye, sir. Make ready all defenses."

Barry set about a series of tasks I'd never understand over the coming minutes, but I fully understood the weapons officer when he said, "All defensive systems stand ready, sir. Radar-absorbing and active jamming is operational. Your ship is ready for war, sir."

With that, the captain turned to me and folded his arms across his chest. "All right, Mr. Fulton. Your boat is now a warship, and the crew is standing by for your orders."

Instead of the confident tone of a battle-hardened warrior, I sounded like a frightened child when I asked, "Where are we going?"

The captain was all business. "Away from the coast of Bulgaria. I don't know how many hornet's nests you kicked while you were ashore, but we're ready to fight them off if they swarm."

"Tell me about the Bulgarian Navy and Air Force," I said.

Barry sighed. "This sounds serious. They have fewer than fifty Russian MiGs refit to NATO standards. Fewer than half of those are airworthy, and even fewer qualified pilots exist in the country. The Navy consists of four frigates, three corvettes, five minesweepers, three fast missile craft, and two landing ships. Have you started World War Three, Mr. Fulton?"

"I don't think so, but why aren't we running for the Bosporus?"

He said, "Your orders were to run and gun. Neither is possible in the Bosporus. We're in open water, making"—he turned to the console and turned back—"sixty-one point five knots over the ground. You wanted to be away from the coast, so I put you away from the coast."

"Forgive my failure of high school world geography, but what's ahead of us?"

"The Kerch Strait and the Sea of Azov."

I suppose the blank expression on my face brought about his next lesson.

"The coast of Ukraine. If you have started a war, we can hide in the Port of Mariupol in a shipyard I know until it blows over. You're not the only one with friends in Eastern Europe."

"Let's hope it doesn't come to that."

Before I could continue, he slapped me in the face with, "Hope ain't a plan."

"May I see a chart?" I asked.

He spun on a heel and motioned toward the digital GPS chart plotter. "You know how to use one of those, don't you?"

I zoomed out and made some rapid measurements. "Can you initially lay off Sevastopol before we cross into the Sea of Azov?"

"I can do whatever you want," he said. "Just remember. When you're calling the shots, you're responsible for the ship, the crew, and everything that happens to both."

I took a step closer to my friend, who just so happened to also be the captain. "What would you do if you were calling the shots?"

He whispered, "If I were in command of this train wreck, I'd put us in the shipyard at Mariupol and report our position to Odessa, the UN, and the Pentagon. We can be high and dry in the shipyard in ten hours. That gives us a plausible alibi. No conventional ship on the planet can be in Mariupol ten hours after she was in the Bay of Burgas, kicking hornet's nests."

Having men of such experienced wisdom around me made my life so much better than I deserved. I said, "She's your ship, Captain. I'm going to go play grownup spy with my team."

He gave me a pat on the back. "You do that, Mr. Bond. We'll have martinis and Cubans before bedtime, and you can tell me all about your little shore excursion."

Inside the combat information center, Weps manned his station with a headset firmly covering his ears, and an array of laptops rested on the console with cables running in every direction. Skipper and Dr. Mankiller patrolled the array, never taking their eyes from the laptop screens.

"What's happening here?" I asked.

Without looking back at me, Skipper said, "We're crawling the hard drives you recovered for anything of value, especially anything mentioning a mass kidnapping. Why are we going east?"

I said, "We're running to Ukraine."

"Why?"

"Plausible deniability"

"Got it."

I asked, "Have you found anything interesting on the hard drives?"

"Oh, yeah," she said. "Tons of stuff, but so far, nothing about a kidnapping."

"You're listening for hostage-taking, not just kidnapping, right?"

She nodded, and I got the feeling I was an unwanted interruption. My suspicion was confirmed when Skipper said, "Why don't you go check on Anya? She's down in sick bay with Dr. Shadrack."

"Yeah, I guess I could do that if you don't need me up here."

She said, "You can go hang over the stern rail with a pistol in each hand for all I care. I'll find you if we come up with something important."

My first stop was back at the helipad and hangar deck, where I found

Singer and Gator, each in the prone position behind a .50-cal rifle covering overlapping fields of fire across the stern. "You guys are taking this battle station thing seriously."

Neither man looked up, but Gator said, "Yes, sir."

Inside the hangar bay, Barbie lay on her back beneath the Huey with a collection of tools lying around her.

"Is everything okay under there?"

"It will be," she said. "How's Anya?"

"I don't know. I've not been to sick bay yet."

She stopped what she was doing and glared up at me. "What?"

"I've been on the bridge with the captain and down in the CIC."

She screwed up her face. "You've done enough, Chase."

"What are you talking about?"

She slid from beneath the chopper. "I get it. You don't want anybody thinking you're going to run to Anya's bedside the instant something happens. That makes sense, but you've done enough to prove that's not what you're doing, so get your butt down to sick bay and make sure your soldier is all right."

I pointed beneath the Huey. "What's wrong under there?"

"I broke an antenna."

"How?"

"When we left Burgas, I clipped a few trees trying to put distance between us and whatever you did in that building."

"Nice work," I said. "I'll take a broken antenna over getting busted for storming a civilian facility in Bulgaria any day."

"I thought so. Now, go check on Anya . . . Chasechka."

On my way to sick bay, I found Hunter and Kodiak in the armory. "Is everything good in here?"

Kodiak said, "Oh, yeah. We're just doing some maintenance, cleaning, and repairs. How's Anya?"

"Why does everybody keep asking me that?"

Hunter glanced across his shoulder. "Because she's *your* responsibility and *our* teammate. We're worried about her. Aren't you?"

I ignored the question. "Are you guys good?"

"We're fine," Kodiak said. "Are we going to debrief the mission?"

"We'll make that happen when we're not at general quarters."

The hatch to sick bay was sealed, so I pulled the arm and stepped through, being careful to reseal it once inside. Anya was sitting on the edge of a bed with an IV in one arm and bandages on both hands, and the entire left side of her face looked like she was trying to hide a cantaloupe in her mouth. The other side of her head and face were bandaged. The portion of her face not hidden behind gauze and tape bore the bruises of unthinkable abuse at the hands of her captors.

I did my best to avoid grimacing. "Hey, there. How are you feeling?"

She mumbled something I couldn't understand, and I cocked my head.

She reached into her mouth and pulled out a wad of bloodstained gauze. "I feel stupid. This is how I feel. I made stupid mistake, and it was stupid."

I said, "I think we covered the stupid part. What's going on in your mouth?"

She held up the gauze. "Is broken and missing teeth."

"Broken and missing teeth?"

"Yes. I bit person trying to interrogate me, and I did not let go until you killed him. Thank you for that, but I was doing fine without you."

"If you call getting taped to a chair and breaking your teeth doing fine, I guess you were."

She tried to smile, and she was still beautiful, even beaten and broken. "Seriously, are you okay?"

"I have maybe broken fingers, and of course problem with teeth, but Dr. Shadrack is very good doctor. He will fix everything."

"I don't think he's a dentist."

She dabbed at her lips with the bloody gauze. "Yes, I suppose this is true, but maybe."

I said, "We recovered a few dozen hard drives from the listening post. Skipper and Dr. Mankiller are going through them now."

"Celeste is very good choice, yes?"

"She's fantastic. Thank you for recommending her."

"Of course. You are welcome. Is my way of making sure you have best of everything, even when I cannot be one of those best things for you, Chasechka."

I smiled and brushed a matted clump of blonde hair behind her shoulder. "I'm glad you're going to be okay."

"Thank you. Even when I do stupid thing and get captured, it feels nice working with you again and also team. Gator person is strong and smart. I was once in love with a young spy just like him, except you were cuter, even with tongue having stitches."

"You're the one who made those stitches necessary, if you remember."

"I remember everything, and I would do many things differently if I could go back to that time, but I cannot."

"What would you do differently?"

She tilted her head. "I would love you perfectly, and you would love also me with same perfection. You had money, and we could have become like dust on wind and lived in place where sun shines always and nobody tries to kill us."

"You think about that a lot, don't you."

She pressed her fingertips to her bruised face. "I do not look so pretty now, but then, I was perfect. This is what you said to me when you touched my face on sailboat when we were both young, and . . . I do not know word for this.

"The word is *stupid*."

Chapter 19
It's All a Dream

Sometimes it's possible to trace a situation back to the singular decision that precipitated the condition. I had the perfect life: a brilliant and beautiful wife, a wonderful home, friends who qualified as family, and a job I was born to do. I wouldn't have changed anything about my life, even if I could have, but it's impossible to entirely dismiss what might've been.

The woman sitting on the edge of the hospital bed, three decks beneath my feet, had been one of the most important elements in my young career as an operative, and from her, I learned lessons that would keep me alive for years to come. I also learned some people leave indelible marks on parts of us that refuse to lay dormant and silent. Sometimes, those marks come alive and carry the wayward mind back to a time of blissful ignorance and willful disregard for the looming reality. Anastasia Robertovna Burinkova would forever be one of those marks, and if the things she said were true, I'd left a similar stain on her.

Too many decisions of enormous weight lay in my future for me to let Anya or anyone else occupy my mind. I was running from a fight that may not have existed, or perhaps I'd fired the opening volley of the greatest war the Earth had ever seen. Only time and radar images would tell.

Two brilliant minds worked tirelessly in the CIC to sift through mountains of information in search of a speck of intelligence foretelling a situation that may never have come to be, but if the chance for us to prevent the atrocity arose, I'd much rather drip an ounce of prevention on the problem than a steaming pile of cure. If any team on the planet could isolate that speck buried beneath the mountain, Skipper and Celeste were the ones, and I couldn't think of anyone I'd prefer to have on the project.

I shucked off my boots and lay back on my bunk with my clothes still on, but before sleep could take me, someone knocked on my cabin door. "Come in."

The hatch swung inward, and Captain Sprayberry leaned through the opening with a bottle in his hand. "It ain't martinis, Double-Oh-Seven, but it'll have to do."

I'd forgotten the captain's plan to have martinis, Cubans, and story time, but I was happy to see him. "Give me a minute to get my boots back on."

I followed my friend down the corridor and onto the stern deck, where a pair of chairs waited for us. I motioned toward the seats, "You did all of this for me?"

He planted himself and said, "I had it done. It's good to be captain . . . most of the time."

I punched cigars while he poured old bourbon. We lit up and listened to the roar of the wind and waves passing the hull of the fastest ship of her size anywhere on any ocean.

A few minutes into our communion, Barry broke the silence. "So, are you going to tell me what you did back there that made it necessary for me to push my tub so hard?"

"We recovered a prisoner."

He took a sip and admired the whiskey inside his tumbler. "That doesn't sound like justification for all of this."

"That was sort of the *Reader's Digest* version. We blew our way into a secure facility, fired a few shots in anger, left a few stacked bodies, and ran home to Momma. That'd be you."

He took a measured draw from his cigar. "Those Cubans sure can grow a tobacco leaf, can't they?"

"Indeed, they can."

Several minutes of silence passed before he asked, "Were they military?"

"Nope."

"Bulgarian nationals?"

"Nope."

"Good guys?"

"Nope."

"Citizens of an allied country?"

"Yep."

"Justifiable?"

"We got Anya back."

Silence reclaimed the night until he said, "That girl sure has caused you some heartache over the years."

"Yep."

"Regrets?"

"Nope."

"I figured as much."

Captain Barry Sprayberry would always be a man of few words, but when the words came, they were rarely wasted.

When the Cubans became nubs and the bottle ran dry, the captain pushed himself from his chair. "Get some sleep, Chase. You've earned it."

Perhaps he was right. Sleep took me within minutes after my shower to wash the cigar smoke and gunpowder from my skin. Unfortunately, sleep couldn't defend me from my own analyst.

After what felt like mere seconds of slumber, Skipper came crashing through my cabin door. "Chase, get up! Remember that place Clark told us about? Culver Cove?"

I rolled over and tried to focus. "What?"

She flipped on the light, and I shielded my eyes. "You've gotta wake up. We found it."

Rubbing the sleep from my eyes, I sat up and dangled my one remaining foot over the edge of the bed. "Slow down. I had a few drinks with the captain, and I'm not ready for DEFCON One."

"Well, get ready," she said. "This thing could be huge."

I pulled on my prosthetic, a pair of pants, and a T-shirt I wasn't certain was clean. "Okay, give it to me."

She said, "Answer my question first."

"What question?"

"Do you remember Culver Cove?"

"Yeah, but only what Clark told us. I don't know any more than that. Why?"

"That could be where the mass hostage event is going to happen. The captured audio mentions something about a Midsummer Retreat, which is a Culver Cove thing. That sounds like an awfully inviting target for someone who wants a couple thousand hostages."

Sleep was suddenly the last thing on my mind. "Have you called Clark yet?"

"Not yet. I work for you, so you're always first."

I stepped into my boots. "Let's take this up to the CIC. Is anybody else awake?"

She led the way. "Just Celeste and me, as far as I know, but I didn't look for anybody else."

We stepped through the hatch and into the CIC, and Weps was still at his station with his headset now covering only one ear and the other cup positioned on top of his head.

I asked, "Are we still at general quarters?"

He looked up. "Affirmative."

"Is Captain Sprayberry still on watch?"

"He is."

I scanned the equipment in front of the weapons officer. "Is anybody chasing us?"

He studied several screens. "Negative."

"I think we can return to normal ops."

"That's not up to me. That order can only come from the captain."

"Let's get him on the horn."

Weps lifted a handset, and I stuck It to my face.

Barry's voice filled the receiver. "Bridge, Captain."

"Captain, it's Chase. Weps says nobody is pursuing us. I don't see any reason to remain at battle stations overnight."

He said, "It's not that simple, but I'll consider your recommendation."

"Thanks, Captain. We may have a break in the case. I'll let you know when I have something concrete."

"Thanks, Chase. Bridge out."

I handed the receiver back to Weps, and he continued doing whatever he was doing when we walked in. As much as I love the water and every ship that sailed, I'd never understand the working of a warship.

I dialed Singer's sat-phone, and he answered after three rings. "Yeah."

"It's Chase. Are you and Gator still on the helipad?"

"We are."

"I just spoke with Weps and the captain. Nobody appears to be chasing us, so I don't see any reason for you two to stay up there all night. You can get some rest."

He said, "If you're ordering us to stand down, we will, but if not, we'll stay here until the captain secures from general quarters."

"Of course," I said. "How's Sniper Junior holding up?"

Singer almost chuckled. "Solid."

I hung up and said, "Okay, Skipper. I'm all yours."

She stuck a headset in my hand. "First, listen to this."

"Can't you send it to my bone conduction device?"

Celeste said, "Sure. Here it comes."

She stepped around Skipper and hit a few keys, and the audio played inside my head. A few seconds into the audio, I waved a hand. "Cut it off. I don't speak whatever language that is."

Celeste stopped the audio. "It's Old Turkic, I think. It's the oldest form of the Turkish language. It died out in the fifteenth century."

"Do you speak it?" I asked.

She laughed. "No, but my computer speaks pretty much every language and dialect ever spoken . . . except Old Turkic."

"Hang on. I've got an idea." I rolled my chair back to the weapons station. "Can you get me the bridge again?"

Weps handed me the receiver. "Bridge, Captain."

"It's Chase again. Do you have any native Turkish speakers on board?"

"What kind of question is that?"

"It's classified."

He huffed. "I'll classify *you*. Why do you need a native Turk?"

"We're working on an intercepted transmission that's apparently in Old Turkic, and the computers aren't doing a very good job with translation. We could use some help."

"Can it wait until morning?"

"No, it can't."

He sighed. "In that case, wake up Ronda No-H and tell her what you need. She'll know."

"Thanks, Captain."

Weps spun in his seat. "May I make a suggestion?"

"Absolutely."

"Call the American Embassy in Ankara. That place is chock-full of native Turkish speakers."

I slapped him on the back. "It looks like you're good for something other than sinking ships."

He shrugged. "I do what I can."

Skipper had the American embassy overnight duty officer on the phone in seconds.

I said, "Sorry to bother you in the middle of the night, but my name is Supervisory Special Agent Chase Fulton with Treasury." I gave him my badge and ID numbers and said, "I'll wait while you verify me."

A series of clicks was followed by, "What can I do for you, SSA Fulton?"

"I need to speak with the station chief or his deputy. Can you make that happen?"

"Which one do you want, sir?"

"Wake up the chief."

"Stand by, sir."

I waited several minutes until a groggy voice came on the line. "Who is this?"

"This is SSA Fulton with Treasury. Are you the COS?"

He groaned. "What do you need, Agent?"

"I need a native Turkish speaker."

"My God, man! You woke me up because you need a native Turkish speaker in Turkey. What's wrong with you, Fulton?"

"That's Supervisory Special Agent Fulton, and I need a native speaker with a TSC."

"What's this about?" he demanded.

"This is about me speaking with a Turk with a clearance."

"Let me explain how this works, Fulton . . ."

I said, "I'm hanging up now, but go ahead and stay awake, Former Chief of Station. The Secretary of State will be the next voice you hear when your phone rings again in three minutes. If you want a pissing match, I'm not the guy you want to compete against."

"Like I'm supposed to believe some Treasury agent can—"

I disconnected and said, "Get me anybody from the Board."

My tone kept Skipper from asking questions, and I was connected with the same face who dispatched us on our mission.

I said, "I'm sorry to bother you in the middle of the night, but—"

He cut me off. "It's not the middle of the night, Chase. It's nine p.m. What can I do for you?"

"Oh, I guess it is. Sorry for interrupting your dinner, but I need the Secretary of State to call the chief of station in Ankara and tell him to give me whatever I want."

"Is that all?"

It may have been sarcasm from him, but I was tired, excited, and mad at a career CIA puke in Turkey. "Yes, sir. That's all I want. We have the threatening transmission, but we need help interpreting it. It's apparently in Old Turkic, and our computers can't translate it very well."

"In that case, stay by the phone, Chase. The COS will call you back any minute."

"Thank you, sir."

The line clicked, and less than three minutes later, the secure line rang, and Skipper said, "Op center." She listened for a few seconds. "He is. I'll ask him if he'll take your call."

She placed the line on hold and grinned at me. "How long are you going to make him wait?"

I said, "I could use a cup of coffee. How about you?"

She nodded. "Yeah, that'd be nice."

"I'll brew a pot."

I took my time measuring the grounds and pouring in the distilled water, and after sufficient time had passed, I picked up the phone. "Is that you, Chief?"

His tone carried a little more respect than it had five minutes earlier. "Dr. Fulton, I apologize for our misunderstanding—"

"*We* didn't have a misunderstanding. *You* had a misunderstanding. Where's my native speaker?"

The next voice on the line was undeniably Turkish. We exchanged pleasantries, established his clearance level, and played the audio for him.

"Play it again," he said.

We did, and after three more times through the audio, he said, "I cannot be certain, but I believe he is saying something like *target selection* or *target choice* and *midsummer retreat*. The verb is uncertain, but the phrase after the word *retreat* definitely means *proceed as planned* or *proceed with plan*. It doesn't directly translate into English, but this is my interpretation. Does what I have told you make sense?"

"Perfect sense, sir. I can't thank you enough. If you'll tell me who you work for, I'll see that your chain of command knows how helpful you've been."

He laughed. "This is not necessary. My chain of command has only one link above me. I am the Turkish vice president."

"In that case, sir, please take down my contact number. I am a man of enormous resources and capabilities in many unconventional areas. If you ever have a need for a man like me, I owe you a favor."

"Your reach is apparent, sir, and I will definitely keep your number somewhere safe. I must ask you . . . Do you know of an event in Burgas, Bulgaria, in the past few hours that left five or six men dead and the offices of an international organization ransacked?"

I said, "Bulgaria is in a state of revolution, if I'm not mistaken, and true revolution always spills blood, Mr. Vice President."

"Indeed, sir. If there's nothing else, I bid you good night."

"And good night to you, as well."

I dropped the receiver on the counter. "That was the vice president of Turkey."

"Yeah, I know. I heard. How did you and I end up in the middle of the Black Sea, talking to the vice president of Turkey, in the middle of the night? Sometimes, I still think of us as a cocky baseball player and a nerdy teenager."

"I know. Sometimes, I wonder if I'm going to wake up and it will all have been a dream."

She grinned. "If you could snap your fingers and make that so, would you?"

"Not a chance. If this is a dream, please let me sleep."

Chapter 20
Marching Orders

I checked the time. "Do you think Clark's still awake?"

Skipper said, "Who knows? But I know how to find out."

He answered on the fourth ring. "Please tell me you've got good news."

"Good evening, boss. I hope we didn't wake you. I've got a lot to tell you, and as a whole, it qualifies as good."

"Start with the bad," he said.

"We killed at least five people in Bulgaria."

"Good guys or bad guys?"

"The guys who took Anya."

"I thought I told you to start with the bad news."

"That is the bad news."

"You look at the world all wrong, College Boy. Anytime bad guys get dead, that's good news. So, let's hear the better news."

"We captured a bagful of hard drives from the listening post, and the big-brained folks found the proverbial needle in the haystack."

He said, "There's no story about needles and haystacks in Proverbs. You need to spend more time listening to Singer. Tell me about this non-proverbial needle."

"I jumped the chain of command and went straight to the Board when I needed a little help convincing the chief of station at the embassy in Ankara to find me a native Turkish speaker, so we might get a little blowback from that."

"I know all about that," he said. "And you did the right thing. Keep talking."

"We're confident the potential hostage-takers are planning to hit the Midsummer Retreat of Culver Cove."

The question I expected didn't come. He asked, "Who are the hitters?"

"We don't know that one yet, but we've got plenty of time to figure it out. The retreat isn't until July."

"Are the brainiacs still listening to the hard drives?"

Skipper shook her head, and I said, "No, they pulled off for now, but we'll get back on it when things settle down."

As if on cue, the shipboard intercom came to life. "All hands, now hear this. This is the captain. Secure from general quarters. Secure from general quarters."

"What was that?" Clark asked.

"That was the sound of things settling down. We were on the run just in case we stirred up enough trouble in Bulgaria to get our pictures on a wanted poster, but it looks like the coast is clear."

"Does that mean you're heading west?"

"Not yet," I said. "We'll have a staff meeting after breakfast—it's still the middle of the night over here—and we'll create a plan. I think we need to get back on the hard drives and glean everything we can from them."

Clark clicked his tongue against his teeth. "There's going to be some fallout from what you did in Bulgaria."

"I know. I hope the Board can protect us from the falling debris."

"They will if they can, but we need to get you out of that part of the world as soon as possible."

I said, "The captain is heading for a shipyard in Mariupol, Ukraine, on the Sea of Azov."

Clark's clicking continued. "I don't hate that idea. Does the ship need any repairs or upgrades?"

"You'd have to talk to the captain about that, but I'm not

sure I want an Eastern European shipyard snooping around on our boat."

"You've got a point there. Let's get you home. Are you on the foils?"

"Yes, we were running hard."

"I recommend coming off the foils and loitering in the middle of the Black Sea for a few hours while we decide what to do. I may want you on an airplane, but we'll make that call tomorrow. Do you have anything else for me?"

"No, that's it. We'll get some rest and get back on the audio. Do you want in on the a.m. meeting?"

"Negative. I plan to be sound asleep as soon as you hang up."

"All right, Sleeping Beauty. We'll talk tomorrow. Nighty-night."

"Oh, that's cute," he said, and the connection closed.

I turned to the analyst. "It's time for you and Celeste to get some sleep. You've been at it for two days."

Skipper stood and moved to a recessed panel beside her console. "Check this out."

With the turn of a knob, the panel swung open, revealing a small compartment with a single bed, chair, small table, and a refrigerator.

She said, "It's my home away from home when I'm away from my home home."

"Home home? That's interesting. I like it. So, this is where you're sleeping when we're on a mission?"

"Yeah. Since we moved the CIC up here, it's too far from my cabin. I want to be right here by the equipment if I need to go to work in a hurry."

"Don't work yourself to death," I said. "You're too important to us for you to burn out."

She smiled up at me. "Practice what you preach, College Boy."

* * *

Breakfast came and went, and the team gathered in the CIC. My body wasn't finished sleeping, but duty called, so I went to work.

"Good morning, everybody. I hope you got plenty of rest. We had some good news overnight. First, nobody's chasing us, so we stopped running. Second, Celeste and Skipper found the missing link. We know the hostage-takers plan to hit the Midsummer Retreat of Culver Cove in Oregon in July."

"July?" Hunter said. "If you're telling me we got ahead of a terror group by two months, we'll cut them off at the knees long before they become a problem for anybody."

I grimaced. "Yes, we're ahead by two months, but the kicker is, we don't know who the terror group is. We only know that they plan to hit Culver Cove and that their transmissions are in Old Turkic, an ancient form of Turkish."

The look on Mongo's face said he was instantly intrigued. "Old Turkic? We have audio spoken in Old Turkic?"

"Yes, it's a short burst, but we have it. Why?"

"I've got to hear it. That's a language that hasn't been spoken since the fifteenth century."

"How do you know this stuff?" Hunter asked.

He said, "I read, you knuckle-dragger. You should give it a try."

Hunter groaned. "I struggle with big words, so I'll stick to my coloring books if I can get Gator to stop eating my crayons."

Gator threw up his hands. "How did I get dragged into this? I was minding my own business, ashamed that I didn't know what Old Turkic was, and you just had to pounce on me."

"Okay, that's enough," I said. "We'll wrestle when this is over. As you can see, we've got a guest with us this morning. Captain Sprayberry has the same clearance as the rest of us, and as far as I'm concerned, he has the need to know for what we're going to discuss. Does anyone have anything critical before we get started?"

Heads shook, so I kicked off the important stuff. "First, Clark wants us back on American soil. We're less vulnerable at Bonaventure than on the ship. No offense to your ship, Captain, but dry land is generally safer than steel at sea."

Captain Sprayberry said, "Do you have Sea-Whiz and anti-ship missile capability at Bonaventure?"

"Maybe we should stick with the boat. Anyway, Clark will make that call later this afternoon after the sun comes up in Miami. We may pick a friendly port and fly home. We'll see, but have your gear packed in case we have to beat a hasty retreat."

Skipper said, "I'll take it from here for a couple of points."

I surrendered the floor.

She said, "We've had the computers sifting through the audio all night, and we haven't found anything else relating to the planned hostage-taking event. We'll keep trying, but what we have may be all we get. We have to be prepared to move on that tiny morsel of intel, so here's what I expect to happen in the next seventy-two to ninety-six hours. The Agency will likely figure out that we have the hard drives, and they'll make a grab for them. By the time that happens, I will have backed up every word, click, tick, and scrape of audio on those drives, so we'll continue to have them at our disposal, even after we turn over the hardware. What we don't want to see is the CIA take over the case."

Kodiak jumped in. "If it's a domestic attack, the CIA doesn't have jurisdiction. It'll have to be the FBI Counterterrorism Unit on American soil."

Skipper said, "Didn't somebody brief you on the penalty for interrupting one of my briefings?"

He said, "No, but I might like it."

"Trust me, you won't. Now, after that brief interruption, here's the rest. The CIA will likely grab the case and work on it as an international threat and pursue whoever they guess the bad guys are. I don't want that to happen. All that does is let the real terrorists know we've got a bloodhound sniffing their trail."

"How can we keep that from happening?" I asked.

"Now, you're interrupting. *My* recommendation is to turn over all of the hard drives we put in the box."

I raised an eyebrow. "Are you talking about knowingly withholding information about a credible terrorist threat from the CIA?"

"Absolutely not. I'm suggesting that we report our acquisition to our handler and follow his direction concerning the acquired intelligence."

She looked at me as if expecting another interruption, but I didn't meet her expectation. Instead, I gave her a wink, and she continued.

"Now, let's talk about the dissemination of what we've learned. I believe we have a responsibility to notify the management of Culver Cove." She paused and then said, "I see a lot of heads nodding, so you must agree. The problem is, we don't know who to notify. There's a shroud of secrecy around Culver Cove, and believe it or not, I can't break in. Whoever does their security is better than me."

Mongo said, "I doubt it."

"So far, it's true," she said. "No matter how hard I dig, I can't get in."

He said, "It's likely there's nothing available electronically on them. If they don't use computers, they can't be hacked."

Skipper's jaw dropped. "I-I mean . . . Who doesn't use computers?"

Mongo said, "People who want to be one hundred percent hack-proof."

Skipper stood in utter silence for half a minute, so I reclaimed the floor.

"So, here's what's going to happen for the next several hours. We're going to drill holes in the Black Sea while we wait for official word from Clark and the Board. If you've got training to do, do it. If you've got equipment maintenance to do, do it. If you need to catch up on your reading—or your coloring, in Hunter's case—do it. If you need me, write down what you need, and I'll come find you after I find the missing three hours of sleep I didn't get last night."

* * *

Sleep refused my invitation and left me standing on the doorstep ringing the bell, so I did what insomniacs all over the world have done for centuries: I went to work. At least my brain went to work. There's always been something magical to me about overlooking the ocean, so I parked myself on the stern deck by the RHIB cradle and listened to the water as the *Lori Danielle* cruised on the docile surface.

What kind of people become members of a club such as Culver Cove, and how can I stick my nose in the door and get a peek?

That thought churned through my mind just like the waters of the Black Sea through the ship's propulsion Azipods. With the vessel and my team in a holding pattern, my thoughts and our floating temporary home made exactly the same progress: none.

Everyone runs home when the rest of the world fails them, and that home is rarely an address. For me, home was Penny, my loving wife, so I dialed the phone.

"Hey! How's it going? Is everything all right? Where are you?"

I couldn't help but smile. The familiarity of her rapid-fire questions felt like a warm blanket. "It's not going anywhere at the moment. We're stalled while the important people above us make the next set of decisions. Things are okay. Anya got hurt pretty badly, but we pulled her out of the fire, and Dr. Shadrack's taking good care of her."

Penny said, "She can always count on you to rescue her when she finds herself in over her head."

That stung a little, but I let it pass. "We're in the Black Sea, but we won't be here for long. We'll have a new set of orders before the end of the day, and we'll likely be back in the States shortly thereafter."

"Does back in the States mean home?"

"At least temporarily. We may even have a couple of months before this thing turns into anything dangerous."

"That would be something new. Every mission you've been on since I've known you has been time-critical."

"There's a first time for everything, I guess. Hey, something just came to me. Have you ever heard of Culver Cove?"

"Yeah, of course. Why?"

"So you know about it, really? Do you know anybody who's a member?"

"Probably, but again, why?"

"Have I told you lately how glad I am to have you?"

She said, "If you hadn't, I'd remind you, but seriously, why do you need to know about Culver Cove?"

"It's part of this mission. In fact, it's at the center of it. Do you think you can get me a face-to-face with an active member?"

"I can ask around."

"Can you keep it close to the vest at first? It would be best if you only asked people you know and trust."

She let out a guffaw. "Yeah, right. How many Hollywood types do you trust? I know what you mean, though, so I'll keep the grapevine short."

"Thank you," I said. "Now, how's the murder investigation going?"

She sighed. "Frustrating, but you wouldn't believe the access the police chief has given me. It's like I'm Tony's detective partner. I keep thinking they're going to give me a badge."

"Handcuffs, too?"

"Stop it, dirty boy. Just come home, would you?"

"I'll be there soon. I'll let you know as soon as we get our marching orders."

"Okay. Tell Anya I hope she gets better soon but looks like a troll when the ordeal is over."

Chapter 21
What Might Have Been

My sat-phone buzzed, and I looked down to see "CIC, now!"

Apparently, I wasn't the only one to receive the message because the whole team filed in with me and we took our seats.

Skipper checked the time and said, "The Board—the whole Board —wants a meeting in three minutes."

I asked, "Do you know any details?"

She shook her head. "None, but Clark says it has to be important. They specifically directed that all personnel involved in the mission be present."

"Bring Clark up."

In a flash, Clark showed up on the number-one monitor. He said, "That was quick. How's everybody doing?"

"We don't have time for that," I said. "What's this about?"

He re-situated himself in his seat. "I don't know, but it must be something big. The only reason I can think of that they'd want every-body involved is a carefully worded briefing. They apparently don't want to take the risk of any detail getting screwed up if we pass down the briefing individually."

"That makes sense," I said. "But are you guessing?"

"I am, but what else could it be?"

Skipper cleared her throat. "It's time, boys."

I leaned back. "Let's do it."

The second monitor filled with a wide-angle shot of seven somber faces, but only one of them was looking directly into the camera.

The same gentleman who launched us on the mission took the floor. "Good morning. Let's get right to it. Ms. Woodley, if you would, please confirm we are live and secure."

Skipper said, "The connection is live, secure, and clean."

"We show the same. Thank you. First, allow me, on behalf of the full Board, to congratulate you on the exceptional work you've performed so far. Mr. Johnson provided a full briefing, and we couldn't be happier with the progress."

As much as I didn't want to interrupt him, my gut wouldn't let me sit in silence. "Excuse me, sir, but are you fully aware of the details of the intelligence-gathering operation in Bulgaria?"

He put on a face of annoyance. "We know more about what happened in Burgas than you do, Dr. Fulton, and we have every confidence that your actions were not only necessary, but also the only viable option given the circumstances. I extend the wishes of the Board for the speedy recovery of your injured operator. Now, may I continue?"

"I apologize. I was simply—"

"Thank you for being forthcoming," he said. "It's now time for phase two of the mission. As you may well assume, we have connections worldwide that allow us to dangle our influence inside a great many organizations. Culver Cove, unfortunately, may not be on that list. We're still exploring options, but I'm confident we will find a way to make the organization aware of the potential threat against its assembly."

That spike in my stomach repeated its previous assault. "I apologize again for interrupting, but I may have a contact inside the Culver Cove organization."

Silence filled the room, and every face from the Board turned immediately to the camera.

The spokesman said, "And who is this contact?"

"I don't have a name yet, but I should have it within twenty-four hours."

"And just how do you plan to obtain the name of this contact?"

I gave him my best Clark Johnson half grin. "I'm certain you remember when you dispatched us on this mission and didn't ask how we planned to execute it. With that same degree of confidence and plausible deniability, I ask that you extend the same courtesy to the next phase of the operation."

"In that case, Dr. Fulton, I have only one question. Do you plan to stack any more bodies, and if so, will those bodies fall on American soil?"

"No, sir, I do not plan to shed any more blood in this phase of the operation, but I can't make the same promise for phase three."

"Very well," he said. "In that case, we shall continue our efforts while you continue yours, and we'll see who grabs the brass ring first."

I gave him a silent nod and a continuation of the Johnson-esque expression of confidence.

"With that behind us," he continued, "the reason we required the attendance of everyone involved in this operation is this. We're dipping our toes into unfamiliar waters on this one, and it's crucial that everyone understand the severity of the fallout should we fail on this new ground."

He paused, seemingly in search of his next line, or perhaps the courage to deliver it. "It appears this potential hostage situation is planned within the continental U.S., with the majority of the hostages likely being Americans. As all of you know, we do not exist. We don't have the freedom to present a public presence inside the United States, and if you or any other operational team mentions this Board, or any of its members, following any operation inside the United States, there will be no evidence found of our existence."

"Are you saying we're not going to deploy if this thing develops in the States?" I asked.

He said, "No, that's not what I'm saying. We'll do everything in our power to prevent this situation from coming to fruition. That has to be our primary goal, and we're open to ideas about how to accomplish that feat."

"This is all starting to sound a little cryptic to me, so I want to make sure I understand our marching orders. You want us to find a way to notify the Culver Cove organization of a credible threat against their little kumbaya hand-holding party in the woods while you and your associates pretend not to exist."

He glanced back at the other members of the Board and then back at the camera. "That is phase two in a nutshell, and we're pleased that you understand."

With that, the screen went black, and we were left sitting in silence in a secure room aboard a ship that didn't exist in the middle of the Black Sea with no justification for being there.

I turned to face my expanded team, but I had no idea what to say.

Mongo, as usual, rescued me. "Who is your contact inside Culver Cove?"

"It's a second-hand contact, at best. In case you don't know who and what the Culver Cove Club is, let me give you a little history lesson." I took a drink of my coffee and continued. "The club was founded in the late eighteen hundreds by a bunch of entertainment types—musicians, poets, playwrights, and actors. They wanted a place they could go and be as weird as they wanted without fear of public ridicule. Thus, the Culver Cove Club was birthed in—where else?— Culver Cove, Oregon. At the time, Culver Cove was a small town with a railroad station, and it was far enough away from California for these hippies and avant-garde dudes to misbehave without risking being discovered doing so in and around Hollywood."

Hunter scowled. "So, that's what this club is? A bunch of Hollywood types who want to dance naked around a campfire?"

"That's what it *used* to be," I said. "It's grown and morphed into quite a bit more in its hundred-fifty-year existence. It was once made up of a few liberal-arts types from the entertainment industry, but the lion's share of the membership seems to now be world leaders, former high-ranking military officers, congressmen, senators, princes, tzars, and the like."

Hunter's expression didn't change. "And what makes you think you've got an in with this crowd? Are you a member?"

I laughed. "Not hardly, but I happen to be married to a modern-day playwright who lives in that world. Even though it's the ultimate boys' club, she likely knows people who are members. If she can get just one of them to have a rational conversation with us, we might be able to crush this whole hostage thing long before it would've happened."

Hunter shot his eyes to Clark, whose face still loomed on the monitor. "Is that cool? To bring civilians into this thing?"

Clark played with his toothpick. "I'm not sure we have any other choice in this case."

Hunter's attention fell back on me. "You said something about retired high-ranking military officers being part of this little treehouse gang. Is that a possible access point?"

I said, "If we knew who they were, sure, but we can't start calling every retired general we can think of and asking if he knows the secret handshake."

Hunter finally leaned back in his chair. "What do these guys do out there in the woods?"

"There's a lot of supposition floating around, but not much hard data. It's kind of like the Masons or Skull and Bones. Everybody likes to believe they know what goes on, but unless you're in the clique, you don't have a clue. Being shrouded in mystery seems to be part of the draw of clubs like Culver Cove."

He shook his head. "Every day, I'm more thankful to be a tiny little nobody who nobody knows."

"Me, too," I said. "And I hope I always get to stay that way."

Gator appeared to have been waiting for his turn to talk, so when the opportunity opened up, he asked, "So, what's next?"

I looked up at Clark on the monitor.

He made a show of taking in a long, deep breath and letting it slowly leave his lips. "Come home, College Boy, and bring that big boat of yours with you. Keep me posted on what Penny learns."

"We're on our way," I said.

But before I could have Skipper disconnect the line, Clark held up a finger. "One more thing. Make sure Anya's all right."

"What's that supposed to—"

Before I could finish my accusatory question, a light on Skipper's panel illuminated, and she turned to a small screen beside the light. Anya's face appeared, and Skipper looked at me.

"Let her in," I said.

Our analyst pressed the combination of keys that unlatched the door to the CIC, and our Russian came through the door, but I couldn't believe my eyes.

I leapt to my feet. "Anya, are you okay?"

She bowed her head and rolled herself forward in the lightweight wheelchair from Dr. Shadrack's sick bay. "No, Chasechka, I am not okay. This is why I am here. I do not want to interrupt your briefing. I received also message to come to meeting, but I could not."

"What's with the wheelchair?"

She maneuvered herself closer to the team. "I am ashamed, and I have come to make to all of you apology."

"What are you talking about?" I said. "You don't owe any of us an apology."

"This is not true. I made foolish mistakes and became prisoner who had to be rescued. I put all of you in danger and could have gotten you killed with my stupidity. You should not have to rescue me. For this, I am very sorry."

To my surprise, Hunter was first to speak up. "You've got no reason to be sorry. You're part of the team, and we'd wade through Hell and half of Siberia to go get anybody on this team. You're no exception."

I'd never seen her so humble, and it almost broke my heart. "Anya, hold your head up. You've got nothing to be ashamed of. All of us have been nabbed. Some thugs stuck me in the trunk of a car and took me for a joyride on I-Ninety-Five. You're not above making mistakes."

She didn't raise her head. "Is not same thing. You are team operator. I am one-person assassin. Is okay for you and any of team to make this mistake, but is not okay for me. I am ashamed, and I am very sorry."

Dr. Mankiller stood from her perch. "If the briefing is over, could Anya and I have a moment?"

Skipper motioned toward her small cabin off the CIC. "You can use my room."

The tech guru and our favorite Russian made their exit, leaving the CIC in silence and me lost in curiosity. Sincerity from Anya had been a rare commodity in the fifteen years I'd known her. There was far more to her performance than an authentic apology. She'd never played the pity card with me, but the rational analysis from a psychological standpoint could lead to no other conclusion.

I wheeled my way beside Skipper. "Is your room wired for sound?"

She stared at the door and shook her head. "No, and you should be ashamed for asking. Okay, *we* should be ashamed for thinking it, but I'd love to know what's going on in there."

"Me, too."

She whispered, "Maybe I'll bug the whole ship."

I winked. "Maybe you should, but stay out of my cabin."

She gave me an evil grin. "What makes you think yours isn't already bugged?"

Mongo took a knee beside us. "We're going to give you the room. Make sure Anya's all right. There's more going on than just shame."

I nodded, and Skipper said, "This is going to sound wrong coming from me, but if Celeste can't do it, you have to do something to make her all right. You're the only one she's got left."

"You're right," I said. "That does sound bizarre coming from you."

She shrugged. "She's a snake, but she's obviously hurting."

Skipper and the team cleared out, leaving me alone in the oversized CIC and praying Dr. Mankiller was a better psychologist than I was. Singer taught me that sometimes prayers are answered with no, and this one fell solidly into that category.

Celeste and Anya came from Skipper's room, and Celeste kept walking.

I planted myself in a seat beside the Russian and leaned in. "Listen to me, Anya. Everything inside me wants to tell you that what happened couldn't be avoided, and we all understand, but that's not how this is going to go. I'm responsible for the team first, and at least for this mission, you're part of that team. I want to know what happened out there."

I didn't believe tears would fall from her eyes. She had far too much self-control to allow that to happen, but her trembling lip told a different story.

She stilled herself. "I was angry."

"Of course you were. Any of us would've been, but that doesn't explain how you got taken."

She barely nodded. "I wasn't focused on mission. I was thinking of something else. I was thinking of you, Chasechka."

She let that hang in the air between us for what might have been centuries before saying, "I was trained to seduce anyone. This is work of Russian sparrow. For me, this is always easy, but not this time. I was going to smile and tilt head only small bit. I was going to touch his arm and lean close when he talked. I was going to play with my hair and do all things I was taught to do at that terrible place on bank of Volga River when I was only young girl."

Is this another attempt at soliciting sympathy and drawing me in?

I said, "One of the truest statements about what we do is that operators rarely rise to the occasion. They most often fall to their highest level of training. That's what you were doing . . . reverting to your training. That's what allows us to accomplish our mission without getting dead."

For the first time, she raised her eyes to meet mine. "No, this is not what happened. I could only think of how it felt when I did these things to you. I did not have to pretend with you, and I do not want to pretend ever again with anyone. I am no longer this person who can do these things."

I swallowed the lump in my throat. "Anya, I shouldn't have asked you to do that. It was . . ."

She wrapped her hands around mine. "Is okay, Chasechka. You could not know if even I did not know. I am . . ."

She paused as if struggling to keep her voice from cracking, so I said, "Human. You are a person, Anya. A beautiful person whose life has been chaos poured over smoldering horror from the time you were an innocent child. I don't have the words to tell you how much I love seeing this humanity in you. The baseball player and the ballerina, both living lives that should've never been theirs. What a pair we make."

The tear I never believed would fall did, and she didn't try to stop it. "What a pair we could have been."

Chapter 22

Homeward Bound

I believed the conversation and counseling session with Anya was finished, but oh how wrong I was.

She closed her eyes, seemed to gather her thoughts, and said, "I was once the girl lion."

What on earth is she talking about?

There's one unbreakable rule shared by psychologists the world over: Never interrupt a patient. Just let them talk. And talk is exactly what Anya did.

The longer she spoke, the cleaner her English became, and I'll always believe a transformation happened before my eyes, on that day in the middle of the Black Sea, when Anastasia Robertovna Burinkova poured out her heart into my hands.

"There was time when I could kill anything I wanted to feed the lions lying in shade on edge of grassy savanna."

Grassy savanna?

"You know this of girl lions, yes? The boy lion lies beneath tree and waits for her to kill something for him to eat. I do not know English word for girl lion."

I whispered, "Lioness."

"Yes, yes. This is word, lioness. I was this for very long time, feeding my boy lion masters while they were lazy beneath trees. 'King of the jungle' they are called, but this is silly. Lions live only in plains of Africa—never inside jungle."

Oh, no. She's wandering off. Should I say something to get her back on course or just continue listening?

"Maybe this phrase, 'king of jungle,' is just like my life: is not true. Is only lie upon more lies until everyone believes. This is not how anyone's life should be. You know of Gwynn, yes?"

"Who?"

"Special Agent Gwynn Davis with Department of Justice. She is my friend, and maybe she is my only friend in all of world."

That stung a little, but I couldn't honestly say I'd been her friend. "Tell me about Gwynn."

Anya smiled for the first time. "She is beautiful person and exactly what I want to be. She is lawyer with gun."

"You want to be a lawyer?"

She squeezed my hand. "No, silly. I want to be American girl, just like Gwynn. She lives in New York City, and we are making one life together."

I furrowed my brow. "One life? What does that mean? Are you in some kind of relationship with her?"

"Do not be silly, Chasechka. Although I was taught to pretend to love women and men for purposes of espionage, this is not how my heart feels. Gwynn is friend only." She released my hands. "I must tell to you something, and it does not mean I am asking for anything from you. Is only something I need you to know."

At that point in my life, I should've been killed a dozen times or more. I'd been lost, blown up, cut, shot, stabbed, beaten, and nearly drowned, but none of that frightened me as much as sitting alone with Anya in the CIC and waiting for the next thing to fall from her lips.

"Chasechka, I have only love inside my heart for you and for no one else. This will always be true, and I will spend every day wishing you felt the same. I told to you that I loved you so many years ago, and that was maybe only thing in my life that was true back then. Do not be afraid, my Chasechka. I will never do anything to hurt you or Penny. But please know inside your heart that I will always be yours."

I sat in silence, staring into the smoky blue eyes that captivated me the first time I saw them, and I was even more lost for words in that moment than I had been fifteen years before. It was clear she didn't expect, or even want, an answer.

She leaned toward me, kissed my cheek, and brushed her badly swollen face against mine. "I will forever love you, Chasechka. And I'm never giving back your UGA sweatshirt."

One of the most serious conversations of my life ended with unbridled laughter from both of us until the joy of the laughter mixed with the pain of her wounds, and she gasped.

I stood and stepped behind her. "I'll take you back down to sick bay. I'm sure Dr. Shadrack wouldn't approve of you being up here like this."

She squeezed her stomach. "He does not know I am here. You will keep secret, yes?"

I rolled her through the doorway and into the corridor. "Forever."

With the good doctor's patient returned to her confinement, I walked away with Anya's confession ringing in my head. It must've shown on my face because Singer stopped in the corridor in front of me and did something so far out of character that I could hardly believe what was happening.

He grabbed two fistfuls of my shirt and shook me. "Whatever she stuck in your head, get it out."

The admonition from Hunter, Clark, or even Mongo wouldn't have been expected, but from Singer, it was astonishing.

I said, "Walk with me."

He released my shirt and stepped beside me. "Where are we headed?"

"To see the captain. But first, I want to talk with you."

"About Anya?"

I said, "No, not just Anya, but she's one of the things. Let's start with phases two and three of the mission. I'm waiting for Penny to make contact with somebody in the Culver Cove group. Maybe we'll get lucky and she'll have a contact we can talk with like real human beings."

"That'd be something new," he said. "In our business, we don't meet a lot of those."

"You couldn't be more right. Let's assume that happens. If we tell them what we know about the pending hostage situation, I would expect them to do one of two things."

He said, "Either cancel the assembly or hire some excellent security."

"Exactly," I said. "If the group is made up of the powerful people we suspect, I think we'll be dealing with some enormous egos and maybe even a heaping helping of disbelief. Sometimes the ultra-privileged have a false sense of security."

He grunted. "It could never happen to me."

"Exactly. Now, let's say they believe us and ask our opinion on who to hire as private security. What should we tell them?"

He scuffed his boot against the deck. "Not us."

"Definitely not us," I said. "We're not security. We're the guys you call when security has already failed."

He said, "I'm glad we agree."

"We almost always do. If they ask, we'll have to recommend one of the big private security firms. Anybody less than one of the big boys is likely to end up dead in a pile somewhere in the Oregon woods, and I don't need that on my conscience."

He said, "Agreed, but I'd go so far as to say that we don't have a recommendation. I don't want the responsibility."

"Same. So, that'll be our plan. If they ask, we'll say we don't have a recommendation other than canceling or rescheduling their little camping trip."

He slowed his pace. "Now, back to Anya. It's clear that she poured something pretty heavy on you. If you want to talk about it, I'm all ears, and it'll go no further."

"I know, and it's not what you're thinking. She just told me that she can't do the sparrow work she used to do. She said that's not who and what she is any longer."

He raised an eyebrow. "That's fantastic. It sounds like she's growing."

"That's what I wanted to talk with you about. She's coming to realize that she's a free human who can make her own choices and carve her own path. I see that as a very good thing. She's becoming more American, apparently by the day."

"There's nothing bad about any of that," he said.

"No, but think about the environment she grew up in. It was the Soviet Union and then Russia after the wall came down. She's never known freedom or had the ability to think for herself."

"I get it, but what does that have to do with you?"

"It has nothing to do with me, but I think it might be good for her soul if you spent a little time with her. She's probably an atheist because that's what she was taught to be. I'm sure she has a lot of questions, and having somebody like you to field those questions could be incredibly meaningful for her. I know it's a lot to ask, but if you're up for it, maybe you could visit with her in sick bay and talk to her about . . . things."

Singer said, "It'd be my pleasure to talk to her about God and the freedom that comes from loving Him *and* accepting the love He wants to give her."

It was my turn to scuff a boot against the steel deck. "Maybe you could start the conversation with something other than hellfire and brimstone."

He laid an arm across my shoulder. "How many sermons have you heard me deliver about fire and brimstone?"

"I don't remember any."

He said, "I learned a long time ago that people are a lot easier to love into Heaven than to scare out of Hell."

"You never cease to amaze me," I said. "I'm going to the bridge to get the captain to point this thing west. Are you coming with me?"

"No, I've got things to do, but when you're ready to talk about what Anya told you, I'm ready to listen."

"I told you . . ."

He dropped his chin. "You told me part of it, but you didn't tell me the part that put that look on your face. We've never lied to each other, Chase. Let's not start now."

I stopped in my tracks. "She told me that I'm the only person she never had to pretend to love, and she said she'd always love only me."

He sighed. "That's some heavy stuff, brother, but so is the commitment you made to Miss Penny. I know the man you are, and so do you. Don't reach for the shiny things the devil dangles in front of us. Cling to the solid rock God provided for us. I don't mean to sound arrogant, but I'm part of that rock He gave you, and so is Miss Penny. You're accountable to us, but most of all, you're accountable to Him. Now, go talk the captain into pointing us toward home, and then go do the same thing for yourself."

"What would I do without you?"

He gave me one of those big brother hugs everybody needs from time to time. "I hope you never have to find out."

Chapter 23

A Long Way from Red Square

Captain Sprayberry saw me coming toward the navigation bridge. "You don't need permission. Come on."

I followed him onto the bridge as the officer of the watch declared, "Captain's on the bridge."

"Carry on," Barry said. "You still have the bridge. I'm just passing through."

He poured me a cup of coffee and led me through the short passage to his cabin. "What's on your mind?"

I took my first sip. "That's better than the coffee in the mess downstairs."

He winked. "That's the captain's coffee. Now, what brings you all the way up here with the working folks?"

"Working folks, huh? I guess that means the rest of us are on a pleasure cruise."

"Something like that. Now, let me guess. You're ready to go home."

"You're good at this game. How do you feel about another trip through the Bosporus?"

He took another sip. "I'm okay with it, but you need to understand that unless it's a matter of survival, we're defenseless in the Bosporus Strait. We can't unmask and start shooting if the local authorities decide they want to detain us."

"Do you have any reason to believe they'd do that?"

He shrugged. "It all depends on how the Bulgarians are reacting to your little field trip ashore . . . and one other huge consideration."

I said, "From all accounts, the Bulgarians have their hands full of a revolution and aren't reacting at all, so I don't think there's anything to worry about from them. I think our heads are in the same place concerning the second consideration, though."

He peered over his glasses. "Ontrack Global Resources."

"Yep. They're not little fish. They've got global reach, just like their name implies, and they've got the resources to put up a pretty nasty fight if they want."

The captain drained his cup. "Want a refill?"

"No, thanks."

He poured himself a second cup and watched the steam rise from the black surface. "In open water, we can fight. We can outgun most navies on the planet, but inside the strait, we're a humble little research vessel with no plausible reason to have been anywhere near the Black Sea."

"That part is taken care of," I said. "Skipper and Dr. Mankiller can whip up any documents you need to justify our position almost any-where on Earth, so if you'll have somebody get with them, you'll have the docs you need."

"That's reassuring, but OGR won't be as easy to fool as the local authorities."

"Do you think they'd try anything in the confines of the strait?"

He said, "There's no way to know, but is your team prepared to deal with them if they decide to board us?" My grin answered his ques-tion, and he said, "I guess that settles it, then. We're heading home. All I need to know is which home."

"Make way for Bonaventure until our orders change."

He carried his coffee back through the short corridor and onto the bridge. "Captain has the bridge. Lay in a course for the Bosporus and point west. The *Lori Danielle* is heading home."

With contract documents in hand, we made twenty-four knots toward the mouth of the strait, and I briefed the team. "All right, gang. Here it is. We're heading home to prepare for what happens next with the possible hostage situation, but we may have another issue on our hands when we hit the Bosporus. The captain seems to think Ontrack Global Resources may retaliate for what we did to their facility and their men in Bulgaria. I can't say I'd blame them. If somebody hit us like that, we'd fight back, too. That's what we need to be ready for. We're going to stand armed watch until we're through the strait and into the Sea of Marmara. If they're going to hit us, that's the most likely place."

Hunter raised his head. "Do you really think they'll try to board an American-flagged vessel?"

I said, "Would you care what flag was flying over the folks who hit us if we were chasing them down?"

He groaned. "Good point. So, what are the ROEs?"

"The rules of engagement are simple," I said. "Defend your ship and her crew against all aggressors with all available means."

That brought smiles to every face in the room. Shooters shoot, and hitters hit, and that's exactly what the men and women in front of me were: straight shooters and hard hitters.

I turned to Singer. "Is anything broken?"

He pointed to his protégé with his chin. "He's the armorer now. Ask him."

"What about it, Gator?"

The new guy said, "All weapons aboard are serviceable, clean, and ready, sir."

"You're starting to sound like the sailors on the bridge with that *sir* stuff. Brothers don't call each other sir, and you've earned your stripes, brother."

He clearly wanted to smile but successfully suppressed it. "Thank you, sir. I mean . . ."

"Quit stuttering, and issue weapons. I want everybody carrying at least three hundred rifle rounds and a hundred fifty pistol rounds."

Hunter coughed. "Expecting a fight, are we?"

"I don't want one, but I'm not afraid of one."

The team sounded like barbarians with their grunts and guttural expressions of agreement.

"All right," I said. "For overwatch, I want whatever Singer thinks he'll need times two."

Singer nodded. "Did you hear that, Gator? The man said times two. That means two snipers, sniper."

Gator didn't make any effort to hide the coming smile. "Yes, sir."

I continued. "We'll be at the mouth of the Bosporus Strait in ten hours. Until then, I recommend getting some rest before we stand to battle stations."

"Now you're starting to sound like the sailors," Hunter said. "We shall be to quarters. Aye, sir."

"I'll quarter you. Get out of here. I've got important stuff to do."

He laughed. "Whatever you've got to do better not include one particular Russian who used to be pretty cute before she got her teeth yanked out and her face beat to a pulp."

"Speaking of our Russian," I said, "she's slowly improving, but her sparrow days are over. We won't be using her in that capacity again."

A hush fell over the CIC until Hunter said, "I was just kidding about her face. Is she going to be all right?"

I nodded and swallowed the lump in my throat. "Yeah, she'll be fine. She's finally learning how freedom feels."

Singer's expression said his talk with Anya had gone well, and that pleased me.

I said, "Okay, get out."

Everyone evacuated except the Baptist sniper. When the hatch closed, he said, "I won't be baptizing her anytime soon, but she's got a lot of excellent questions. And you were right. It turns out you were the first person to ever mention God to her fifteen years ago."

"Really? I don't remember that conversation. In fact, what she and I did back then wasn't exactly godly."

"Spare me the details," he said. "She's got a lot of healing to do, both inside and out, but she's a long way from Red Square, also both inside and out."

I pulled open a shade over one of the portholes in the CIC and stared out over the Black Sea. "I can't imagine the life she's had."

"Neither can I, but the part you're imagining is behind her now. She's an American, and she's got more going on than you know."

I turned from the porthole. "Oh?"

"Yep. She told me she's working with the DOJ out of DC, and she bought some kind of adventure-tourism company in Bonaire."

"Bonaire? What kind of company?"

"Apparently, it's dune buggies, helicopter rides, and dive trips for tourists."

I furrowed my brow. "What on Earth would make her buy a company like that?"

He tapped his index finger on the center of my chest. "You. She said you made her fall in love with the Caribbean, and that's where she's the happiest."

"Maybe she'll give us a job flying helos and leading dive trips when we retire."

"Maybe she will," he said. "While I've got you, I need to bring you up to speed on your boy."

"My boy?"

"Yeah, Gator. He's really taking to the gun side of our business. If he's not sleeping or eating, he's studying weapons manuals. I think we should send him to armorer's school when we get some downtime."

"How about his sniping?" I asked.

"He's a natural, and we're lucky to have him. When you don't need him kicking down doors, he's going to be a fine overwatch."

"I'm counting on it."

He left the CIC with a nod, and I turned back to the porthole. The room felt strange with one of the shades open. During classified briefings, the room had to be shielded from the outside world in every way possible, including transparent windows like the porthole. When prying eyes weren't a concern, there was no reason to leave the shades down, so I opened all eight of them and let the sunlight filter into the otherwise claustrophobic space. I couldn't stop thinking how the same thing was happening inside the mind and soul of the former Russian assassin lying on a hospital bed a few decks below. For the first time in her tortured life, she could see and feel the sunlight of freedom pouring into a space that had been dark, solitary, and barricaded against everything and everyone outside.

* * *

After a restless nap and a visit to the bridge, I made my way back to the CIC, where I found Skipper lost in a world of electronic information.

Without looking up, she said, "Oh, good. You're here. I picked up a piece of intel you probably want to know."

I parked myself in a chair beside her. "Let's hear it."

"Through means that *may* have been a little questionable, legally, I discovered some financial activity in Kavala."

I leaned in, but the look on my face apparently told the story.

She said, "You don't know where Kavala is, do you?" I shook my head, and she sighed. "It's a port city in Northern Greece on the Aegean Sea."

The atlas in my head did a reasonably good job, but I was pleased to see a map appear on Skipper's monitor.

"It's right here," she said.

The proximity of the city to our route was close enough to make me care about the money OGR spent at the edge of the sea.

"First, tell me about the money, and then tell me how you found it."

She said, "I'll do the first thing, but you don't want to know the second thing."

"I'll take it."

186 · CAP DANIELS

She said, "Just before sunup this morning, Ontrack Global Resources bought one point five million euros worth of MGD."

"What's wrong with that? We buy a lot more fuel than that when we top off the tanks for this ship."

She leaned back in her chair and crossed her arms. "Ontrack Global Resources doesn't own any ships."

"Oh. Now, I really care."

"Yeah, I thought you would. I also thought of the next question you're going to ask, and I wrote the answer on the back of that piece of paper." She pointed to a small scrap of plain white paper.

I lifted the paper and flipped it over to read "Green Alliance Cooperative."

"What's Green Alliance Cooperative?"

She said, "The answer to your other question, which would've been, whose ship did Ontrack Global Resources fuel up in Kavala?"

"Okay. You know me too well sometimes, but now I want to know who or what Green Alliance Cooperative is."

She pulled up a website. "And the answer is a huge, worldwide environmental activist group who spends a ton of money trying to stop commercial fishermen from killing whales and sharks in the Pacific Ocean."

"The Pacific?"

"Yep, you guessed it. They're a long way from home. There's plenty of commercial fishing in the Aegean, but not enough whales to justify the GAC having a ship in the area."

"Could it be innocent?" I asked.

She crossed her arms again. "Could we be a legitimate research vessel? Sure, but we're not."

"They're not going to hit us in the Bosporus, are they?"

She didn't change her position. "Probably not, but it sure looks like they've paid somebody to use their ship in the Aegean Sea at the same time we're going to be there. Coincidence? I think not."

"Do you have any idea how much it would cost to replace you?"

She huffed. "You'll never have enough money to pull that off."

"We're still going to stand ready through the strait, but I need your focus to be on that ship. What's her name?"

"The *Better World*," she said.

"Of course it is."

Chapter 24
Pilot Stuff

As I stepped onto the navigation bridge, I suddenly wished someone would call out, "Chase is on the bridge," but until I became captain, it wouldn't happen.

The sun was hanging low in the western sky, somewhere over Greece and Albania, as our bow slipped into the eastern mouth of the Bosporus Strait. The captain stood with a pair of binoculars pressed to his face and was scanning the ever-narrowing passage through Turkey.

Determined not to interrupt whatever Captain Sprayberry was doing, I leaned toward the oldest young person on the bridge—a thirty-ish woman with more decoration on her shoulder than anyone else in sight. "Why don't we have to use a pilot through the Bosporus?"

"We do," she said. "But only at night."

"It'll be night very soon, right?"

She smiled. "Yes, sir. It will be."

"So, when and where will the pilot come aboard?"

"To be honest, sir, I don't remember the last time he got off."

My confusion must've been obvious, so she chuckled and said, "Captain Sprayberry holds a pilot's license for the Bosporus Strait, among several other unique bodies of water around the world."

"I guess we should think about upping his salary, huh?"

She shrugged, but the captain said, "Yep, you should." He lowered the long eyes and said, "It looks like it's time to send out the crossing guards."

"They're already deployed," I said, "That's why I'm here. We're on channel six, and Skipper and I are also isolated on seven if you need only her or me. I'd appreciate a heads-up call on anything that doesn't smell right."

The captain said, "Nothing smells right in this part of the world, but we'll be sure to sound the alarm if we see anything we don't like, and we'll monitor six and seven from here, as well."

"May I assume the status of the ship is unchanged?"

He nodded. "She's shipshape, but we're limited to eight knots for our tonnage in the dark through the strait, so expect two hours for the passage."

"Thanks, Captain. We've got some new information that leads us to believe we may be more likely to be intercepted once we're in the Aegean than in the Bosporus."

He lowered his chin. "Do tell."

I explained the information Skipper discovered, and he said, "I agree with your assessment. It would be a death warrant to hit us in open water, though. If I were planning to board us, I'd do it at the exit of the Dardanelles Strait into the Aegean. That's where we'll be most vulnerable."

"Show me," I said.

He brought up the nautical chart and ran his finger down the narrow strait of water separating two chunks of the country of Turkey.

I asked, "Are you a pilot for the Dardanelles Strait?"

"No, but there's no requirement for a pilot unless we're an oil tanker in the dark."

"And what's the speed limit?"

He said, "Twelve knots in daytime and eight at night for our tonnage."

I studied the chart and ran the math in my head. "Can you put us at exit of the Dardanelles before noon tomorrow?"

He glanced over the chart. "Sure. How long before noon?"

"Before I answer that one, let me ask you a question. Do you have a team of six to ten shooters on board who can stand watch when we exit the Bosporus and before we enter the Dardanelles?"

"Absolutely. We wouldn't want your Green Berets to miss their beauty sleep."

"Exactly. We'll stand watch through the Bosporus and surrender security to your team as soon as we hit the Sea of Marmara."

Almost before I finished, he was on the radio arranging the security watch. After a stream of naval jargon I didn't understand, he said, "Expect my team to relieve yours in two hours, and we promise not to sneak up on you."

"Good plan. Thanks, Captain."

"Sure, no problem. Now, get off my bridge. I've got some pilot stuff to do."

The passage through the famed Bosporus Strait was uneventful, and I'm pretty sure the captain pushed the speed limit at least a little in a few places. I guess that was part of his "pilot stuff."

Just as promised, we were relieved right on time, and my team hit the sack after a briefing on the new plan. We were back on our feet and locked and loaded when the captain stuck the bow into the Dardanelles Strait for the three-hour passage. The *Lori Danielle*'s security forces were standing their posts like the rock-solid force they were. Each man briefed the position and conditions flawlessly as my men assumed responsibility for the exterior security of the ship.

The Dardanelles is wider and straighter than the Bosporus, so although longer in nautical miles, the daytime passage felt more comfortable. No signs of trouble arose, even though we were expecting unwanted visitors.

When we were clear of the strait and well established on the Aegean, I pressed the button on my radio. "Nice work, guys. This is where it could get dicey. The captain thinks this is the most likely spot for a strike, so stay on your toes."

The second I released the button, Skipper's voice resounded in my skull. "Chase, the *Better World* just shut down her AIS off the southern tip of Lemnos."

"Give me a little help on the geography."

"Forty-five miles ahead."

"Tell me you can still track her, even with her system shut down."

I could almost see her exasperation. "Of course I can, but not for long. She'll be out of satellite coverage in fifteen minutes, but I've got a pair of long-range drones ready to fly."

"Send them," I ordered, and seconds later, a pair of birds the size of coffee tables lifted off from the helipad and powered ahead.

"Airborne," Skipper said. "It'll take eighteen minutes for the drones to arrive on station above the *Better World*. That'll only leave a few minutes between the satellite passage and our own coverage."

"Nice work, Skipper. Keep me posted, especially if they turn to bear on us."

She said, "I think they're hovering and tracking us to see what route we'll take around the Greek Islands. Do you want me to have the captain shut down our AIS?"

"Stand by. I'm on my way to the CIC."

I ran and fired up the processor between my ears. By the time I pushed through the hatch into the CIC, I'd changed my mind forty-seven times. "Get the captain on the line."

"Bridge, Captain."

I caught my breath. "Captain, it's Chase in the CIC. The *Better World* is running dark and loitering just south of . . ." My pause led Skipper to point to the island on the screen, and I continued. "The island of Lemnos. Do you know the island?"

"Ask better questions, Chase. I'm the captain."

"Sorry. We've got a pair of drones in the air to keep an eye on her, and I'm looking for input on our next move."

He said, "By input, I assume you mean other people's ideas, even though you probably won't take their advice."

"Exactly," I said. "So, let's hear yours."

"We've got three options, and the first two begin with shutting down our automatic identification system. The first is running the coastline, where there will be far too many witnesses for the bad guys to mess with us. Second is running north of Lemnos and down the western side of the Aegean. That's open water, and we can outrun them, even if they find a way to track us."

I said, "Neither of those is a bad idea, but let's hear option number three."

"We can leave the light on and run straight at them. If they want to dance, we'll strike up the band."

As badly as I wanted to jump in the ring with those guys, I chose discretion, the better part of valor. "Let's go dark and run the coastline."

The captain said, "There's one disadvantage to that plan. We can't run on the foils. There will be too many curious onlookers, and we don't need a picture of our beloved girl flying above the waves all over the internet."

I laid a finger against Skipper's arm. "Do you have specs on the *Better World*?"

She typed furiously, and soon, the screen in front of her filled with every piece of technical data available on the ship. I scanned the page and said, "She can make nineteen knots. Even in displacement, we can outrun her with ease."

Captain Sprayberry said, "Just because we can outrun the ship doesn't mean we can outrun her launches, and we'll be in relatively calm seas near the shoreline. That means their go-fast boats won't struggle."

I leaned back, closed my eyes, and let the scenario play out on the movie screen in my head. When I'd watched the slow-motion encounter unfold several times, I said, "Run the coast at five miles offshore and make fifteen knots, but leave the AIS running. I want to dangle a little bait for them and see if they'll bite."

"You're the boss," he said. "I just drive the boat."

"You make pretty good coffee, too,"

He chuckled. "Come on up for a cup anytime you'd like. And keep me posted on the save-the-world boat, or whatever she's called."

"Skipper will keep you up to date if it looks like the *Better World* wants to dance with us."

An alarm sounded from somewhere in the room, and Skipper turned to a pair of small monitors to her left. "The drones are on station. Number one is in high orbit at twenty-five hundred meters, and number two is at a thousand. You can see both of their camera feeds on these monitors."

I said, "A thousand meters? Is that high enough to avoid being seen or heard?"

She cocked her head in obvious disbelief. "Really? Go outside and listen. Do you really think anybody on the deck of a moving ship could hear a pair of electric motors as big as my fists?"

"Okay, okay. They can't hear it, but can they see it?"

She shook her head. "Have you not met our resident mad scientist? Celeste designed a film to coat the drones that morphs to match the color of the sky above it, so it's practically invisible from the ground. She calls it 'adaptive camouflage,' and it's awesome."

"She's worth her weight in gold," I said.

Skipper glared up at me. "That better mean I'm worth Mongo's weight in diamonds."

"Oh, no. You're worth far more than that."

She leaned toward me. "You want to pick a fight with Ontrack Global Resources, don't you."

"No, but I won't be disappointed if they pick one with us."

"You should've been a Viking. You know that, right?"

"What do you mean by should've been? I *am* a Viking, baby."

"Then turn around," she said. "I'm going to braid your hair, Thor."

* * *

Captain Sprayberry made the turn to the south with the western coast of Turkey still visible to the east, and the *Better World* stuck her bow in the wind on a course to intercept us.

Skipper said, "It looks like you may get to burn and pillage something after all."

Before I could respond with something perfectly savage, Dr. Celeste Mankiller came through the hatch and into the CIC. "I've got an idea!"

"I like it when you have ideas," I said. "Let's hear it."

"We're running from the OGR ship, right?"

I said, "Not exactly. We're actually playing a little game of mouse and cat with them."

"Are you the mouse?" she asked.

"For now."

"Cool. I like it. How about making them believe there are a dozen of us mice running around out here?"

Skipper froze. "Oh, I can't wait to hear this."

Celeste said, "Try to stay with me. The AIS system is basically an autonomous satellite-coded discrimination system, so it's pretty dumb, right?"

She stared between us as if I were supposed to have some idea what she was talking about.

I said, "Forget it. We're not capable of staying with you. Don't explain it. Just tell us what you want to do."

"Well, like I said, it's a dumb system. It just reports what it receives without performing any data verification. Generally, it's just a pass-through satellite system. I can tell the satellites to report as many of us as you want. I can even have it believe other ships are us. Think about what that'll do to the cat."

"The cat?" I asked.

She raised her eyebrows. "Yeah, the cat in your game of mouse and cat."

"Oh, yeah. The cat. I love it. How long will it take you?"

"I can write the code in ten minutes and debug it in probably twenty, so maybe thirty minutes, tops."

Skipper said, "Oh, this is amazing. Tell me how I can help."

Celeste wasted no time. "Get me an AIS transmitter."

Skipper leapt from her seat and bolted from the room while Celeste situated herself in front of a computer and disappeared into a world I'd never understand. The world I did understand, however, called to me in a voice that may have been stronger than the wizardry inside Dr. Mankiller's head. Apparently, I didn't keep the voices contained well enough to avoid disturbing the master at work.

She shot a look over her shoulder. "What?"

"Nothing."

She groaned. "You said something. What was it?"

"I don't know what I said, but what I was *thinking* was a plan to unleash the mouse on the unsuspecting cat."

She stopped typing. "What are you talking about?"

I rolled closer. "Please tell me you can make us appear to be somewhere we're not without our actual AIS transmission being on."

"Of course I can do that. That's the whole point of this exercise, isn't it?"

"It is, but I thought you meant you could mask us so we could escape."

She said, "Exactly."

"I don't want to escape. I want to pounce."

A mischievous look overtook her, and she waggled a finger. "You're a dangerous man, Chase Fulton. And I like it."

Skipper burst through the hatch with a device in her hands that I couldn't identify, but Celeste apparently understood it well.

She had a dozen screws removed and the guts of the unit on her lap in seconds, and then she studied a pair of circuit boards and laughed. "Oh, yeah. This is way easy."

I motioned toward the pile of electronics and mouthed, "What is that?"

Skipper said, "According to the engineers, it's an automatic identification system. It turns out we have several of them on board, but I can't imagine why."

"Maybe people like Celeste take them apart whenever they see them, so we need plenty of spares."

"Could be," she said.

I stood. "I'm going to brief the captain on our plan."

Skipper stopped me. "What exactly is our plan?"

I pointed toward the genius in front of the keyboard. "She'll tell you. I'll be back."

I found Captain Sprayberry exactly where I expected to, and he still had a pair of binoculars in his hands. "Do you ever put those things down?"

He held up the glasses. "Not when somebody's interested in shooting up my ship and my crew. I even sleep with them sometimes."

I said, "I have a plan, and you're going to like it."

"Do I get to sink the *Brighter Tomorrow*?"

I laughed more than I should have. "Her name is the *Better World*."

He rolled his eyes. "Oh, I know her name, but the chances of you getting me to call her by her real name are way low . . . unless you let me sink her."

I spent five minutes briefing him on my plan and the role Celeste's electronic magic would play.

When I finished, his eyes lit up. "If that doesn't work, can I sink her?"

It was still funny to me. "Yes. If my plan fails, you can sink her, but not until all of my men and I have safely disembarked from her."

He gave a sharp single nod. "I've never wished for one of your plans to fail before this moment, but I'm keeping my fingers crossed."

Chapter 25
Pirate Games

Celeste exceeded her own expectations and had her program running like a top by the time I returned to the CIC. She looked like an excited child holding a report card full of straight A's.

"Does it work?" I asked.

She huffed. "Does it work? What kind of question is that? Of course it works, and it works even better than I thought it would. Somebody should've built a more secure system for the AIS network. It's way too easy to mess with."

"For you," I said. "For those of us who are mortal, the system seems perfectly fine."

"It won't after today," she said. "Did the captain approve of your plan?"

"Sort of, but he's hoping we fail."

She shivered. "What? Why?"

"Because I told him he could sink the *Better World* if my plan didn't work."

"Oh, then I understand. We should really find something for him to sink. He's earned it. Don't you think?"

"I do, indeed, but I'm not a big fan of sinking an environmental activist vessel. There's a lot of bad press that comes along with that."

Skipper said, "Maybe, but they're harboring pirates, and that's not exactly good juju either."

"Excellent point," I said. "Now, let's get the ball rolling."

Celeste spun until she was centered on her keyboard. "Just say the word, Dirty Bird."

"Dirty Bird?"

"I don't know. It just fell out of my mouth. I can't explain it."

I said, "Let's start by placing a phantom track directly on top of us at the same instant you shut down the real AIS."

She rubbed her hands together. "That's what they call the old switcheroo in my world."

"You're just full of 'em today. Can you pull off the much-loved switcheroo?"

"It's already done," she said, "and there was less than a one one-hundredth of a second delay between the two, so no human eye could detect it."

"Excellent. Now, make the tag match our speed and direction, and make it continue the track we're on right now. I'm initiating the pull away."

"You got it," she said.

I picked up the bat-phone, and Batman himself answered. "Bridge, Captain."

"Captain, it's Chase. Initiate the pull-away maneuver."

He didn't acknowledge me other than to give the command of, "Helm, reduce speed to one-two knots."

The helmsman answered, "Reduce speed to one-two knots. Aye, sir."

The captain said, "Speed coming off. Stand by for the turn."

I couldn't resist, so I said, "Speed coming off. Standing by for turn. Aye, sir."

I could almost see Captain Sprayberry shaking his head. "No, Chase. Just don't."

I wasn't finished, though. "Aye, sir."

He ignored me and said, "Helm, come right to two-seven-zero degrees."

The helmsman answered, and the *Lori Danielle* began her turn to the west and toward a *Better World*.

I watched our AIS icon and associated data block on the screen in front of Celeste continue southward at eighteen knots while our GPS position slowly drifted behind and eventually turned westward.

"Is it working?" I asked, almost holding my breath.

Celeste didn't take her eyes from the screen, but she said, "Oh, it's working . . . and even better than I expected."

"Can you plot the *Better World* and her track on that screen?"

She struck a few keys, and every ship in the Aegean with an AIS system slowly populated the screen. "How's that?"

"Beautiful," I said, "but where's the data from the *Better World* coming from if she turned off her AIS?"

Skipper said, "I'll take that one. We're getting her position, track, and speed from the GPS in the drones. You may be really great at gunfights, but we're just as good at the tech stuff."

I said, "I disagree. You two are better at this than I'll ever be at gunfighting. Let me know when we're eight miles in trail of the *Better World*."

"You got it, boss."

I headed for the hatch, but Skipper stopped me. "Wait, Chase. This is Penny calling."

I spun on a heel and sighed. "This isn't a great time."

Skipper asked, "Do you want me to let her know we'll call her back?"

I stepped back across the room. "No, just show me how to answer it."

She tossed me a headset. "Just put that on and press the round button on the right earpiece."

I followed her instructions and pulled the microphone to my lips. "We're really busy, so make this quick."

She said, "Hello to you, too. Listen, I've got some news on Culver Cove."

Suddenly, everything else seemed less important. "Let's hear it."

"My producer on the investigative report I'm doing on the murder is a guy named Anton Blaire, and he's a member of the club."

"You've got to be kidding me."

"Nope, not kidding. Are you too busy to talk about it right now?"

I glanced at the monitor and back at my watch. "I've got two minutes, so go."

"Anton Blaire is a pretty big deal. He's produced two of my movies, and he's got a great reputation in the industry. He's a high-net-worth guy with a lot of connections. I asked him about Culver Cove, and he clammed up at first, but after a little verbal judo, he said he knew of the club, so I kept pushing."

She paused, and I said, "Keep talking."

"Sorry," she said. "I had to take a breath. What are you doing that's so important?"

As the impatience in my chest rose beyond the reasonable limit, I said, "We're chasing down an environmental activist ship that has a team of commandos on board who want to take us out."

"And you're chasing them? I don't get it."

"It doesn't matter right now. Finish telling me about this Anton guy."

"Anyway, he finally agreed to talk to me face-to-face about the club, but not on the phone."

"Did you make that happen?"

"Stop asking so many questions. I thought you were in a hurry."

"Sorry. Please continue."

"Yes, I made it happen. He's a card-carrying member, and I have his attention. He agreed to talk with you, but not on the phone."

"What's this guy got against phones? You can take him to the op center and call on a secure line to the ship. We can even do a secure video call."

"I told him all of that, but he won't do it. He's insistent on a face-to-face conversation or nothing at all."

My world suddenly felt like a ticking time bomb, and I closed my eyes in a wasted effort to calm my churning mind. "Uh, let me think . . ." After thirty seconds of listening to the blood rush to my brain, I said, "If we survive the day, we can be in Athens tomorrow. Have this Anton guy on an airplane—a nice airplane—for Athens. It doesn't matter what it costs. We'll bill somebody."

She gasped. "What do you mean, *if* you survive?"

"Sorry. I was just thinking out loud. It'll be fine. They're just hired goons, and we'll shut them down in no time. Just get your producer friend on a plane."

"I'll do what I can, but no promises."

"Tell him to meet me in Athens or prepare his buddies in the club to become hostages. I have to go."

She said, "I love you!"

I repeated the affection and tossed the headset back to Skipper.

She caught the set and said, "Well, that sounded interesting. Are we heading for Athens when this is over?"

"I hope so."

* * *

I gathered the team on the stern deck and briefed the plan. I did a terrible job explaining what Skipper and Dr. Mankiller pulled off with their computer magic, but the guys got the picture.

"So, here's what we're going to do. I'm calling it a game of mouse and cat. We're going to sneak up behind the *Better World* with our radar-absorbing system churning away. That should make us practically invisible to their surface radar. I've got no reason to believe they have any other means of detecting us in their wake. We'll deploy the RHIB and run them down."

Gator frowned. "Won't they see the RHIB on radar?"

"Probably not," I said. "Its low profile should keep us mixed in with the swells. We'll ingress over the stern rail and make our way to the bridge. If we encounter resistance, we'll use only the required force to overcome the resistance. Lead in the air is not an option unless we know we're about to die. There's a legal term for what we're doing, and it's called piracy."

Singer lowered his chin, but he didn't open his mouth.

I continued the briefing. "We'll take the bridge and stop the ship. That'll get the attention of the team of hitters who are planning to play pirate games of their own. When they come out to investigate, we'll roll them up and make them understand they're playing out of their league."

The faces of my men didn't share my level of excitement, and for the first time in the years we'd been together, I began questioning their willingness to follow me onto the battlefield I'd chosen.

I said, "Somebody speak up. You don't look excited about this mission."

They looked between themselves, and Singer finally said, "Chase, we'll follow you through the gates of Hell, but we need to know this isn't an ego trip for you. If what you described about Dr. Mankiller's computer program is true, we could slip these guys and be halfway across the Atlantic before they know we're gone. Boarding a ship at sea with hostile intent is a serious violation of international law."

I said, "So is sneaking into Bulgaria and shooting up a private business, but that didn't stop us."

He softened his tone. "We did that to save Anya. If we cross that rail, we're guilty of piracy, and if we're forced to press a trigger, we'll be guilty of a lot more than that. I, for one, just need to know that we're doing this out of necessity and not out of a need for you to prove you're better than the Ontrack Global Resources guys."

I said, "We *are* better than them."

Singer shrugged. "Maybe we are, but tell me who their hitters are. Are they former—or current—Spetsnaz, British SAS, Norwegian FSK, American Delta Force?"

I leaned against the rail. "Okay, I get it. We don't know exactly who we're messing with."

"Or how many," Singer said.

I sighed. "Or how many. But here's my rationale. If we let them catch us, they're going to board us and gun us down. Whoever they are, they have an egress plan. They'll disappear, and no one on Earth will ever believe that a Dutch-registered environmental activist ship was involved in an attack on an American research vessel on the Aegean Sea."

I paused long enough for my message to sink in before continuing. "That leaves us only three options. First, we could run, and we would escape temporarily, but that wouldn't stop them. They'd keep coming for weeks, months, maybe even years. Second, we could lie in wait for them to run us down and board us. We'd have no choice other than putting them down if they came aboard. We all know that scenario forces us to kill them. Option number three is what we've been talking about. We make a preemptive strike, show them we're not a bunch of amateur chumps, and let them live. They get the message and leave us alone. Which of these three scenarios do you guys like best?"

"There's a fourth option," Mongo said from way in the back.

"Let's hear it."

"We could lie to them."

"What are you talking about?"

"We could get within radio range, have Celeste make us look like a Hellenic Coast Guard vessel, and radio them to say we intend to board them because of reports of potential acts of piracy."

Heads nodded, and I considered the option. "What if they tell us to go pound sand?"

Mongo said, "Then we let them be the sand we pound."

I lowered my head and swallowed my pride. "Okay, suddenly, this is a democracy. If you're in favor of Mongo's plan, raise your hand."

Eyes darted among the team, and hands slowly made their way into the air until mine was the only hand not raised. I waved a finger across my team. "This is why we're a family and not just a team."

With that, I raised my hand into the air, joining my brothers in the unanimous vote in our newly formed democracy before heading for the CIC.

Chapter 26
Showtime

"I've changed my mind," I announced as my left boot hit the deck inside the combat information center.

Skipper seemed to ignore the declaration, but Dr. Mankiller pulled herself from her workstation and stared up at me. "What are you talking about?"

"We're not hitting the *Better World* . . . unless they make us. The game has changed from mouse and cat to masquerade."

That was enough to get Skipper's attention. "I thought you might come to that conclusion before we boarded a sovereign vessel in international waters with hostile intent."

I frowned down at her. "If you knew I was screwing up, why didn't you stop me? It's not like you to sit in silence when I'm on the verge of doing something stupid."

"It's not stupid," she said. "It may become necessary, and I didn't want to pull you out of that place your head goes when you're planning a tricky op."

"In the future, pull me out of wherever I am if I'm headed down the wrong road. We've been together too long to tiptoe around each other."

Skipper smiled and gave me that cute little smile that hadn't changed a bit since the first time I saw her nearly twenty years before. The memory of those innocent years when classes were a distraction and baseball was the center of the universe for me at UGA washed over me, and I couldn't stop myself from wondering what cosmic forces contrived to put that bratty teenage girl and me on a half-a-billion-dollar warship halfway around the world.

The snap of her fingers pulled me from the moment. "So, what's this masquerade you want to pull off?"

"Sorry. I was thinking about—"

She rolled her eyes. "Yeah, I know. The Russian in sick bay, but I need you to think about what we're doing up here."

"No, it wasn't her. Believe it or not, I was thinking about you and me, but you're right. We'll have plenty of time for that later. For now, I need you to find me a Hellenic Coast Guard ship that would likely detain the *Better World* in open water."

Her innocent smirk turned into a mischievous grin. "Ooh, I like this. Give me thirty seconds."

Thirty seconds, I thought. I expected half an hour, but I should've known better.

Before I finished doubting her timing, she said, "Got one."

She pulled up a picture of a Grecian Coast Guard vessel that looked more like a missile frigate than a patrol boat. I studied the picture, and she said, "We'll be the *Fourni*, a Sa'ar-class patrol boat. She's an Israeli-built, fifty-eight-meter, five-hundred-ton converted missile boat. The Greeks bought her from the Israelis prior to the two-thousand-four Olympics."

"She sounds perfect," I said. "But isn't the real *Fourni* on patrol somewhere?"

"That's the best part. She's suffered a minor electronics fire and has been in port for eight months undergoing a refit, and it's time for her to be back on the water. But, wouldn't you know it, there's some mix-up between the contractor and the Coast Guard about payment, so she's stuck in port. I doubt the captain of the *Better World* knows that, though."

"That's a pretty big gamble," I said. "What if he does know?"

"There are some other smaller options, but the *Fourni* is the only ship in the inventory the *Better World* would have any reason to stop for. Everything else is small coastal patrol boats."

"The *Fourni* it is," I said. "How long until we're in their wake?"

Celeste said, "Half an hour if nothing changes, but I recommend making something change."

"What are you saying?"

She pointed to her screen. "I've kept our false track on a consistent track for over an hour, and it's a logical time for it to make a turn. I'd like to turn the electronic track and see if the *Better World* makes a course correction to intercept."

"Do it," I said.

Her fingers went to work, and soon, the symbol representing the fake *Lori Danielle* turned southwest. We held our breath and bored holes in the screen, staring at the *Better World*, until Celeste clapped her hands. "There it is! She made the turn. It's working like a charm."

I laid a hand on her shoulder. "Get the new course information to the captain, and plot a new course to fall in behind her."

"It's already done. We patched into a monitor on the bridge so Captain Sprayberry sees everything we see."

"With the new course, are we still half an hour out?"

She typed some commands. "Twenty-six minutes."

"Perfect. Now all we need is somebody who can sound like a Greek Coast Guard captain."

Skipper said, "That shouldn't be too tough with a crew as diverse as ours. I'll get on it."

The next ten minutes of my life were spent briefing the captain on the new plan, and his reaction both disappointed and thrilled me. He listened intently as I laid out the plan to pretend to be the Hellenic patrol boat to, hopefully, make the skipper of the *Better World* turn around and head back to port.

When I finished my briefing, he said, "It ain't gonna work, but it'll be fun to try. What will you do if they go all stop and invite us to board them?"

"That's the best possible option. It's not piracy if they open the door and invite us in."

He laughed so hard he almost shot coffee through his nose. "Oh, it's still piracy, but it's piracy while impersonating a lawful authority, and that makes it worse. I'm going to buy a maritime lawbook for you to study in your downtime."

"Downtime? What's that?"

He checked the chart plotter. "All right, hotshot. Get off the bridge and go to work. I'll have you in position in twelve minutes. I assume you're bringing Mr. Papadakis up from engineering to play Coastie."

"Skipper's working that angle, but I suspect you're right. We'll go hot from the CIC when we get in position."

He motioned toward the bow. "Look out there."

I turned, peered through the glass, and offered up a little prayer of thanks. "Oh, that's perfect."

"I thought you'd like it. In that rain, we can park this thing on his poop deck and he'll never see us."

"In that case, let's snuggle up, but stay out of visible range."

"You got it. Now, go!"

I abandoned his bridge and met Skipper back in the CIC. A crewman in white coveralls I'd never met stood beside her at her console.

Skipper said, "Hey, Chase. This is Ernie Papadakis. He's the second engineer and a hundred percent Greek."

I shook his hand and briefed him on the plan. The more I talked, the more he smiled. When he finally spoke, my heart sank.

I said, "Uh, you don't sound Greek."

His smile broadened even more. "I can sound Greek or Italian or Turkish or Spanish. I can be whoever you need on the radio, but I'm all Greek when you see my face."

We wrote the script for the radio call, and Ernie practiced several times until I was convinced he was pure Greek, through and through.

The captain came over the speaker. "CIC, Bridge. We are in position five miles in trail of the *Better World*. It's showtime."

208 · CAP DANIELS

I said, "Thanks, Captain. Here we go." I motioned toward the script. "Okay, Captain Papadakis, do your thing."

Ernie pulled on the headset and adjusted the microphone. In his native Greek, he said, "*Better World, Better World*, this is the Hellenic Coast Guard patrol ship *Fourni*. You are ordered to reduce speed to dead slow and respond to this order."

He paused, and we waited. Her speed didn't change, and no one responded, so Ernie read the script again.

The *Better World* didn't slow, but she did answer the radio.

Someone said, "Vessel hailing the *Better World* in Greek, we are an English-speaking crew. Please repeat your call in English."

Ernie cleared his throat and spoke in his best Greek-accented English. "*Better World, Better World*, this is the Hellenic Coast Guard patrol ship *Fourni*. You are ordered to reduce speed to dead slow and respond to this order."

Seconds later, the voice returned. "Coast Guard, we are a sovereign ship in international waters, and we've committed no violations of any law. What is the reason for your order?"

Ernie looked up at me, and I pointed toward the script. He spoke into the mic. "We have an international warrant authorizing us to escort you back to your previous port of departure for suspected conspiracy to commit piracy on the high seas."

Silence filled the air for over a minute while the captain of the *Better World* likely considered his options.

Finally, he said, "Under whose authority is the warrant written?"

Ernie widened his eyes. "We don't have a script for this one."

Skipper typed furiously and scanned the screen in front of her. "Tell him the warrant was issued by the Areios Pagos."

The Greek chuckled and said, "I'll give it a try, but the Supreme Court of Greece doesn't issue maritime warrants."

"Have you got a better idea?" she asked.

Ernie sighed. "*Better World*, the warrant is under the authority of the Areios Pagos."

Everything was silent except the screaming voices in my head. Everything inside me wanted to climb over the stern rail of that ship and pin those guys to the deck.

It may have been thirty seconds or perhaps ten years before the *Better World* answered, but when it came, it didn't disappoint me.

"Coast Guard, the legal office of our parent company, Green Alliance Cooperative, does not acknowledge nor recognize the authority of the Areios Pagos in international waters."

"What now?" Ernie asked.

I didn't hesitate. "Keep 'em talking if you want. I'm taking my hoard of Vikings over the rail. We're going to shove a rifle muzzle down their throats and see if they recognize that authority."

Chapter 27
A Little Piracy

When my boots hit the stern deck of the *Lori Danielle*, the rigid hull inflatable boat was already connected to the crane, and my team of unstoppable warfighters were poised in the RHIB and waiting for me to complete the lineup.

A pair of deckhands handled lines from the bow and stern of the RHIB as the crane operator lifted us over the rail and deposited us into the waiting sea below. Disco pressed the starters the instant the hull hit the water, and the twin turbo-charged engines drew their first breath of the day. The davit lines fell away, and we roared from alongside the ship. Disco managed the boat—with the same precision he flew everything with wings—as the rain sliced into our faces at fifty knots and the hull cut across the swells toward the unsuspecting *Better World*.

We had no radar-absorbing or jamming capabilities in the RHIB, but our low profile made us nearly invisible to surface radar. God's gifts of fog, rain, and low clouds gave us the remaining stealth we needed to make our approach. Our radar pinpointed the environmental ship ahead, but eerily, there was no sign of the *Lori Danielle* to our stern. Her ability to hide from some of the best radar systems in the world gave her abilities few vessels possessed. When the battle ended, she would show herself and give us a target for home. But before we could return victorious, an unknown challenge lay before us: there was no way we could know the number of fighters we'd face onboard the ship. We knew next to nothing about the anti-piracy capability of the vessel, but if we made every move correctly and played our hand with precision, we'd be aboard and prowling her decks before the crew of the *Better World* realized just how unwound their world was about to become.

We pierced the wall of grey, and our target's green hull lay dead ahead. Singer and Gator lifted line rifles with grappling hooks protruding from their muzzles just as Disco plowed over the roiling wake of the ship. The two shooters watched as the mighty green wall grew ever closer, until Singer gave the order, "Send it!"

Both rifles fired simultaneously, and the titanium hooks exploded from their muzzles. An instant later, the hooks fell across the top rail of the stern, and Gator and Singer hauled in on the messenger lines until the narrow boarding ladders locked in place inside the mechanism of the pullies on the hook shackles. They yanked the ladders until they were certain they would hold even Mongo's mass, and they turned, awaiting my command.

The words were already out of my mouth by the time their eyes met mine. "Execute! Execute! Execute!"

A billion things go through an operator's mind in the opening plays of a mission, and the most bizarre thought came to mine in the moment. Gator and Singer looked like trapeze artists climbing the single-footed ladders to their lofty perch. The difference was, we'd be performing without a safety net. Our sniper team disappeared across the rail, and I knew without seeing them that they were kneeling with rifles raised and scanning for targets.

The roar of the engines and disturbed water around the hull of the ship made even our mandible comms useless. We were reduced to hand signals, and Singer gave his. Next up the ladders were Hunter and Kodiak, but we didn't wait for a second signal. Instead, Mongo and I mounted the ladders and rolled across the stern rail seconds later.

To my disbelief, no one greeted us on the deck as we made our way forward. Kodiak slid the blade of his knife into the tubes of the RHIB nestled in a cradle on the port side of the vessel. On the starboard side was the emergency evacuation lifeboat resting on its angled frame, waiting for a frightened crew to climb aboard and pull the release to abandon their sinking ship. We weren't going to sink her, but if everything went my way, we were going to plant a massive helping of terror into their souls in the coming minutes.

We broke into two assault teams. Mongo, Gator, and I took the starboard side while Kodiak, Singer, and Hunter broke left. We stepped through the first hatch we reached to avoid exposing ourselves on the waist of the vessel. The corridor was empty, but incandescent bulbs burned in caged overhead fixtures, making me wonder why an environmental activist vessel wasn't using LEDs.

Focus, Chase. Focus.

We moved forward, clearing each compartment as we came to it, until we reached the crew mess. I had no interest in scaring the cook out of his apron or dealing with a dozen hungry crewmen, so I pressed against the hatch until I could see inside. My theory on the number of diners was high. I only counted seven men, none of them armed, sitting at a table with bowls of something in front of them. I carefully allowed the hatch to close, and we continued our movement toward the bow.

The next hatch was labeled "Conference Room" on a conventional door instead of a hatch. I examined the door closely and silently signaled for the camera. Mongo pulled the device from his pocket and slipped it into my palm. I slid the fiber-optic lens beneath the door and squinted at the two-inch display. What I saw sent my heart racing and anticipation pounding inside my head.

Withdrawing the barely visible lens, I gave the signal to retreat, and the looks on the faces of the men behind me reminded me how foreign the concept of retreat is for any of us. Only I knew how brief our fallback would be.

We made our way into an empty compartment, and I called team two. "Sierra Four, Sierra One."

Hunter answered immediately. "Go for Sierra Four."

"Say position."

He said, "We're one deck above the engine room with no contact yet."

"Meet us on the starboard side, six compartments forward of the aft hatch."

"We're moving now. If we don't find resistance, we'll be there in less than two minutes."

His estimate was spot-on. Kodiak, Singer, and Hunter stepped through the hatch with weapons raised, but they lowered them the instant they identified us as friendlies.

I said, "We found the fighters. They're in the conference room sixty feet forward on the left."

"How many?" Hunter asked.

"I counted nine, but there could be more. My view was restricted by a low wall astern of the door."

"Door?" Kodiak asked.

"Yes, it's a conventional door, not a waterproof hatch."

"Locked?"

I grimaced. "I didn't check. I just probed the bottom with the fiber-optic camera."

"No problem. We'll get through it even if it is locked. Were they carrying?"

"Some of them may have had sidearms, but I didn't see any rifles. They were kicked back and eating. They're obviously not expecting to be hit."

Hunter said, "Okay, we can take nine without any problem if they don't start shooting. Are we gunning or just rolling them up?"

I said, "Stay off the triggers if possible, but don't suffer any losses. We want to get their attention and give them the opportunity to change their minds about how they want to die."

Hunter nodded. "Let's do it. What's the stack?"

"Let's go unconventional," I said. "I want Mongo through the door first. His size will keep their eyes on him while the rest of us flood the room. Kodiak is number two. Start issuing commands the instant we crush through the door."

"Do you want them on the ground?" Kodiak asked.

"Absolutely. I'll bring up the rear. The rest of the stack doesn't matter. Just don't let them draw. We don't want a gunfight if we can avoid it."

Singer shuffled close to me. "Are you okay for this one, Chase?"

I locked eyes with the sniper. "I'm better than okay. Let's do this."

Mongo led the way from the compartment and into the corridor. Twenty paces forward, he pressed an enormous palm on the knob side of the door to the conference room and applied enough pressure to check the latch. It didn't budge, so he gripped the knob and checked over his shoulder.

Starting with me, each of us squeezed the shoulder of the man in front of us until Kodiak nodded, and Mongo twisted the knob. It didn't turn, but the twenty square feet of wooden door was little more than an annoyance for the big man. His shoulder and left hip made quick work of the barrier, and he was inside the room and breaking right with his rifle trained on the collection of mercenaries. We alternated directions until the whole team was in position, forming a half circle around the wide-eyed team at the table.

Kodiak turned on his drill sergeant voice. "Hands in the air now! Do it! On your knees facing me, right now!"

Surprise, speed, and violence were on our side. It was obvious that no one at the table expected six armed commandos led by a giant to step through the door, but one of the men made a terrible decision. Instead of following Kodiak's commands, he drew a holstered pistol and began the practiced presentation of the weapon on target. I was that target, but before he could level the weapon and press the trigger, Gator put a pair of .300 Blackout rounds through the man's right shoulder, sending him spinning from his seat and his pistol skidding across the floor.

I was surprised and thankful for both Gator's reflexes and precision, but what most impressed me was his action immediately following the shooting.

He studied the scene, apparently to make sure no one else had any ideas of drawing a weapon, and then asked, "Can I take care of him?"

My answer was no, but not because I didn't want the wounded man to survive. Singer was already halfway to the downed fighter with his trauma kit in hand. The rest of us held our positions and started a cattle line.

I said, "Mongo, you're on the door. Everybody else, disarm, cuff, and shackle everyone except the wounded man."

Kodiak took the closest man by his arm, stood him up, and searched him. Out of his pockets came a pair of knives, a lighter, two pens, and a small flashlight. Kodiak put the man on his knees and cuffed his hands and ankles. Hunter was next, and the second man's pockets produced a similar haul with the added bit of spice in the form of a compact pistol.

"Look what we have here," Hunter said, pocketing the gun.

When Hunter turned back to his intended prisoner, the room exploded with activity. Hunter's man threw a flying elbow intended for my partner's jaw, but he ducked the coming blow and sent an uppercut to the man's chin, melting him like butter.

Every other mercenary leapt from his seat and closed the distance between us. One fighter drew a pistol from a concealed holster, but Gator landed a boot to the man's wrist, sending the weapon skittering across the deck.

Mongo abandoned his station at what was left of the door to join the fight, and the big man was the epitome of a force multiplier. Having his strength and size in the fight changed the odds. The heftiest of their men faced off, giant against giant, but Mongo showed no signs of backing down. He knocked away the first punch the man threw and jammed an attempted knee strike. A hammer fist to his opponent's collarbone reduced his will to continue the fight, and a left cross to the jawbone destroyed his ability.

What happened inside me in the next seconds of my life during the fight was something I'd never be fully capable of explaining. Instead of standing my ground and letting the fight come to me one man at a time, I leaned in and slipped my rifle's sling across my head, turning the nine-pound weapon into a bludgeoning hunk of plastic and steel. I landed the stock against the first victim's jaw, sending blood and spittle flying as he absorbed the blow. After the follow-through, I delivered the butt of the rifle directly beneath the man's nose, splitting his lips and destroying at least half a dozen of his teeth. As he began his slow trip to the deck, I struck again, breaking his nose and extending his coming slumber.

With rage in my eyes, I spun to see the glistening blade of a fighting knife swinging toward my face. I sidestepped the strike, caught the attacker's wrist with one hand, and drove my rifle into the back of his elbow. The agonizing cry exploding from his mouth did little to cover the crack of the bones as his elbow came apart, but a broken arm couldn't satiate the bloodlust boiling inside me. I struck two blows to the man's face, adding his lost teeth to the count.

The fight around me seemed a million miles away, and everything in my periphery faded in a misty white cloud as I focused every ounce of rage and cruelty directly into every man I faced. There may have been only three, or perhaps three hundred, but no matter how many came, I dispatched each of them with punishment beyond description to their mouths, faces, and especially their teeth.

With sweat pouring from my face and more fire than I'd ever felt inside my chest, an enormous arm encircled my shoulders and chest, trapping me against a mighty oak. No matter how I struggled, I couldn't break free, but I wouldn't surrender. I wouldn't secede. There was too much power screaming to explode from my body for me to allow my captor to prevail until I heard Mongo's gentle voice.

"Chase, take it easy. It's over."

Chapter 28
Hit the Batter

Mongo spun me in his arms and shook me. "What's wrong with you, man? Calm down."

I should've been able to make the simple diagnosis, but in that moment, I was the opposite of a psychologist—I was an animal. But I forced myself to breathe and find a way to calm myself.

When the muscles of my arms and shoulders relaxed, Mongo let go of me and stared into my eyes. "Are you okay?"

Suddenly, I was both thirsty beyond description and exhausted in the same instant, so I stuck the dispenser of my CamelBak between my teeth and drew in a long swallow. "Yeah, I'm good."

"What was that about?"

I looked away. "Sorry. I just got excited. That's all."

He huffed. "I've seen you excited, and that wasn't it. Get yourself together and go talk to the captain. We'll babysit these guys 'til you get back."

I slung my rifle around my neck and shoulder and turned to Hunter. "You're with me."

He fell in beside me as I stepped back into the corridor outside the conference room.

He whispered, "You okay?"

"I'm good."

"I've never seen you like that. I'm glad Mongo was there 'cause I don't think any of the rest of us could've stopped you. You were out of control."

Analyzing my own behavior and lack of rational thought in that moment was almost impossible because it was so easy to lie to myself about what was truly driving me. It was easy to write it off as fear for my life or the belief that the men in that room constituted a nearly insurmountable threat, but neither of those things was true. The ugly truth lay in my need to do to them what they'd done to Anya. The broken teeth, the battered face, and the ruthless punishment all had to be returned. Even though they weren't the men who hurt her, they were part of the same team, and in the game I played, the sins of the brother are the sins of the team.

Hunter and I found the navigation bridge and tested the door. It was unlocked but closed.

Hunter asked, "How are we going to play this?"

"It depends on how they react to seeing a pair of armed commandos stepping onto their bridge."

He said, "You do the talking, and I'll try to look scary."

"Oh, sure," I said. "Take the easy job."

I gripped the knob and eyed my partner. He gave me a nod, and we pushed through the door with our rifles at the low ready position. Everyone on the bridge turned in shocked disbelief when the two of us materialized in their space.

I patted the air with a palm. "Everybody, stay calm. We're not here to hurt you, and we don't want your ship."

The captain earned an instant measure of respect when he took two steps toward me and waved everyone on the bridge behind him. He maintained his composure while some of the younger officers wore terror in their eyes.

The captain said, "Who are you, how did you get on my boat, and what do you want?"

I let my rifle hang from the sling to be as unthreatening as possible.

"I'll answer one of those questions, Captain. What I want is to provide you with some information you don't have."

He lowered his chin. "Nothing happens aboard my boat that I don't know about."

I glanced back at Hunter. "We came aboard."

"What do you want?" the captain demanded.

I took a step closer to him to use the psychological advantage of my height over the chubby, sixty-something sea captain. "Your passengers are mercenaries in the employ of a company called Ontrack Global Resources. Those mercenaries intended to use your vessel as a pirate ship to hunt down and assault my team and me."

"That's preposterous. Those men—"

I stopped him in his tracks. "It doesn't matter what you believe those men to be, Captain. They are hired killers with a mission, and you don't want to be any part of that mission. I assure you. Now, listen closely. Those men—all nine of them—are bound and gagged in your conference room. One chose to attempt firing on us, and we returned fire, injuring him, but he is non-critical. I'm confident your ship's doctor can have him back on his feet by the time you deposit them back ashore."

He took a step backward. "What are you talking about?"

I slowly shook my head. "Stop playing games with me, Captain. You ignored the lawful order of the Hellenic Coast Guard, so we had no other choice but to confront both you and the mercenaries you carry. Turn your ship around and deposit those men back ashore, and there will be no further action taken against you, your ship, or your company. This is nonnegotiable, and it is your only warning. If you choose to disregard my instructions, prepare to deal with not only the loss of your vessel, but also your crew, and possibly your own life."

Before he could protest, Hunter and I backed through the door and into the corridor.

"Sierra Six, Sierra One. Mission complete. Move to the lifeboat."

Singer said, "Roger, One. We're moving."

Hunter and I sprinted to the stern deck and climbed aboard the lifeboat in its launching cradle. Kodiak pulled the safety pins and cycled the lever, releasing the orange and white emergency vessel. We slid down the rails and plummeted onto the waiting sea below. The engine started on the first attempt, and we motored away from the ship.

I called Disco. "We're afloat in the lifeboat and heading zero nine zero. How 'bout an upgrade?"

He said, "I'm on my way."

He picked us up four minutes later, and we lashed the lifeboat's wheel hard over so the boat would make continual circles until it ran out of fuel. The captain and crew of the *Better World* shouldn't have had any trouble finding and retrieving their little orange boat, but we wouldn't be there when it happened.

When I stepped from the lifeboat and aboard the RHIB, Disco said, "While you were off playing patty-cake with the save-the-world bunch, I did a little thinking."

"That's something new for you," I said.

He shook off the jab. "Our radar can't see the *Lori Danielle* as long as she's stealthy, but if she unmasks, the radar on the *Better World* will be able to see her, too. To work around that issue, Skipper and I came up with a plan. We've got about half a mile of visibility in this rain, so she's feeding the ship's real-time coordinates to our chart plotter on the RHIB. It'll be just like flying a GPS approach. The satellites will guide us all the way home."

"Nicely done," I said. "Now, get us out of here before we melt."

He couldn't pass up the opportunity, so he said, "Don't worry, my friend. What you're made of floats."

We made the five-mile trip back to the *Lori Danielle* in just over fifteen minutes, and it felt good to be back home. We showered, changed into warm, dry clothes, and reconvened in the CIC.

"How'd it go?" Skipper asked.

Hunter said, "Gator almost got a kill, but he missed."

"I didn't miss," he said. "I intentionally shot around his body armor and away from his head. Chase told us not to kill anybody."

"That's not exactly what I said, but you did the right thing. Keep it up. Those quick hands of yours probably saved somebody's life over there."

Gator nodded but didn't say another word.

Skipper said, "Okay. Other than Gator missing, how'd it go?"

I motioned toward the monitor. "I suspect we'll know soon. If the *Better World* turns around and heads for a convenient port, I'd say it went extremely well. However, if they chase one of the ships they think might be the *Lori Danielle*, maybe we didn't make the impression I'd hoped."

"They're turning," she said. "But there's no way to know if they're turning for a port."

"While we're waiting," I said, "let's do the after-action review."

The team took seats, and I propped up on the edge of the console. "The launch and delivery were flawless. There's nothing to change there. Once on board the ship, movement was solid and teamwork was spot-on. Does anyone have any input on the first portion of the mission?"

Heads shook, so I continued. "When we hit the conference room, we could've been softer, but I think announcing our presence in that room was crucial. Those guys were hard-core hitters. We couldn't afford to walk in there with our hats in our hands. Nice command of the room. And nice work, Gator. I'm disappointed I didn't see the gun in time to react. I guess I'm getting old."

"We're all getting old," Mongo said. "But that doesn't make it excusable to miss a drawn pistol. We're all better than that. Every one of us should've put a bullet in that guy. I'd like to say one more thing about the shooting, if you don't mind."

I said, "Sure, go ahead."

"When did we start shooting to wound?"

"That was going to be my next point," I said. "Gator, we all appreciate your reaction time and shot placement, but we send bullets downrange for only one reason, and wounding isn't it. Next time, make sure it's two in the high A-zone and one in the T-box. Got it?"

Gator nodded. "Got it."

I took a long breath. "Now it's time for me to hold up a mirror. I went off the rails, and it's inexcusable. I let emotion override prudent battlefield mindset, and I owe each of you an apology. When one of our team is brutally attacked, my instinct is to punish the perpetrators of that attack tenfold for what they did to one of ours. I'd like to stand here and tell you it won't happen again, but I'll never intentionally lie to any of you. I don't know if I possess the wherewithal to overcome that punisher characteristic inside me. It's easy to preach to young operators and tell them to never make this job personal, but teaching it and living it are two different worlds. I'll make this promise to you, though. I'll work on it, but ultimately, I need your help to keep me focused on mission completion and not retribution."

The room was silent for a long moment before Skipper jackhammered that silence. "She's turning!"

The chairs emptied, and the team poured forward, surrounding the monitors. We held our breath as the *Better World* slowly maneuvered through a turn to starboard and then relaxed as she rolled out, heading north and back toward Kavala.

"Whatever you did over there must've worked," Skipper said. "It looks like they're bugging out."

A sigh of relief escaped the team, and I said, "Keep watching. If she goes anywhere other than Kavala, I need to know."

"Of course," Skipper said. "I'll program the tracking software to keep us posted on any course changes."

"Back to the AAR," I said. "The exfil was flawless. Overall, I'm extremely happy with the outcome, but not so happy with my execution. Does anybody have anything else to mention?"

After a few seconds of silence, Mongo said, "Is Penny's producer meeting us in Athens?"

I hadn't forgotten that element of the mission, but it wasn't on the top shelf of my brain, either. "Let's find out."

Skipper had the phone on speaker in no time, and Penny's voice filled the air. "Hey, Chase. Please tell me this is the call telling me everyone survived and we're still on for Athens."

"That's exactly what this is," I said. "Did you talk your producer into the trip?"

"I did. We'll land at Athens International at one fifteen local time tomorrow afternoon."

"Private or commercial?"

"Private."

I said, "Good. Gun Bunny will pick you up at Signature Aviation and chopper you back to the ship."

Penny gasped. "We're doing the meeting on the ship?"

"We are. Having the talk aboard the ship lends an air of validity to our intel. Meeting in a hotel room doesn't have the same flavor as meeting in the combat information center aboard a warship."

"Perception is fact," she said. "I'll see you tomorrow."

"See you then."

Skipper cut the line and asked, "Are you really bringing a civilian into the CIC?"

"I'm at least bringing him aboard the ship. I want him to understand the severity of our message and our offer to help."

She said, "I think it's a great idea. I can make sure we don't have any classified material or equipment exposed if you want to bring him in here."

"Let's plan for that," I said. "This is definitely an impressive room."

"That it is," she said. She closed her eyes and sighed. "Listen, Chase. I talked to Dr. Shadrack while you were on the mission. Anya isn't doing well. You should probably go down and talk with him."

That was a boot to my gut that I didn't need, but I hustled my way to sick bay. Instead of heading straight into Dr. Shadrack's office, though, my feet took me to Anya's bedside, where I found her somewhere between barely awake and almost dead.

She reached for my hand when her sleep-filled eyes met mine. "Chasechka."

Hearing her voice so weak and childlike broke my heart, but I tried to maintain my composure. "Anyechka, I'm sorry I brought you into this. I would've never intentionally gotten you hurt."

She tried to smile, and in her native Russian, softly whispered, "Anyechka . . . I like this." She squeezed my hand and continued in Russian. "Singer came to me right after mission on other ship, and he told me what you did. He told me how you broke the faces and teeth of those men for me."

I stared at my boots and did my best to answer in Russian. "I shouldn't have . . ."

She squeezed again and almost smiled. "*Spasibo*, Chasechka."

I planted half of my butt on the edge of her bed. "I want to tell you a baseball story."

It may have merely been my imagination, but she seemed to perk up for an instant.

I said, "When I was playing ball, if a member of the opposing team did something to hurt one of our players, it became my job as the catcher to make sure a fastball hit that player nice and hard the next time he came up to bat. The price for hurting one of my teammates is always high and always painful."

Chapter 29
Cooking with Greece

Anya drifted off to sleep, or unconsciousness, somewhere in my story, and her hand slipped from mine. To see her lying there, broken and bruised, sent daggers of fury slicing through my soul. Knowing I was the reason she was lying in that sick bay bed with those injuries was my fault, and I couldn't forgive myself no matter how much she would insist I wasn't responsible.

Dr. Shadrack ambled from his office. "I thought you might show up. How'd the operation go?"

"It was a success," I said. "What's going on with Anya?"

He squeezed one of the three IV bags hanging above her bed. "She developed a serious infection inside a sinus cavity beneath her left eye. I don't have the facility or skill to continue treating her here. We have to get her to a hospital within the next twenty-four hours."

I looked down at the strongest woman I'd ever known, lying unconscious and beaten almost beyond recognition. "Is it critical?"

"It's more than critical, Chase. It's potentially fatal if we don't get her into the hands of a competent surgeon."

"We'll be in Athens in less than twelve hours. I'll arrange for a medevac anywhere in the world. Just tell me where to send her."

"Give me an hour, and I'll have a name and address of the best facility I can find."

"Is she in pain?"

He said, "She would be, but I'm keeping her medicated beyond her body's ability to recognize and react to pain. On top of that, I'm pouring antibiotics into her as quickly as she can accept it."

I stared down at her and sent up a silent prayer at the same moment Dr. Shadrack laid a hand on my shoulder. "She'll most likely live if we get her to a good facility quickly, but she's got a long road ahead of her. They did a lot of damage. Somebody should make them pay."

"You can consider that box checked, Doc. The men who did this to her drew their final breaths in Burgas, and the team we encountered today left the fight in at *least* Anya's condition. Maybe worse."

"I'll get you the name as soon as possible."

I left sick bay and found Singer sitting on the stern deck with a rifle lying across his lap. "Mind if I join you?"

He looked up. "It's not very comfortable, but you're always welcome."

I took a seat beside him and immediately agreed with his description of the position. "Planning to shoot somebody?"

He ran a hand across the weapon. "No, I just think better with a rifle in my hands."

"What are you thinking about?"

"This mission. So far, nobody we've hit in this operation has been an active combatant, and that's weighing on me a little. Have we turned into hired guns?"

"We've always been hired guns."

"Yeah, but this one's different," he said. "They hit Anya, and we had to get her back, but we're the ones who put her in harm's way. The guys we hit on the other ship were mostly unarmed."

"They may have been relatively unarmed, but they were on a mission to intercept us and take us down. We stopped that before it could happen."

He let his finger trace the trigger guard of his rifle. "How many civilians have you trained to shoot?"

"I don't know. Maybe a few dozen. Why?"

He asked, "How many of those did you teach to avoid a gunfight at all costs?"

I sighed. "All of them."

"Exactly. We could've avoided that fight."

"You may be right," I said, "but I made a battlefield decision, and it probably saved innocent lives."

He removed the bolt from his rifle. "You're probably right. How's Anya?"

"Not good. She has an infection from the injuries to her face, and Dr. Shadrack says we have to airlift her out to a real hospital."

"I know all of that. I want to know how she is."

I gave his question a great deal of thought before saying, "She accepts it."

"Just like any of us would."

I said, "It's a little different inside her head, but generally, yeah, she'll deal with it just like we do."

He inspected the bolt and inserted it back into the weapon. "So, what's next?"

"A stop in Athens so we can talk with Penny's producer and get Anya on a medevac."

The sniper and I sat in silence, watching the wake of the *Lori Danielle* part and then resettle behind the ship.

He finally said, "I'm thinking about spending some time at the monastery where my brother lived."

My heart sank. "But we need you."

He smiled. "Maybe that's why God sent Gator to us."

"He may be a great shot and have the academics of sniping memorized, but he's never—"

"Don't worry. I won't leave you without a sniper. He's still got a lot to learn, but he's got the goods."

I closed my eyes. "I can't imagine the team without you."

"I'm not talking about walking away right now. I'm considering spending some time at the monastery to meditate, pray. It says, 'Thou shalt not kill,' Chase."

"Come on. We both know that means commit no murder."

He raised his eyes and stared directly into mine. "What's the difference?"

* * *

We made the passage to Athens in just under ten hours, but that block of time was as torturous as any period of my life. The thought of operating without Singer perched someplace high above the rest of us and killing anyone who dared encroach on us sickened me beyond description, but the deepest agony lay roiling in my troubled soul. I'd relied on Singer as my spiritual and moral anchor for more than a decade. Without his wisdom and direction, I feared what good existed in me would devolve into the vindictive creature I proved to be the day before. The loss of a man of Singer's value would be a blow that I feared the team may not survive.

My ringing phone pulled me from my stupor.

Skipper growled, "Where are you?"

"I'm in my cabin. Why?"

"We need you."

"Who needs me, and where?"

She groaned. "Okay, Anya needs you, and she's still in sick bay."

I sat up, pulled on my prosthetic, and subconsciously checked myself in the mirror.

When I got to sick bay, Dr. Shadrack stepped in front of me. "She's not as bad as she looks. I administered some medication to make the transport more pleasant for her. She won't know you're here."

"Then why did Skipper tell me Anya needed to see me?"

"I have no idea. I've not spoken with her, and Anya's been sedated for hours."

Maybe I imagined Skipper telling me Anya needed to see me. Maybe

Singer's announcement sent me over the edge. Maybe I'm not fit to lead this team of men who deserve the focus of the best man on point. Maybe all of this is too much for both Singer and me.

I stood in astonished confusion and finally asked, "Did Skipper arrange for the medevac?"

Dr. Shadrack said, "It wasn't necessary."

"What do you mean? Of course it's necessary. She's obviously in need of the best care she can receive."

"Relax," he said. "She'll get that care, and it'll be in Athens. Barbie is waiting on the helipad to transport her now."

"Are you going with her?"

"No, I don't speak the language, and I don't have privilege at the hospital. If I went, I'd be nothing more than a visitor."

I said, "Somebody has to go with her. We can't just drop her off at their door with a return address label on her."

"Again, just relax, Chase. I've taken care of all of that. An attaché from the American embassy will meet us there and take responsibility for Anya."

"We're turning her over to the embassy?"

He raised an eyebrow. "Do you have a better idea?"

"How about Ernie Papadakis?"

"Who's that?"

"He's one of the engineers, and he speaks several languages, including Greek, Russian, and English. We should send him."

"Fine with me," the doctor said. "I just want her in front of the right doctor in the right facility right now."

The next ten minutes of my life were spent arranging to have Second Engineer Ernie Papadakis escort Anya through the medical process ashore. The captain approved it before Ernie knew I made the request. Big Bob, the chief engineer, was a little less understanding.

He growled at me. "Sure, take my second-in-command the day we've got four cylinders to rebuild. Just send me the best man on your crew to fill in for him while you've got Ernie."

"Mongo is my number-two man, Bob, and I'm certain you don't want him down here taking up the space of three average men."

He waved a filthy rag at me. "Fine. Whatever. Take him, but you better have his butt back down here before we move this tub another foot."

"Thanks, Bob. I'll do what I can."

With the negotiations complete, Anya, Dr. Shadrack, Ernie, and I boarded the Huey for the short flight to Attikon University Hospital in Athens. Gun Bunny made the rooftop landing look like child's play, and a team of scrubs-wearing medics rolled Anya from the chopper and into a corridor of the hospital, while the rest of us followed closely behind.

Between the efforts of Dr. Shadrack and our Greek engineer, the receiving doctor seemed to understand Anya's condition.

In his decent English, the doctor said, "We will have surgery for her today if she is stable."

I pulled Ernie aside. "Do you have money?"

"Yes, I have both euros and American dollars."

I stuck a black card in his hand. "Use this for whatever you need. Do you have a charger for your sat-phone?"

"I do."

I leaned close to him. "You check in with Skipper every six hours or whenever anything significant happens. Got it?"

"Yes, sir. I understand."

"Thank you for doing this, Ernie. I trust you far more than I'll ever trust an embassy diplomat."

My watch said it was almost time to meet Penny and her producer at Signature Aviation at Athens International.

I asked and was granted permission to fly from the left seat. I needed a task to get Anya out of my head, and flying the Huey was just what the doctor ordered. We touched down on the ramp outside the FBO just before a Gulfstream G550 taxied up.

The customs and immigration officer made short work of stamping their passports, and I threw my arms around my wife for the first time in what felt like an eternity. Even when she let her arms fall to her sides, I didn't want to let her go. I was coming apart at the seams, and she made everything better.

When the embrace finally ended, she motioned toward a distinguished-looking gentleman in a perfectly cut Italian suit. "Chase, meet Anton Blaire, the senior production manager at the studio."

I offered my hand, and he shook it like a man should. It was firm, confident, and bore no hint of Hollywood. "Pleasure to meet you, Mr. Blaire. I'm Chase Fulton."

"The pleasure's mine, Chase. And please call me Anton. I understand you and I have some rather pressing business to discuss."

"We do, indeed. That's precisely why I'm here."

He nodded. "Would you like to make use of the conference inside the FBO, or would you be more comfortable aboard the jet?"

"Actually," I said, "let's talk somewhere with a little more privacy and a lot more security." Concern filled his face as I pointed toward the Huey and said, "That's our ride, if it's not too crude for you."

He smiled. "Not at all. I paid for college using the G.I. Bill, so this will not be my first time aboard the old workhorse."

We boarded the Huey, and I reclaimed my seat up front. Barbie managed the radios while I flew us back to the ship. My landing was rocky compared to her practiced hand, but Barbie offered a pleasant "Nice job" when all the pieces stopped moving.

I led the way to the newly relocated combat information center, where I found Skipper, Dr. Mankiller, Captain Sprayberry, and the weapons systems officer entranced by something on Skipper's monitor.

That collection of people focused so intently on the same screen at the same time could mean only one thing, so I held up a hand to halt Anton and Penny. "Wait here. We may have a situation."

Chapter 30
About My Father's Business

Penny and Anton stopped in the corridor, and I approached Skipper's console. "This doesn't look good. Is everything all right?"

Weps glanced over his shoulder. "Oh, yeah. Everything's fine. We're just analyzing our position in case our friends from Ontrack Global decide to float another poison balloon our way."

"So we're not under attack from some alien force we didn't know existed?"

Weps chuckled. "Not that I know of, but if that happens, I'll be sure to tell you."

"On second thought," I said, "I don't really want to know if that happens. I'd rather have them beam me up and probe me than deal with a shootout with little green men."

Weps's absence of a sense of humor showed its ugly head, and I asked, "Will it bother you if I conduct a meeting at the conference table?"

"Not at all. In fact, we're just finishing up. I'll brief you on the situation when you're finished with your meeting."

I invited the guests into the room and motioned for Penny and Anton to have a seat. Right on cue, the rest of the team strode through the door in full tactical gear and focus etched on their faces.

I stood, and Anton followed suit. "Mr. Blaire, this is the tactical team who will likely become a valuable part of your life very soon."

The look in his eyes belied the confidence of the businessman beneath the bespoke suit and polished manner. He shook hands and offered polite greetings to each man. Penny didn't share Anton's impression of the team. She knew them all too well, and she was probably forcing back a giggle or two as our family played the part of the battle-hardened warrior.

We reclaimed our seats, and I began the briefing. "Can I get you anything, Anton? We've got a lot to discuss."

He waved a hand. "No, thank you, Chase. I'm anxious to get started."

"In that case, let's waste no more time. You told Penny you were a member of Culver Cove. Is that right?"

"It is," he said. "She asked, and I denied all knowledge of the club, as we're bound to do as loyal members, but her persistence changed my position."

"Very well. I'm glad she was persistent because what we have to discuss is of the utmost importance to the safety of that organization. Your annual Midsummer Retreat is scheduled, as usual, for the month of July. Is that right?"

"It is. The retreat has been held in July for over a hundred years, even through the war years."

"I'm as crazy about tradition as the next guy, but what we have to tell you may change that greater-than-a-hundred-year tradition."

He leaned back in his chair and scoffed. "Ha. I doubt it. But please, continue."

I cleared my throat. "Some time ago, an unnamed intelligence agency picked up a piece of radio traffic representing a direct threat to the Culver Cove Club. It seems that a terrorist organization plans to take everyone at the retreat as a hostage. We have no idea why they want to do that or even if they have the means to pull it off, but the threat is credible and quite real."

The confidence behind his eyes continued but appeared to crack at the edges. He said, "We have extremely high-level security on hand at every gathering, and the Midsummer Retreat is one of the most highly guarded private events in the country every year. I'm afraid whoever these people are have no idea who they're dealing with."

"Forgive my confidence, Mr. Blaire, but look at the men at this table. Every man you see has proven himself in the face of battle against unimaginable odds and has come out alive on the other side . . . multiple times. We represent over two hundred years of tactical and covert operations experience and training. Tell me, Mr. Blaire, how many of your security guards have those credentials?"

I gave him a moment to examine the eyes of the men around him, and he leaned forward. "What are we talking about here, Chase? Let's get this thing down to brass tacks, shall we?"

It was my turn to lean in. "The facts are simple, sir. You and your organization are in enormous danger if you hold your retreat this year, and it is highly unlikely that your high-paid security personnel have the training and experience to deal with an attack of this magnitude from some of the world's deadliest terrorists."

"Wait a minute," he said. "Are you telling me there's going to be another terror attack on the United States, and you believe it's going to happen at our Midsummer Retreat?"

"That's precisely what I'm telling you, sir. And I'm recommending that you cancel this year's retreat."

"That's preposterous. Our entire organization is built around that retreat, and canceling is out of the question. It's unthinkable."

"Is it as unthinkable as becoming a hostage and possibly being killed by a group who thrives on violence and striking terror into the hearts and minds of the American people? Are you so confident in your hired security that you'd risk your life and the lives of the other members just to continue a century-old tradition?"

He lowered his head as if either in prayer or deep thought. When he looked up, he said, "Give it to me straight. Is this real, or is it merely a threat to frighten us?"

"It's more than real, Anton. It's assured. We gathered the intel ourselves and nearly lost one of our operators, who is now in surgery in

Athens. This operator is one of the best in the world, and she was attacked, abducted, and tortured nearly to the point of death by these people. We liberated her and stacked the bodies of the perpetrators. That's who and what we are, Mr. Blaire."

He sat as if piecing together the puzzles of the universe, then he waved a hand through the air. "So, that's what all of this is? Some kind of CIA or military spy ship?"

"Not at all. We're not members of the military, although many of us have served in uniform. We're not associated in any way with the Central Intelligence Agency. And this ship isn't an asset of the federal government."

"So, you're contractors, like Halliburton or Blackwater."

"Neither. We're a team of some of the finest warfighters on the planet who've devoted our lives to the preservation of freedom and destruction of tyranny."

"Who pays you?"

I leaned back. "We're getting off track, Mr. Blaire. You and your organization are in potential peril. I have indisputable evidence of a planned attack against you and your Midsummer Retreat. Let's focus on that. Are you in a position within the organization to influence the schedule of the retreat?"

He appeared to snap out of a trance and turned to Penny. "So, this is why you write about this world so well."

My wife nodded once and focused on the man. "It is, and everything Chase is telling you is one hundred percent true. He wishes only to preserve your life and the lives of the attendees of your retreat. At the very least, you owe your members full disclosure of what you learned here today, and any rational man would take that information and cancel the assembly this year."

He chewed his lip for a moment. "Look at this from my perspective. A screenwriter flies me halfway around the world, to meet a team of whatever you guys are, aboard a ship that looks like something out of a movie that screenwriter created. Then you tell me that Culver

Cove, one of the most well-guarded secret societies on the planet, is going to be the target of a terrorist attack, so I should cancel our Midsummer Retreat. This all sounds ridiculous and paranoid. What's keeping me from thinking that *you* are the real terrorists trying to destroy one of history's great underground societies?"

At that moment, it occurred to me that the count was off, and I stopped caring what Anton Blaire believed. "Where's Singer?"

Shoulders raised and eyes scanned the room, but nobody said a word.

I slammed a fist onto the table. "Somebody tell me where Singer is!"

Mongo spoke in his soft, confident tone. "We don't know. I assumed he was on an assignment from you."

I spun to Skipper. "Find him!"

When I turned back to Anton, he was whispering behind a cupped hand to Penny, but in that moment, my thoughts abandoned Culver Cove's problem. My problem was a missing sniper and a team who had no idea where he was.

"Excuse me, Anton. We need to cut this meeting short. You have all the information I can give you. What you decide to do with it is your responsibility, but if you don't tell the other members of your little boys' club about the imminent attack, their lives are on you. My conscience is clear."

He rose from his seat. "I'd like to be returned to the airport. Unless, of course, you're holding me hostage."

"You're not a hostage," I said. "But you'll have to wait until we find our missing man before I can authorize the chopper to leave the ship."

Skipper said, "Uh . . . Chase. The chopper's already left the ship."

"What?"

"Yeah, she's back inbound now, and I think I found Singer."

I rolled my chair beside Skipper's console. "You *think* you found him?"

"His sat-phone is inside the hospital in Athens, but why would he be there?"

"He's trying to scare the hell out of Anya."

"What are you talking about?" she asked.

"I asked Singer to talk with Anya about what happens to us when we die, and I asked him to do it gently since she was probably raised to believe in nothing but Mother Russia."

"Is she going to die?"

"Sooner or later, but it's the possibility of the sooner part that has Singer concerned. He probably believes it's his responsibility to prepare her for eternity, just in case."

Gator had apparently been listening to the conversation, and he said, "Remember when Jesus got lost at the temple and his parents asked him where he'd been? He said, 'I've been about my Father's business,' or something like that. I guess that'll probably be Singer's answer when you ask him why he ran off."

Skipper said, "You've been spending too much time with Singer. You're starting to sound like him."

"He's a great teacher, but I'll never be that wise."

"Don't sell yourself short," I said. "You're doing just fine so far."

Persistence is the mark of desperation at times, and I had reached the point of utter desperation with Anton Blaire. I rolled back to the table and continued pleading my case. "I understand why you're opposed to canceling your retreat, but please hear me out."

He cocked his head and said, "Is this Singer person your chaplain?"

"What?"

"You called him Singer, right? Is he the chaplain?"

I scratched my chin. "No, he's our sniper."

"Your sniper . . . Interesting."

I said, "Let's focus. It's important for you to understand the severity and the reality of this threat."

He sighed. "Listen, Mr. Fulton. Canceling the retreat isn't going to happen. We've never canceled it before, and I can't imagine a scenario that would justify canceling it in the future."

"That scenario is here. That's what I'm trying to make you understand. If you're not willing to listen and take this threat seriously, please give me a way to contact the person in charge of security for your event. Because of what I know involving this threat, I have the responsibility to do everything in my power to protect the potential victims, and you *are* one of those potential victims."

He bowed his head as if finally considering the dire warning. When he looked up, he said, "Your passion is admirable, Chase, and believe me when I tell you I'm not taking your words lightly. I'm merely weighing them against everything I know. I'll tell you what I can do."

"Let's hear it."

"I can have a conversation with the leadership, share the information you provided, and pass along your recommendation to cancel the retreat. I have no reason to believe they will even consider canceling, but I will run it up the chain—as they say in the service."

I leaned in. "Tell me this, Mr. Blaire. If they don't cancel, knowing what you know now, will you still attend the retreat?"

Chapter 31
Fix What I Broke

I caught Gun Bunny before she could put the helicopter away. "We need to talk."

She froze. "Did I do something wrong?"

I led her inside the hangar bay. "No, you didn't do anything technically wrong since we've never discussed this before now, but I was caught off guard when I couldn't find Singer. On top of that, Skipper didn't know the Huey was gone. So, with that in mind, let's come up with a protocol for airborne operations during a mission."

Her shoulders relaxed. "Good idea."

"I need to know before you and the chopper leave the boat when we're on an assignment. You and that bird play critical roles in the operation of this team, and as team lead, I need to know the status and location of all of my assets. Secondarily, you're the only person on the team who can make that thing dance, regardless of conditions—"

She interrupted. "Disco is pretty good."

"Yes, he is, but not like you. You're the pilot. He's the emergency backup pilot."

She said, "You do okay, too."

"No, I don't, so don't flatter me. Can we agree on those parameters?"

"Sure, and I should've asked if you okayed the flight before I took Singer to the hospital."

"It's all right this time, but in the future, let's stick together."

"You got it," she said. "By the way, do you plan to have a similar conversation with Singer?"

I kicked at an imaginary pebble in front of my boot. "He's over there witnessing to Anya before they cut her face open to scrape out the infection, so I think I'll cut him a little slack on this one." She nodded, and I said, "Are you up for another run to the airport?"

She glanced through the hangar and then back at the Huey. "Yeah, but give me two minutes, if you don't mind. I had a lot to drink at lunch."

"We'll be ready to go when you get back."

I strolled out of the hangar bay and said, "Let's load up and get you back to the airport."

Anton stepped aboard, but Penny paused and said, "Uh, are you . . . I mean, where's Barbie?"

"Oh, you don't think I'm capable of flying you back to the airport?"

She laughed uncomfortably. "Yeah, I know you're capable, but I—"

"Just get on the chopper, you crazy thing. Barbie's coming back."

She took my arm. "Let's talk first." We stepped away from the Huey, and she asked, "Did you hear what Anton was saying to me when he was whispering in the CIC?"

I rolled my eyes. "I can't hear thunder, let alone anybody whispering."

She stepped closer. "He was firing me."

I turned for the chopper, but she grabbed me.

"No, wait. He changed his mind after you came back to the table. I think it was that line about him still attending the retreat that did the trick, so I was only temporarily unemployed."

"That was a good line, wasn't it? Maybe I should be the writer in the family, and you should chase bad guys all over the world and shoot them in the face."

She said, "Sounds like good work if you can get it."

"Does that mean I should let him live?"

She gave me the smile that melted my heart the first time I saw it. "For now."

Barbie returned, and we dropped Penny and Anton off at the airport, where their Gulfstream waited patiently for their return.

I kissed her goodbye on the ramp and said, "You can stay, you know."

She cocked her head. "I'd love to, but Tony and I are about to break the murder investigation wide open, and I have to be there."

"Oh, so now it's Tony *and* you conducting the investigation. Did somebody deputize you?"

She put on her wicked grin. "Maybe, and maybe I've got handcuffs. I'll see you when you get home, sailor."

I waved. "Don't shoot anybody in the face."

She shrugged and yelled back, "No promises."

Back on board the Huey, Barbie asked, "Do you want me to drop you at the hospital so you can read Singer the riot act?"

Part of me wanted nothing more than to be there when Anya woke up from surgery, but my responsibility lay with my team back on the ship. I'd already made a horrific battlefield decision because of the Russian, and I vowed I wouldn't make another.

"No, let's get back to the boat. I've got work to do."

She studied me for a moment. "Are you sure?"

I swallowed the indecision in my throat and nodded.

She touched down like a feather drifting to the ground, and I helped fold the blades and pull the Huey into the hangar bay. "Thanks for everything today, Barbie. You're a real asset to the team."

She gave me a mock salute. "Just doing my job, boss."

Back in the CIC, Skipper met me with her hat in hand. "Chase, I'm really sorry for not keeping track of the Huey. It won't happen again. I'm on my way to talk to Barbie right now."

"Relax," I said. "I already talked with her, and she's not leaving the ship again without ensuring that both you and I know she's leaving."

"I'm still sorry. It was my fault."

"It was nobody's fault. We'd never developed a protocol until now. It's solved, and it won't happen again."

"Okay, but I'm still sorry. What's the plan? Are we waiting around for Anya or what?"

"I haven't decided yet. What's your thought?"

She twitched her nose. "I don't know. Part of me thinks we should be here for Anya, but we really need to be back in the States to continue the mission."

"Let's do both," I said. "We'll hang on the hook right here until Anya gets out of surgery, then we'll pour on the coals and head for home."

My sat-phone chirped, and I answered without checking the screen. "This is Chase."

"It's Singer. You should probably come to the hospital."

Chills ran down my spine. "I'm coming."

"What was that?" Skipper asked.

"It was Singer. He said I should probably come to the hospital."

She logged off her computers. "We're coming, too."

I was pleased to see the signage inside the hospital written in both Greek and English. We found Singer and Ernie Papadakis in a surgical waiting room, both with their heads bowed and eyes closed. I froze at the door and waited for them to finish. Ernie looked up first and nodded, and the burning question felt like daggers inside my chest.

When Singer whispered "Amen" and opened his eyes, I slid onto the seat beside him. "Is she all right?"

"No, she's not all right. It's far more serious than Dr. Shadrack thought. I don't understand everything the surgeon said, but he came out just before I called you to update us on the surgery."

"What did he say?"

"He originally told us the surgery was primarily to clear her sinuses of the infection, but when they opened her up, they found some bone fragments penetrating the sinuses and something called superior sagittal sinus thrombosis."

The daggers in my chest turned to molten lava as I relived the hours I'd spent learning the anatomy of the brain I thought I'd never use. "That's a blood clot in the brain's sinus channels. Essentially, it stops blood from leaving the brain and going back to the heart."

Singer nodded. "That's what the surgeon said."

I grimaced. "Did he say . . ."

Singer slowly shook his head.

One of the fiercest warriors I've ever known was lying on a surgical table with pressure building around her brain and fragments of broken bone piercing tissue that should protect the frontal lobe from every-thing a person would normally encounter in their life, but I put Anya in a position so far outside the realm of normal that I'd likely gotten her killed from the punishment she received. It was my turn to pray.

When I closed my eyes, I sat there in silence, furious with myself for what I'd done to Anya and for what I'd asked her to do for me. Noth-ing short of a miracle was going to return her to the life she'd known only days before, and I was responsible for that.

How Singer knew is a mystery I'll never solve, but he leaned close and laid his arm across my shoulders. With wisdom dripping from ev-ery word, he said, "God doesn't care how much you blame yourself. He just cares that you trust him to fix whatever you broke."

That's when the tears came and the conversation with God began. I don't remember what I asked for. I don't remember what I wanted. Maybe turning back the hands of time so I could leave Anya out of the mission was what I wanted, but un-ringing that bell could never hap-pen. My sin was committed, and absolution wasn't coming. Being for-given isn't the same as un-committing the crime. The consequences remain, regardless of the amnesty. Anya would still be punished for my decision. Even if the surgery was successful, there would be damage that couldn't be repaired. There would be a price to pay, and she would pay that price. Forgiveness from above wouldn't mean Anya could ever for-give me for what I'd cost her . . . for what I'd taken from her.

The passage of time in that room had no measure. It could've been minutes or centuries before the surgeon dragged himself through the door. His shoulders sagged, and his hair stuck to his scalp, plastered there by sweat and time. His gait was that of a man who'd crossed a desert, and the clean scrubs he wore couldn't hide the battle he'd fought.

Everyone stood, and the surgeon's weary eyes searched the new faces for a familiar one and finally fell on Singer and Ernie. The doctor poured himself onto a chair beside our sniper and wiped his brow. All of us waited, praying for good news but fearing the truth.

His English was good, but exhaustion drew out his words. "She is alive, and she will stay alive, but we cannot know the severity of the damage to her brain. She will be in a coma for several hours, but someone will come for you when she is awake. She will be in neurological intensive care overnight, but you may see her two at a time after eight tomorrow morning."

Singer turned to me, but nothing I could ask would change the revelation, so I simply said, "Thank you, Doctor."

He nodded, rose, and left us staring at each other. Sometimes, silence is thunderous in its echoing torture, and in that moment, I wanted nothing more than to hear anyone say anything. Deep within my heart, I wanted to hear Singer's voice, but it was Ernie who broke both the silence and the tension when he checked his watch and said, "Everybody speaks English, so I'm going back to talk to the engines that know my voice so well."

Singer and I stayed, but the rest of the team choppered back to the ship, where Ernie's engines waited to feel his touch and hear his voice again. We slept minutes at a time as exhaustion overcame us, but neither of us was willing to leave the room.

As the sun crept through the blinds, I stretched and stumbled toward the coffee pot. Eight o'clock came, and we made our way to the intensive care ward and labored through the linguistic fog until we found a nurse with enough English to direct us to room seven.

Inside the room, Anya lay with her head bandaged, an IV in one arm, and monitors of every description recording everything going on inside her body. Singer stood on one side of the bed while I stepped to the other. I took her right hand in mine and held it gently. She opened her eyes and stared directly into mine for several seconds without a word. Then, she turned her attention to Singer, and he smiled.

He said, "Welcome back. We missed you."

She stared deeply into his eyes and said, "Chasechka, you look so much different than I remember."

I froze in place as she studied Singer's face. Neither of us knew what to do or say until she slowly turned to me, winked, and smiled.

I let go of her hand. "You had us worried."

"Why would you worry? I have many things to live for. Is too early for me to die. Besides, was funny joke, yes?"

"It's funny now," I admitted. "But I think you scared both of us nearly to death."

She reached for the sniper's hand. "I love you, too, Singer, but this is because you were worried I would go to Hell if I die. Now you know I have already been there, and I will never go back . . . thanks to you."

"Not thanks to me," he said. "I just told you the truth. You made the decision."

I said, "I never thought you'd be this alert when you woke up."

"I have been awake for hours. Doctors came to me in middle of night when I was first time awake. They were pleased with outcome of surgery, and I have been taking small nap maybe two or three times waiting for you."

"So, you've been planning to mess with me for hours?"

"No, plan only came to my mind when I heard both of you walk inside room. I will go to better room with not so many interruptions today and maybe leave hospital in few days."

"We can stay until you get out," I said.

She smiled again. "No, my Chasechka, do not do this. You go home to wife Penny, where is right for you to be. I will be okay. I am big girl."

Singer said, "I'll stay. We've got a lot to talk about, and I've got a lot more to tell you. If that's all right with Chase, of course."

Chapter 32
Ides of May

Back aboard the *Lori Danielle*, I finally got a few hours of quality sleep until Skipper banged on my door. "Chase! Wake up. I need you."

I didn't bother checking my watch. "Let me put my leg on, and I'll be right there."

"No, I'm coming in. You better have some clothes on."

She pressed through the door as I swung a leg and a stump over the edge of my bunk. "Good morning."

She looked away. "I know it's fine, but that thing still freaks me out a little."

"You should have to carry it around every day. I'm constantly freaked out by it. What's so important that you couldn't let me have another hour of beauty sleep?"

"You're pretty enough already," she said. "I just got off the phone with Anton Blaire, and he wants to have a face-to-face with you."

I yawned and pointed toward the cup in her hand. "Give me whatever that is."

She scowled. "It's herbal tea. Lemongrass and gingerroot, I think."

"Does it have caffeine?"

She held it toward me. "Yeah, I guess."

I drained the mug and pulled on my boots. "When and where?"

She took back her mug. "As soon as possible, and somewhere secure."

I kicked off my boots, and she frowned and said, "What are you doing?"

"Charter a flight out of Athens for the team, minus Singer. I'm going back to sleep." She started to protest, but I held up a finger. "Is the flight chartered yet? If not, go away."

She stormed from my cabin, and I fell back into the world of perfect slumber, sans boots and prosthetic.

Sometime later, I awoke from natural causes and hopped my way to the head. Showering on one leg isn't easy, but thankfully, the shower in my cabin contained a bench on which I could sit, or more often, place my stump and shower like a normal human. It was, in fact, one of the few things in my life that could be considered normal.

By the time I found food and my way to the CIC, things aboard the *Lori Danielle* were buzzing.

Skipper said, "Good, you're finally up. Everybody's ready to go, and the charter is booked. I even checked on Anya for you."

"For me? What does that mean?"

She cocked her head. "Stop it, Chase. You're not fooling anybody. They moved her to a private room. Are you paying for that, by the way?"

"Not that I know of, but she was injured on an officially sanctioned operation, so it is our financial responsibility."

She scribbled something on a notepad. "I'll talk to Ronda and make sure that happens. Anyway, Anya's doing better. Her cognitive function is good, and there are no signs of amnesia. She's a strong woman, and those surgeons must be really good."

I smiled. "I suspect Singer might disagree about the source of her improvement, but I'm glad to hear she's feeling better."

She continued. "So, nobody's taking any gear home. They said you wanted to build up the onboard armory. Is that true?"

"Yeah, I should've told you. I'm sorry."

She checked off an item on the pad. "No, don't be sorry. I just wanted to make sure. Let's see . . . What's next?" She consulted her pad. "Oh, yeah. I briefed the captain, and he's going to make way for Miami as soon as we disembark."

"Why Miami?"

"Because that's halfway between St. Marys and the mouth of the Panama Canal, sort of. That way, depending on which coast we need the ship, he can easily divert north or south. I thought it would be the most efficient route while we figure out the next steps."

"I like it. If I'm not careful, nobody's going to need me around here anymore."

"That's not true," she said. "Well, maybe it's a little bit true. Perhaps I should work on my gunfighting skills so you can retire."

"Retirement sounds nice. How's the pay?"

"That's out of my hands. You'll have to take it up with Clark."

"Wait a minute. Is Clark in charge of my retirement plan?"

She giggled. "Clark doesn't remember what he had for breakfast. He's not in charge of anything. Oh, I almost forgot. Did you know Anya speaks Greek?"

I laughed. "Of course she does. What made you think of that?"

"I told Ronda to give Ernie Papadakis a bonus for translating."

"Good idea," I said. "It sounds like you thought of everything."

"Almost everything. There's still one little dangler I've not cleaned up. I'm still tracking the *Better World*. She did return to port, but based on the footage from the security cameras, the hitters from On-track Global never got off the boat."

"Thanks for staying on top of that, but those guys aren't going to hit anything except the emergency room for a while."

She raised an eyebrow. "Yeah, I heard what you did. Chivalry is all cool and whatever, but . . ."

"I know, I know. It won't happen again."

"Yes, it will. You're not good at holding back in anything you do, and when Anya's involved, well . . ."

"Let's move on."

In the shipboard equivalent of being saved by the bell, the radio came to life. "CIC, Bunny."

Skipper picked up the mic. "Go for CIC."

"Request permission to depart for lift number one."

"Depart at will," she said. "Lift number two will be ready upon your return."

I motioned toward the radio. "Is that the new departure protocol?"

"It is. What do you think?"

"I like."

She secured the radio, shut down the computers, and locked the consoles. "Ready?"

I stood beside the helipad as Gun Bunny finessed the Huey onto the big white H. Although we couldn't jump high enough to touch the rotors, we all ducked as we approached the chopper. I took one last look over the stern deck, where Singer and I had our conversation about his potential departure, and a sick feeling rose into my gut.

"Let's go, Chase! We're going to miss the plane."

I could barely hear Skipper's voice over the engines and wind, but I pushed my concerns beneath the surface and stepped aboard the helicopter.

We boarded the Dassault Falcon that Skipper arranged for us, and Disco settled into one of the plush leather seats. He said, "So, this is what it feels like to ride in the back. I could get used to this."

I gave his boot a kick. "Don't get any ideas, Fly Boy. We need you up front."

He huffed. "Oh, well. At least I have the best view from up there."

We crossed the Atlantic in comfort, and once again, we were transported through time and space, far enough to leave our bodies wondering why our clocks refused to agree with our heads. Skipper wasted no time firing up the op center back at Bonaventure, and she had Anton Blaire on the phone only minutes after closing the door.

"Hello, Mr. Blaire. Chase Fulton here. I understand you'd like to have a chat."

"Oh, hello, Chase. I thought I told you to call me Anton."

"Very well. Anton, it is. When and where would you like to meet?"

Sounds came through the phone as if he were checking his environment for listeners. "Have you ever heard of the town of Culver, Oregon?"

"I think that name may have come up in some recent research. Would you like to meet there?"

He said, "I would. There's a private airstrip about fifteen miles west of the town of Culver. It's more than adequate to accommodate your Gulfstream, and we have fuel available."

He gave me the coordinates for the private airport, and I asked, "When would you like to meet?"

"I must admit, we're in a bit of a hurry. Would you be available for dinner this evening?"

I checked my watch, but it was a wasted effort. The poor device had no idea what time zone it was in. "That can be arranged, I suppose."

"Excellent. Please plan enough time to tour our facility. It's important."

I was instantly intrigued. "I'll do that, and I'll bring a few colleagues with specialty knowledge."

He paused for a moment. "But they are members of your group or team, right?"

"Yes, you will have seen them before. I believe I understand what you're asking, and we'll be more than happy to work with you."

"Thank you for your discretion, and I'd like to apologize for my lack of—"

I cut him off. "No apology is necessary. I understand. We'll see you in about four hours. May I call you at this number when we arrive?"

"That won't be necessary. I'll be waiting for you at the airstrip."

"There's one more thing," I said. "Our time and travel are expensive."

"You'll be well compensated. I assure you."

"Do you need an estimate?"

"Not at all. It will not be a problem."

Skipper disconnected the call and asked, "Was that what I think it is?"

"Probably. I think he wants us to provide a risk assessment and security plan for the retreat."

"And you're going to do it?"

I yawned. "I'm tired, but yeah, we're going to do it. Round up the team, and tell them we'll be wheels-up in thirty minutes."

No one grumbled when we boarded the *Grey Ghost* for Oregon, but everyone except Disco and me slept like babies on the way.

We landed at an uncharted private airport in the middle of nowhere, Oregon, about a hundred miles southeast of Portland. The runway was over a mile long, with hangars for several dozen airplanes. I taxied to the parking apron in front of what appeared to be the operations office for the field. A fuel truck arrived before we opened the Gulfstream's door, and a trio of SUVs followed only seconds behind the fuelers.

We descended the stairs, and Anton Blaire stuck out his hand. "So good of you to come, Mr. Fulton. I hope your flight was pleasant."

"Don't mention it, Anton. Just make sure your check doesn't bounce."

He chuckled and said, "That's not likely," and then motioned toward the lead SUV. "Shall we?"

We split the team into three vehicles and drove from the airport through a triple-gated sallyport with eighteen-foot fencing.

I examined the gates and fence. "Are you keeping people out or in?"

He said, "Perhaps both. That's why you're here. But before we begin, may I assume everyone understands this is of utmost privacy? Nothing we discuss may leave this place."

"In the world in which we live and operate, those are always the rules."

"Thank you for that. Now, here's what I'm asking of you. I'd like for you to see the retreat grounds and existing security measures already in place. Afterwards, I'd like for you to tell me what additional measures are necessary and whether you and your team have the ability to provide security for the retreat."

I re-situated in my seat. "I wish you'd told me that was your request when we spoke on the telephone this morning. I could've saved you a lot of money and us a lot of time and airplane fuel. The recommendation I made overseas remains my recommendation. We're not interested in contracting with you as security consultants or providers for your Midsummer Retreat. No security firm in the world would accept the risk that's associated with that event if they had the intel we have."

"Forgive me, Mr. Fulton. I failed to mention that based on your warning overseas, the board of directors has made the decision to move up the date for the retreat to the third week of May."

"Again, call me Chase. I'm happy to hear you're taking the threat seriously, but May fifteenth is ten days away."

"That's right. We're continuing electronic correspondence as if the retreat is still scheduled for July as a ruse, but the actual retreat will occur, as you say, in ten days."

"And are you planning to hire your previous security contractor?"

"We are not," he said. "As far as they know, the original date is still the planned date."

After eye-checking Mongo, I said. "In that case, let's take the nickel tour."

We stopped, and I briefed the whole team on what was happening. I said, "I like the fact that we're in three separate vehicles. We'll have a powwow after the tour and compare notes."

Back inside the lead SUV, I watched the scenery pass by as Anton spoke.

"The gate to the left is the primary entrance for those who drive to the retreat. Everyone who flies in uses the same runway you just used, and they come in the same way we did." He showed us several rows of cabins. "This is where most of our members live during the retreat. The others either choose to camp using their own RVs, or they stay in the lodge. We're headed there now."

I took copious mental notes as the security flaws in the property stacked up. We pulled to a stop outside a three-story log structure that could've been a five-star resort anywhere on Earth. Anton led us inside, where, if possible, the interior was more impressive than the outside. I tried to show no reaction, but the beauty of the place was awe-inspiring.

We made our way into an elegant dining room with several long tables, and Anton motioned toward the end of the first table, where several rolls of paper rested with rubber bands holding them in shape.

He pulled the rubber bands from four rolls and let the papers unfold. "These are high-definition aerial photographs of last year's event."

We gathered around and studied the photos carefully while Anton unrolled the remaining shots.

He said, "And these were taken two days ago. If these aren't sufficient, we have a helicopter available for you to see the retreat grounds from the air."

I stepped toward the current photos and submerged myself in them. A few minutes later, I said, "These are more than sufficient. Give me a relatively accurate head count for this year's event."

"Perhaps four hundred, but likely no more than that."

Mongo perked up. "Wait a minute. According to last year's shots, it was well over a thousand."

Anton said, "That was last year, when we had a regularly scheduled retreat. With the last-minute date change, the attendance will likely be cut by at least two thirds."

I took a step back from the table. "All right, Anton. We've seen enough. Give us a little privacy for half an hour, and we'll tell you how fearful you should be of the ides of May."

Chapter 33
The Clowns and Me

Anton pointed toward a pair of doors. "You're welcome to the gallery."

The team and I stepped through the door and closed it behind us.

Skipper was first to speak. "Is this some kind of cult?"

I took a seat. "I don't get that vibe. I think they're just a bunch of rich kids who don't like being told they can't play on their own playground."

Heads nodded, and I said, "Let's hear it. What's the weak link?"

Hunter said, "Too many people know too much."

Echoes of agreement confirmed his opinion, and I said, "That's not a variable we can change. It's always going to be the weakest point of the security plan. How about access?"

"Access isn't bad," Mongo said. "The fence is obviously wired, and I spotted enough subterranean leads to convince me they have a nice inner ring of sensors."

Gator's eyes flitted back and forth between Mongo and me as if he were anxiously awaiting permission to go to the little boy's room, so I said, "Let's hear it, Gator. What did you see?"

He blurted out, "A hundred sixteen cameras and a ring of what looked like microphones about forty yards inside the fence line."

Kodiak said, "Good eyes, kid, but I counted a hundred and eighteen."

"Then you're probably right," Gator said. "I probably missed two."

"He's messing with you," I said. "Nice work. Now, what I didn't see that's a real problem is watchtowers."

Mongo nodded. "Exactly. There aren't any now, and there weren't any in last year's pictures."

I said, "If we do this, we're bringing in overt watchtowers with pairs of wide-eyed shooters in every one of them."

"Where are we going to get these wide-eyed shooters?" Skipper asked. "We're not exactly an army."

"We'll put Clark on that," I said. "If all else fails, we can piece together enough gunners who can stay awake for a thousand bucks a day."

"We should've brought Singer," Hunter said.

I knocked on the table. "He'll be my first call if we decide to take this one. What do you think?"

Mongo leaned in. "Can we guarantee that we can stop an assault?"

I bit my lip. "We can never make that guarantee with any assignment, but can you think of anyone who can give them a better foundational security team than we can?"

Hunter said, "I don't like it. Whoever the potential attackers are, they're going to get word of the change of schedule, and they're still coming if they can pull it off."

I said, "They'll have the same problem we have right now. Can they get it done in ten days?"

"There's a lot wrong with this one," Kodiak said. "But we didn't join the Army, go to Ranger School, then Special Forces selection to say, 'Eh, this mission is screwed up, so I don't want it.'"

That seemed to be the pep talk the team needed. Between the grunts, hoo-ahs, and a bunch of other Green Beret noises I couldn't identify, the spirits of the team seemed to soar until Gator stuck his finger in the air and said, "Uh . . . I never did any of that stuff."

"Neither did I," I said, "but I'm game if you guys are."

A chorus of, "We're in," came back, and I turned to Skipper. "Let's hear your thoughts."

She held up her phone. "Clark already has twenty confirmed skilled shooters and three dozen grunts if we need them."

"Does that mean you're on board?"

She said, "I was on board when dude rolled out the hi-def aerials. Let's do it."

I led the team back through the double doors and found Anton sitting beside a man in an exceptional suit and no tie.

They stood, and Anton said, "Gentlemen, meet Lieutenant General Michael Biggs, U.S. Army retired. He's been head of the security committee for almost a decade."

I stuck a hand in his. "Nice to meet you, General. Are you the decision-maker for the physical security of the retreat? Do you write the check?"

He shook my hand, but not with enthusiasm. "I wouldn't say that I'm the decision-maker, per se, but my vote certainly carries more weight than some others."

I turned to Anton. "I'm sorry. I misunderstood. I thought we were working with the decision-maker today. Our hourly rate isn't insignificant. Am I making my pitch to a committee, the two of you, or just one of you?"

Anton cleared his throat. "Uh, well, technically, I have the authority to speak on behalf of the club, but General Biggs's insights and input are extremely valuable."

The general stiffened. "I'm afraid I didn't catch your name, son."

"Son? Oh, are we establishing dominance now? If so, have a seat, Daddy. I'm going to talk with Mr. Blaire."

We all need a hobby, and mine had long been watching self-important personalities explode. The fuse was lit, and I couldn't wait to see the show.

I sat, and my team formed a semicircle around me. "Mr. Blaire, your retreat ground has a great many attributes that make it relatively easy to defend against a conventional force. The physical security is easy enough. We can provide entry and exit control, perimeter defense, and background checks on each attendee."

The general stuck his three-star collar into the conversation. "Back-

THE SHEPHERD'S CHASE · 257

ground checks are out of the question. That's simply not done, and I won't allow it."

Oh, goody. It's time to cut the fuse and relight it a little closer to the powder keg.

"Oh, gosh. I'm so embarrassed. I misunderstood. I thought you took the security of your event seriously and wanted to make sure the attendees could fellowship in safety without worrying about being held hostage, killed, or worse. You clearly want to avoid hurting anyone's feelings, and in that pursuit, you're willing to forgo reasonable security measures."

It worked.

General Biggs burst from his seat. "What makes you think you can waltz in here without me doing a complete background check on you and every clown standing behind you pretending to be a tough guy? Huh? You listen to me, you little . . ."

The general stopped talking when I pulled a card from my pocket, wrote a name and number on the back, and slid the card toward him.

He glared down at it. "What is this?"

I locked eyes with him. "That's the number for Mr. Bradford Rawlings III. Give him a call, tell him how important you are, then describe me to him. When that's finished, have a seat, and we'll continue."

The general spent three minutes on his phone, and two and a half of those minutes were spent with him listening instead of talking. When he returned to the table, his powder keg was less susceptible to my spark. "Mr. Fulton, I've been assured that you are, indeed, far more than qualified for this mission, and I apologize for being defensive."

Anton glanced down at the card still lying on the table and back at me with his eyebrows narrowed and the plump bulge of flesh above his nose wrinkled and furrowed.

Before he asked, I said, "Bradford Rawlings III is the chairman of the Board who originally dispatched me on the mission to determine the validity of the threat against your organization. He has not only the ear of the president of the United States, but also that of every cabinet member and senator who's sober enough to understand the reality of the dangers in the world in which we live. If you'd like to know more, I'm sure the general can fill you in."

"That's not necessary. Please continue."

I glanced back at the team and said, "My clowns and I will provide the best security available for your assembly. We will be limited only by the restrictions placed on us by you and the organization you represent. If you don't want background checks, we can't be responsible for an internal attack. If you don't want perimeter guards, we can't be responsible for infiltration from the outside. If you don't want—"

Anton held up a hand. "I get the picture. In reality, how likely is it that this threat is internal?"

"That's impossible for me to answer. I don't have a roster of attendees. If you have a group who speak Old Turkic and have connections with terroristic groups in the Middle East, I'd say the likelihood of the threat being internal is relatively high. If you don't have such a group in your ranks, the chances of it being internal fall greatly."

He turned to Biggs. "Do we have such a subgroup within the likely attendees?"

"We do not."

I said, "In that case, we'll provide security for you under the following conditions. First and foremost, we are thoroughly and completely autonomous, meaning that we report to no one on the ground or within the organization. Once we begin providing security, everything regarding that security will be known only to me and my team. No one else will have access to our security plan, procedures, tactics, size of force, capabilities, or equipment. You and your organization will bear no legal responsibility for anything my team and I do in the process of providing that security. If it becomes necessary to implement deadly force, the fallout will be ours and ours alone."

I paused as the first half soaked in, and then I continued. "Finally, there will be no fee for our service from us." I slid Rawlings's card from in front of Biggs and toward Anton. "If reimbursement is required, that demand will come from this man. And when all of this is over, chances are you'll never see or hear from us again."

He tucked the card into his pocket and offered his hand. I shook it, and he said, "The job is yours. Tell me what you need from us to get started."

I turned back to Biggs. "General, sir, if you wouldn't mind providing the previous year's security plan and protocol, that would be of enormous value to us. And I apologize for being argumentative earlier. As you know well, we're men who live our lives in an arena littered with bureaucratic nonsense, and men like you and me don't have time for nonsense."

He said, "Understood, and I'll have those plans in your hands within the hour."

"Thank you, sir."

To my surprise, General Biggs slid a binder and an enormous ring of keys across the table. "Those are the existing access codes and key logs for the property. Members will begin arriving in nine days. If you need me for any reason, my contact information is inside the binder."

I passed the items to Skipper, and she passed them to Mongo without ceasing her incessant texting. When I glanced at the screen of her phone, the instructions to Captain Sprayberry still lingered.

Proceed to Coastal Oregon with greatest haste.

Everybody needs a Skipper in their life.

Anton and General Biggs departed, and I turned to my team. "Well, clowns, what do you say we put up the big top and get this circus underway?"

Chapter 34
Woodstock and Burning Man

"We need Singer on a plane right now," I said.

Skipper rolled her eyes. "It's already done. I recalled him as soon as I knew we were taking the job."

"When was that?" I asked.

"The minute Gator ran out of fingers and toes while counting cameras. I was terrified he was gonna take his clothes off, so I gave him a notepad and pen."

I said, "You're clearly way ahead of me already, but the next steps are getting the extra help headed west and finding the nearest equipment rental company."

"You were right," she said. "I *am* way ahead. Clark is gathering the troops, and I'm working on finding lifts we can use for watchtowers now."

We ran at full steam for the next six hours until the sun and our bodies were done for the day.

Hunter said, "I don't know how long we've been awake, but I'm out of gas."

"Me, too," I said. "Let's commandeer a few rooms in the lodge for the night and get some rest."

When we made it back to the massive lodge at the center of the camp, I was surprised to see two vans parked by the loading dock.

"We're on it," Kodiak said as he and Gator dismounted with hands on their pistols.

I took the rest of the team through the front doors so we could clear our way to the loading docks from the inside. With pistols drawn, we moved in two-man teams, working every room and dead space as we progressed. Disco and I pressed through the double swinging doors to the kitchen and raised our weapons in unison.

I ordered, "Hands up, now!"

Five terrified people in white aprons and hats threw their hands into the air, and someone screamed, "Don't shoot!"

Gator and Kodiak moved into the kitchen from the opposite end, adding even more terror to the eyes of our unexpected guests.

I lowered my weapon. "Who are you, and what are you doing here?"

"We're the caterers, and we're here to serve dinner for you," a woman said, her voice cracking with every syllable.

Still uncertain, I asked, "Who sent you?"

"Mr. Blaire," she answered.

I signaled for the team to lower their weapons and holstered mine. "I'm sorry we frightened you. We weren't expecting anyone to be here."

The woman grabbed her chest as if having a heart attack. "Next time, we'll blow the horns and bang the pots and pans together."

"That's not necessary," I said. "We'll be expecting you next time."

They fed us in the gallery, and every bite was magnificent. It could've been our empty stomachs talking, but it tasted like Michelin Star dining from start to finish. With the adrenaline drained from our bloodstreams and our stomachs full, we crashed as if we hadn't slept in days. The jet lag would force our bodies to sleep for hours to begin the process of acclimating to the new time zone . . . whatever time zone it was.

* * *

"We need Clark," I said as I polished off my omelette served by the same crew as the night before.

Disco wiped his mouth. "Yes, we do. I'll fly solo to the East Coast and bring him back with me when I pick up Singer and the ground troops."

The airlift began and continued for two days using two airplanes—our *Grey Ghost* and a borrowed C-130 from an agency of the federal government I'd never heard of—but finally, every piece of gear we could need and every capable body we could put to use were on the ground in Oregon and ready to go to work.

Singer directed the placement of the rented lifts to act as watchtowers. Dr. Mankiller and Skipper built a secure network for the video cameras. Gator's count was correct. The hanging microphone strands we spotted on our initial tour turned out to be specialized listening devices capable of filtering out natural sounds and targeting noises as light as human footsteps that shouldn't be in the environment. Those were nifty little gadgets, and Celeste made sure their network was just as secure as the video feed.

We brought in a mobile command post borrowed from the U.S. Marshals Service built on a tractor trailer and turned it into our op center. After six solid days of working everyone's fingers to the bone, one of the finest security elements in the world was in place and almost ready to protect the elite membership of the Culver Cove Club Midsummer Retreat.

I called the whole team together outside the op center. "Listen up!"

The crowd quieted, and I spoke loud enough to be heard in the back. "Nice work, everybody. We're two days ahead of schedule because of your hard work, and I appreciate every one of you for digging deep to make it happen."

Somebody in the back yelled, "You're paying us. It ain't like we volunteered."

"True," I said. "And if this goes off without a hitch, your paychecks will be even heavier than you're expecting."

That elicited a cheer, and I said, "Don't get too excited yet. We need to run a couple penetration drills."

That elicited a round of groans.

"I know, I know. But you can't play without practicing, so let's get a couple dress rehearsals under our belts before we rest up for the real thing."

We ran a day and a half of penetration drills using Singer, Kodiak, Gator, and Hunter as opposing force players. The rest of the team, including Clark, graded the response of the security force and made small corrections to their tactics until it was flawless. Of the ten attempts to penetrate the compound they made, only two were successful, and those were early on day one.

Our meeting reconvened, and every shooter was assigned to a team to be directed by one of my operators. Clark would command the op center while I ran the team leaders and reported directly to him. With the squad assignments made and the twelve-hour rotation schedule posted, the physical security was in place, and it was time to get technical.

Skipper and Celeste reported that all systems were functioning as expected, and nothing unusual showed up on any of the background checks.

Skipper laid her hand on a stack of papers. "This is the felony stack. There are eleven of those. None are violent offenders, and all received early parole. Two of them even scored presidential pardons."

I let out a whistle. "Impressive."

She shrugged and motioned toward a much larger stack. "That's the misdemeanor, bankruptcy, and general mischief stack. You can look through it if you want, but it's mostly drug stuff and DUIs. It's hard to believe how many rich people have filed bankruptcy."

"How about connections in Turkey?"

"A few of the retired military have some limited overseas connections, but there's nothing deep."

"How many total attendees?"

"Four hundred and twenty-six, but according to Anton, that number is flexible depending on last-minute availability. He says to expect three to five percent variation from that number."

264 · CAP DANIELS

"Okay," I said. "What are we missing?"

She leaned back in her chair. "Four hundred happy campers doing whatever they do out here in the woods."

Clark pulled me aside. "Let's have a chat, College Boy."

I followed him to the minuscule office at the end of the op center.

He said, "Your final question has me worried. We're missing something, and it's haunting me. I need you to plow through that big brain of yours and think about how you'd hit this compound if you were the bad guy."

I propped myself on the edge of the small desk. "I've been doing that for a week, and I've covered every base I can think of. Have you talked to Mongo?"

Clark said, "I had this same talk with him, and he said the only remaining weakness he can find is the catering."

"The catering?"

"Yeah, he says it'd be easy to turn this thing into a Jim Jones Kool-Aid party if the caterer wanted to do it."

"He's right," I said. "But we ran full backgrounds on everybody on the catering and service staff. It's not like we can run every plate through a gas chromatograph to look for poison."

"I get it. I'm just telling you what I know."

* * *

Campers arrived in droves, and Dr. Mankiller's facial recognition system tied each of them to the list of confirmed attendees. Our perimeter security was all but impregnable, and the arrival went off like clockwork.

Day one of the circus looked like Woodstock and Burning Man had a lovechild and named it Culver Cove Club Midsummer Retreat. Multimillionaires danced naked in front of bonfires ten feet tall, and every imaginable illegal substance flowed like a waterfall. With everything, I expected the upper echelon of society to be crumbled before midnight. It was chaos of the highest order, and I, for one, lost all interest in ever becoming a member of that illustrious club.

At breakfast on day two, I found Anton Blaire eating peanut butter and using a celery stick like a spoon. He had a pair of feathers stuck in his hair and a loincloth draped around his waist.

He shoved the celery into the peanut butter and held out the glistening blob toward me. "Want some?"

I held up a hand. "No, thank you. I ate several hours ago. Listen, I wasn't prepared to watch what's happening here. I should've debriefed you more thoroughly, but it's becoming clear that we'll have some medical casualties who need to be evacuated if this thing continues the way it's begun. We have measures in place for that, but it looks like we may have underestimated the volume of that particular service."

He held up another globule of brown goo. "Are you sure you don't want some?"

"I'm sure. I need to know the number of medical evacuations that were conducted last year at this event."

"Relax, man. It's just some high-stress individuals letting off the steam that's been building up for a year. Nobody's going to die. They'll chill out after a couple of days. It's always wild the first night."

At the end of day number two, Anton's prediction became reality. The drug use slowed, and the energy lessened, but not by much. The medical station I put in place to treat injured security forces became a walk-in clinic for the rich and famous. Our combat medics saw parts of their favorite movie stars they never thought they'd see, and more IV bags of normal saline were hung than in any hospital in America. Defeating dehydration turned out to be the greatest battle we faced in the first forty-eight."

Just before midnight, I stumbled into the op center and collapsed into a chair. Before I could resist, I became the most recent recipient of a needle in the arm.

Singer said, "You look like you've been through the war. This'll make you feel better."

"Thanks. Aside from the general chaos, what are you seeing out there?"

He took a seat beside me. "Honestly, it's a lot better than I expected. I was just talking with Celeste and Skipper about radio chatter, and nobody's talking about this thing."

"Nothing out of the Middle East?"

Skipper pulled off her headset. "Nothing anywhere. It's like all these big shots just vanished from the Earth and nobody cares."

Clark chimed in. "I guess it makes sense when you think about it. A lot of these guys live at the extreme highest levels of whatever they do. They're going to burn out sooner or later. Maybe a week in the woods acting like a flower child in the sixties is what keeps them sane."

I pointed through a darkened window. "Look out there. What about that makes you think anybody in this camp is sane?"

He said, "You know better than anybody that you can only burn the midnight oil at both ends for so long before somebody has to give the piper a pie."

Clark's wisdom made more sense than anything going on in the maelstrom of crazy happening just outside our trailer, and I mumbled, "You can say that again."

Sleep took me, and I loved her for it, but the sun insisted on coming up again. The madness began to form a sense of organization, and I feared I'd adapted to the new normal. Nothing about that made me feel good about myself.

The calamity continued its gently waning arc as the days played out, until Gator came to me early on the morning of day number four.

"Chase, I'm sorry to bug you, but I'm pretty sure we've got some missing people."

Chapter 35
Now You See Me

"How do you know?" I asked our newest teammate.

Gator grimaced. "I don't know for sure, but there seem to be some faces missing that were pretty prominent in the first few days. I can't put my finger on it, but do you remember that lesson you gave me about noticing what I'm not seeing?"

"I remember."

"It's like that. They should be here, but they're not."

"Can you name any of them or describe them?"

"I definitely can't name them, but there's a couple of guys who stood out. The first one was tall and thin with bushy hair. He reminded me of Kramer from *Seinfeld*."

"It's not ringing any bells for me," I said.

"Maybe this'll do it," he said. "He always wears a shirt unbuttoned and no pants."

"Oh, that guy."

"Yep. And the other one is a little guy with really black hair. It has to be a dye job. He wears enormous glasses and walks sideways when he's high."

"Come with me," I said as I led him to the op center.

"Tell Skipper what you told me."

He replayed the story, and Skipper pulled up some security footage on a monitor and pointed toward a chair. "Scroll through the video until you find one or both of them."

Gator obeyed and soon said, "Got him!"

Skipper spun, and Gator pointed to Kramer on the screen.

She said, "Give me a minute to run facial recognition."

A few seconds later, she said, "His name is Lamar Griggs, and he owns a fund management firm on Wall Street."

"Oh, a big money guy," I said.

Skipper typed and finally said, "You could say that. He's worth about one point six."

I frowned. "One point six million? That's not a big player. We're worth more than that."

"*Billion*, with a B."

I tipped my cap. "That's not our tax bracket. What about the other guy?"

Skipper turned to Gator and raised her eyebrows.

He said, "I haven't found him yet, but this guy sets off an alarm. I think he's missing, too."

"Give me a minute, and I'll find him," Skipper said. She ran the program, and results hit the screen in seconds. "That's Rodrigo Pilar. He's a fine wine broker from Portugal. His net worth is . . ." She paused and then typed furiously. "That can't be right."

"What is it?"

She said, "It says here that his net worth is one point four billion. But a billionaire wine broker? That doesn't make any sense."

"He must sell a lot of wine," Gator said.

Skipper was burning up her keyboard and finally relaxed. "Okay, here it is. This makes more sense. It's family money. They were in the worldwide shipping business."

"Like real ships or trucking?" Gator asked.

"According to this, they were into everything from front porch delivery to bulk cargo, all over the world. It's odd that I've never heard of them."

I cocked my head and stared at the ceiling. "Do you find it odd that we've got two missing guys, and both are worth over a billion dollars?"

"And there's another guy," Gator said.

Skipper nabbed the shot and quickly had the man's data in front of her. "That one is easy. I could almost do his from memory, but I won't. He's another high-net-worth guy. His name is Bidar Sharone. He's an Israeli who owns a bunch of diamond mines. Hang on, and I'll give you his numbers."

A few seconds later, she said, "Oh, the diamond mining business is better than I thought. We're looking at one point eight for him."

I didn't like the feeling in my gut. "Is there a way to compare video footage from day one to day three and look for missing faces?"

Skipper groaned. "Uh, maybe, but I'll have to write some code. It'll take a while."

"How about Celeste?" I asked. "Can she do it?"

Skipper checked her watch. "She's sleeping, but she'll be here in an hour."

"Go wake her up," I said. "If this is what I'm afraid it is, we don't have any time to waste."

I gave Gator's shoulder a shove. "Good eye, sniper. Have you told anybody else about this?"

His eyes fell to the floor. "No, but I guess I should've told Singer. I was afraid I was just being paranoid, and I didn't want him to know. That's why I came to you."

"Listen to me," I said. "Never be afraid to tell any of us absolutely anything you see, hear, suspect, feel, dream about, whatever. Don't keep secrets. I hope I'm wrong, but I think our attack is happening right under our noses, and your eyes saw it first."

Skipper was back with Celeste long before I expected, and the mad scientist pushed past me and situated herself at a keyboard in the corner.

I stepped behind her. "Can you do it?"

"Not with you breathing down my neck."

I stepped away, and five minutes later, she spun in her chair. "Try it now."

Skipper ran the program, and images flashed on the screen in front of her like a strobe light.

I was mesmerized. "Is it working?"

"Keep your shirt on," Skipper said. "This is a lot of data and graphics to crunch, and it's not like we have a supercomputer out here."

I tapped my foot on the ground and incessantly glanced at my watch until Skipper said, "It'll be thirty minutes or more. Go do something, and I'll call you when and if I get a list."

I grabbed Gator's shirt. "You're with me."

He gave no resistance, and five minutes later, we were sitting in front of General Michael Biggs. "I'm sorry to bother you, General, but since you were the security manager—"

He stopped me. "No, I wasn't the security manager. I was merely in charge of *hiring* the security manager. I was chair of the committee."

"Either way, we've got an issue, and I'd like to have your input before we sound the alarm."

"What is it?"

"People are missing."

He frowned. "Missing? What do you mean, missing?"

I said, "People who were here on day one aren't here anymore."

"How do you know? Are you taking a head count every day?"

"No, sir. It's just observations."

He sighed. "This is exactly what I was afraid would happen when you and your merry band of door-kickers took over. I knew you'd overreact to environmental variables you don't understand."

"What are you talking about?"

He pointed toward the window. "Look out there. You've got a bunch of over-fifty, overworked, overstressed, overweight overachievers doing every drug you can name in the middle of the woods and dancing naked around bonfires. They're not soldiers like you and me. That kind of extreme lifestyle breaks down, and they end up sleeping for twenty hours at a time. They're sleeping it off in their cabins. Stop being so paranoid, and for God's sake, don't go knocking on doors and invading the privacy of the men who've earned that twenty-hour coma. You're here to guard the gate and run off the reporters with cameras. Nothing more. Do you understand?"

Gator said, "But, General—"

I grabbed his arm and stood. "We're sorry to have disturbed you, sir. It won't happen again."

Biggs turned away as if we'd never been there, and we hit the door.

Gator spoke up the instant we hit the ground. "I'm sorry about that. I didn't mean to butt in like that, but he's wrong."

"I know," I said, "but an ego like his isn't something you can argue your way out of. Just let him believe he's right and pretend to be respectful. We'll work around him and do our job. You're doing fine."

When we climbed the steps into the op center, Clark plowed through the door with half a sandwich in one hand and the other half mostly in his mouth. He mumbled something that sounded like, "I was just coming to find you," so we followed him back into the trailer.

With the sandwich gone, his communication skills improved dramatically. "Skipper got too many hits."

I planted myself beside the analyst. "How many?"

"Too many," she said. "We have to tighten the parameters, so this is going to take a lot longer than we thought."

I leaned back and spun to face Clark. "Should we put out an order to report *not* seeing people?"

He said, "You're the psychologist. What do you think would happen if we tell everybody to do that?"

I sighed. "It would be a disaster, but let's put it out to our team."

Clark nodded his approval instead of talking through another sandwich that mysteriously appeared out of nowhere.

I keyed the radio. "Attention all Sierra elements. Switch to secure seven and check up."

Each of my team reported up on the new frequency in seconds, and I said, "Keep your eyes open for faces that should be in the crowd but

272 · CAP DANIELS

aren't. We may have a situation building, but we're still collecting data.

aren't. We may have a situation building, but we're still collecting data. Expect a full briefing at shift change. Acknowledge by call sign."

Each team member gave their call sign, and I watched Clark devour a Yoo-Hoo in one gulp. He wiped his mouth with his sleeve and said, "Give it to me, College Boy. What do you think's happening?"

I glanced at Gator, and Clark said, "He can stay. He needs to learn how your crazy brain works."

I said, "Somebody is grabbing the high-net-worth guys one at a time, and they're monitoring our reactions."

Clark cut me off. "How?"

"How are they grabbing them, or how are they monitoring us?"

"Both."

"I don't know how they're picking them off, but Skipper isn't the only computer genius in the world. They could be flying high-altitude drones with hi-def cameras or even piggybacking on a satellite or two. Our comms are hard to intercept, but it could be done with enough equipment and know-how."

He said, "All right. Now tell me about the why."

"I don't know yet," I admitted. "But now we know what to look for. We just have to make a top-ten list of the highest bank accounts in the camp and keep them in sight without showing an obvious reaction."

Clark rocked back and forth for a while and said, "I'm somewhere between your know-it-all general and your theory on this thing. Either of you could be right, but your plan to keep an eye on the real players should tip the scales for me."

"So you think I'm wrong."

He shook his head. "I didn't say that. I'm just not convinced you're right . . . yet."

"Good enough. I'm going to find Anton. He needs to know what's going on."

Clark reached for my leg. "No! He doesn't need to know. Not yet. If we're going to disguise our reaction just in case somebody's looking, we don't need to tip Anton off to anything. He'll be impossible to control."

"What about General Biggs?"

"Don't worry about him. He's not going to react. He won't be the one who blows our cover. He's too cocky to believe they were ever a target in the first place."

I leaned way back and closed my eyes as the machine in my skull churned away.

As I built the list of next steps in my head, Skipper said, "Okay, I can get that for you."

I shook my head and opened my eyes. "What?"

She said, "I'll get the list of cabin and room numbers for you. That's what you asked for, right?"

"How did you know that?"

She rolled her eyes. "Chase, everybody knows you think out loud."

"No, I don't."

I scanned the room to see every head nodding in agreement.

"We'll deal with that another time," I said. "For now, get that room-number list and find the billionaires."

"I'm on it," she said. "But what if it's not just the billionaires? What if we just happened to notice them first?"

Chapter 36
Birds of a Feather

"Stay on the code Celeste wrote," I said. "We need a roll call without anyone knowing we're doing it."

I left the trailer thinking about Clark's instructions to leave Anton Blaire out of the situation, but I couldn't swallow it, so I turned and pulled open the door. "Hey, Clark. Let's go for a walk."

Before he reached the bottom of the stairs, he said, "This is about Blaire, isn't it?"

"It is. I don't feel good about keeping him out of the loop since he's the one who hired us and I'm the one who talked him into it."

He stopped and turned to face me. "You're only half right. You talked him into it, but he didn't hire us. The Board directed us. If Anton writes a check, it'll be to the Board, and we'll get paid, regardless whether he writes that check. You're looking at this from the wrong angle."

I considered his position. "Okay, you're right. He didn't technically hire us, but I still feel an obligation to him."

"Of course you do. That's why you're so good at this job, but think about this. What if he's in on it?"

"In on the scheme to kidnap billionaires?"

He said, "Yeah, why not? If you go running to him on a theory that has very little, if any, evidence to support it, it'll accomplish one of two things. If he's in on it, it'll notify him that we're all over it. And the second option is for us to lose all credibility if any one of the three so-called missing dudes shows up hungover, hungry, and looking for more nose candy."

I shook it off. "Okay, I'll defer on this one, but that doesn't mean I agree."

"Give it thirty-six hours. After that, it's all yours. Make all the moves you want and call in the National Guard if you think you should."

"I think we'll leave those guys out of this, but a lot can happen in thirty-six hours."

He slapped me on the back. "You're right about that, my friend."

I huffed. "Did you really say nose candy?"

He laughed. "Call it whatever you want, but I'm thinking about signing up for this group. If I can dance naked at a campfire and not go to jail, that's my kind of people."

I gave him a shove. "Get out of here, Dancing Queen. I've got work to do."

There are environments when security personnel should be blatantly obvious—bank lobbies, concerts, and places like that where the mere presence of an armed guard deters misbehavior. But the environment in which I stood did not fall into that category. The men in the camp neither wanted to see nor encounter anybody outside their social class, and certainly not an armed guard dressed like a freedom fighter. With the exception of the riflemen perched high in the lifts around the perimeter, I never wanted any member of Culver Cove to know we were there. I considered my force to be an invisible shield between the club and the rest of the world.

With that in mind, I walked the perimeter, checking on everyone I encountered. They were alert, attentive, and doing their job like the ardent professionals they were. That pleased me until I realized Singer was missing for the second time in one operation, and that did the opposite of please me.

I grabbed my mic. "Sierra Six, Sierra One."

Nothing.

"Sierra Six, Sierra One."

The silence only served to pour salt in my open wound. "Sierra Six, this is Sierra One. Report!"

The bone conduction device in my jaw sent the sound of two mic clicks to my brain, and I sprinted for the op center. I burst through the door. "Get me Singer's location!"

Skipper didn't put up a fight. She brought up an electronic map of everyone's position and jabbed a finger at the screen. "He's right there near the access point from the airport."

"Do you have a drone in the air?"

"Of course."

"Get me eyes on that location."

She brought up an aerial view on a second monitor, and I studied the picture. "What's he looking at?"

She zoomed in and followed his line of sight. "I don't see anything except the airport, but he's obviously glued to something or somebody."

I called Gator, and he showed up in seconds. "Do you know what Singer's doing out there?"

He squinted at the screen. "No idea, but I can run out there and find out if you want."

"No, stay here. You may see something I miss. Take a look at the airport. Is there anything out there that shouldn't be?"

He studied the monitor and asked, "Can you give me a side angle on that white vehicle between the third and fourth hangars?"

Skipper maneuvered the drone into position, nearly two miles above our heads, and zoomed in on the vehicle. "That's a catering truck."

Gator said, "Yes, it is, and that doesn't make any sense at all."

I scratched my neck. "That wouldn't stop Singer from answering his radio, though, would it?"

Gator tapped on the screen. "Nope, but *that* would. Zoom in right there."

Skipper did as he said, and soon, an array of parabolic directional microphones came into focus.

My heart sank. "Somebody's listening way too hard."

Celeste said, "If those aren't our long-range mics, my PEW-PEWS will take them out and probably deafen anybody who's listening."

"Are you serious?" I asked.

She said, "Sure. They're pulsed energy weapons. Sound is the ultimate definition of pulsed energy. One little love tap from one of my rifles, and those things become giant paperweights."

I poked Gator with a pen. "Hey, Eagle Eye, you and Skipper find every one of those parabolic mics. I'm going to see my priest."

As I approached Singer's perch with Celeste's Pulsed Energy Weapon Prism Enhanced Warfighting system, I called him on the comms. "I'm thirty yards east with the PEW-PEWS."

He didn't have to answer. I watched him turn his head to look my way. He dropped a ball of 550 cord from his elevated position, and I tied the line to the sling lug of the weapon. The high-tech rifle left my hands and slowly rose until Singer cradled it like a baby in his arms.

The weapon made very little sound as it warmed up. When Singer pulled the trigger, absolutely nothing obvious happened, but Skipper had a different story.

Through the magical electronics in my skull, her voice rang loud and clear. "Sierra One, Sierra Ops, the catering van departed simultaneously with the shot from Sierra Six."

As I tried to put the puzzle together in my head, I said, "Roger. Say additional targets."

She said, "Negative additional targets."

"Keep looking," I ordered.

Singer leaned over the edge of his perch and lowered the weapon to me.

I caught it and said, "It must've worked. The catering van boogied out the instant you fired."

He said, "I know. I saw it. What's going on over there, Chase?"

He climbed down, and I said, "Gator picked up on some missing faces in the crowd, and it turns out the three he identified are all billionaires. That can't be a coincidence."

"I knew he was up to something. I wonder why he came to you instead of me."

I said, "We talked about that. He was afraid he might be mistaken, and he's terrified of disappointing you."

Singer sighed. "That's my fault. I can't keep the fact that he's a civilian in my brain. I keep treating him like a Ranger instead of a football player, and this is what happens."

"Don't beat yourself up. You're building one heck of a spotter out of that kid."

"Yeah, but I've got to find a way to teach him not to be afraid of me."

"You'll figure it out. Let's head back to the op center and see if they've found anything else for you to shoot."

Gator looked up first when we walked in. "There are no more. I've scoured every picture from every angle. That was the only listening array."

Singer laid a hand on his protégé's shoulder. "Well done. I'm proud of you. But don't ever be afraid to come to me."

"Did you notice the missing faces, too?" Gator asked.

Singer shook his head. "No, I missed it. That's why you and your young eyes are so valuable to this team and to me."

I stepped back through the door and wormed my way behind the trailer to find a private spot to sit and think.

Figure it out, Chase. Directional long-range listening devices, a catering truck, missing billionaires, a retired three-star general who thinks I'm an idiot, a Hollywood producer, and a bunch of uber-wealthy fruitcakes getting stoned out of their minds and acting like savages. What is going on out here?

I squeezed my temples between the heels of my hands and begged my brain to put it together.

Maybe I'm overacting. Maybe the general is right. Maybe I'm the one who needs a break in the woods to dance naked and sleep for twenty hours in a row.

Back inside the trailer, I asked, "How's the facial recognition search coming along?"

Celeste said, "I reprogrammed it to look for faces that appeared on the first two days of whatever this is and create a database of those faces. Then I had the computer process that database against a database generated on days four and five. I know it sounds simple, but it's not."

I said, "Nothing about it sounds simple. Keep talking."

"When I ran the two databases against each other, I came up with two lists. The first one is a list of thirty-eight people who don't appear in both databases."

"That sounds promising," I said.

"Yeah, that's a good list. We'll come back to that one in a minute. The second list is the interesting one. There are six faces on it, and they are faces that appear on days four and five, but not on days one and two."

"That is interesting," I said. "Are they late arrivals?"

Celeste said, "I thought the same thing. Only two people arrived after day two, and both of them are on that list, so I culled them, leaving four faces we can't identify."

"When was the last time any of those four were caught on camera?"

She said, "I don't know, but that would be a nice piece of data. What I want to know is how those four people got in here without being detected and are not on the official roster."

"Do any of those four ever appear together on camera?"

"Nope."

I let out a long breath. "That's not good. We've been infiltrated, and we missed it."

"We didn't miss it," she said. "We just didn't catch it early."

"Let's focus on that first list. Of the thirty-eight faces, how many are billionaires?"

"Five."

"Do we know their cabin or room numbers?"

It was Skipper's turn to join the party. She handed me a printed list. "We do."

I immediately stuck it in Singer's hand, and he and Gator vanished.

I said, "All of this high-tech stuff is nice, but sooner or later, somebody has to kick down a door."

Clark grinned. "I say we start with the catering van doors."

I said, "My thoughts exactly."

"Birds of a great mind have feathers together, College Boy. Everybody knows that."

"Indeed, they do."

Chapter 37
That's One Way to Do It

As the shadows grew longer and the coming of post-dinner bonfires loomed, Gator, Hunter, Kodiak, and I made our way in utter silence behind the lodge and to the loading dock, where four catering vans waited like sitting ducks. Unfortunately, door-kicking wasn't in our near future. All four vans sat with doors wide open, inviting us to stroll on in.

Hunter and I stood watch while Gator and Kodiak crawled through the vehicles.

Gator said, "You can't imagine how good it smells in here. I'm looking for morsels that fell off of whatever they unloaded out of this thing."

"Stop scrounging, and find something we can use," Hunter said.

A pair of men wearing aprons and pushing two oversized carts burst through the doors from the loading dock.

I stepped around the corner. "Get small, boys. We've got company."

Hunter slid beside me, and our two snoopers froze in place inside the vans. The aproned men shoved the carts across the concrete loading dock, and they clanged their way into the back of the vans. Kodiak groaned as the cart collided with his rib cage, but he kept the volume low enough for the two men to ignore.

When the caterers pushed their way back through the loading dock doors, I said, "Get out of there, guys."

Gator slithered from the van, but Kodiak didn't appear. Instead, he spoke through our open-channel comms. "Uh, you're not going to believe what I found."

"What is it?" Hunter asked.

Kodiak said, "I'm not sure, but you guys need to see it."

I shot a look back across the loading dock before sprinting to the van. Kodiak was kneeling on the floor of the van with a hinged panel raised about 45 degrees. Beneath the panel was a void just large enough to hold a pair of adult men. Two oxygen bottles rested in brackets inside the compartment, and ratchet straps lay neatly arranged in the center of the space.

The doors rattled as another duo of caterers came through with two more carts. We spread like rats when the lights came on, and the two men climbed inside the vans, started the engines, and drove away.

When we regrouped behind the lodge, our roll call fell short.

"Where's Kodiak?" I asked.

Although he wasn't with us, his voice joined us. "I'm inside the van. I didn't have time to get out."

I forced down the panic rising in my chest. "Skipper, are you tracking Kodiak?"

"Negative. Something is blocking his tracking device."

"That doesn't make any sense. Why can we talk to him but not see him?"

Skipper said, "Celeste understands it, but it's too complicated to explain."

"Does your drone have night vision?" I said.

"Not really, but we've got a good moon. I'm tracking the van."

"Don't lose it! Kodiak's life may depend on it."

"I'm on it," she said. "What's the plan?"

I closed my eyes so tightly that flashes of light behind my eyelids were almost blinding.

Think, Chase. Think!

I ran through the thousands of possible outcomes of the scenario, and nothing I could come up with ended well. Finally, I said, "Stop 'em at the gate! We've got to get Kodiak out of that van."

"It's too late," Skipper said. "They're already outside the gate and heading west."

"We're on our way back to the op center."

We sprinted across the open space between the main lodge and the alcove where we hid the trailer.

"Get everybody armed, and have the trucks ready."

By the time we sprinted into the parking area beside the trailer, the rest of the team was already loaded inside a waiting SUV with the engine running. The three of us dived inside, and Clark threw gravel in every direction as he accelerated out of the parking area. Disco handed out rifles, magazines, and body armor.

Clark yelled, "Get the gates open!"

Skipper said, "It's already done."

"They're not open!"

"They will be when you get there."

I looked over the seat back. "Don't hit the gate. We can't kill it. It's too solid."

Clark said, "I know, I know." He hit the brakes hard as the gate started its slow rise out of the roadway, and he growled, "Get out of my way!"

The gate finally rose enough for us to clear, but the second and third gates were still on their slow rise. I could almost taste Clark's impatience, but there was nothing we could do. If we hit the gates, the vehicle wouldn't survive, and Kodiak would be on his own.

Clark lowered his window and yelled, "Get those gates out of my way, now!"

The troopers manning the gate threw up their hands, and one yelled, "They're electric. I'm doing the best I can."

We cleared the second gate by a fraction of an inch, but not the third. It caught the corner of the windshield and sent us sliding sideways, and a hundred thousand airbags exploded inside the vehicle.

White powder filled the air, but the truck was still running. The airbags inflated and deflated just as quickly, and all four windows went down in a desperate effort to clear the airbag powder from inside the SUV.

Clark completed a sliding three-sixty and pinned the accelerator to the floor just as our headlights aligned with the road. The shattered safety glass of the windshield looked like a million tiny spiderwebs running in every direction. Clark stuck his head out the window, and Mongo did the same from the passenger's side.

Each of us coughed and yanked our shirts over our mouths and noses until Hunter kicked out the back glass of the SUV, and the airflow sucked the torrent of powder out of the vehicle's newest vent.

"Give me some directions, Skipper."

Clark's tone softened from psychopath level back down to smooth operator, and Skipper said, "Make the next left. They're about a quarter mile in front of you."

Clark said, "Can you do something about that windshield, Mongo?"

Before he could draw another breath, our giant blasted the demolished windshield from its mounts and sent it sailing across the top of the battered truck.

"That's one way to do it," Clark said as he re-situated his glasses on his face and pulled his head back inside the vehicle.

The air rushing through the wind tunnel our SUV had become felt like the blast from a jet engine, but nothing would stop us from recovering Kodiak from inside that van.

"You're coming up on the building now," Skipper said in her disembodied voice inside my head.

"Where?" Clark asked.

She said, "There's an awning on that big building on the left. They went beneath the awning, and I lost sight of them after that."

The building was tall enough to be a two-story building, but it looked industrial, as if it might've been a warehouse. The awning was actually a large, covered entryway leading to an even larger roll-up door. The windows were several feet above the ground and appeared to have been painted black from inside. Even if they weren't painted, seeing inside them from the ground would show us only the ceiling of the interior.

Clark drove past the awning and turned at the next street. The building standing alone somewhere in the middle of Oregon looked out of place, but it would've fit right in somewhere in St. Louis. There was no signage or employee parking. The structure was an anomaly, to say the least.

As we circled the building, Mongo said, "It looks like there's only two doors, plus that roll-up in the back."

"That's what I saw, too," Clark said. "What's the call, Chase? Are we going in hot?"

"Why aren't there any cars parked outside?" I asked.

"Good question, College Boy, but answering a question with a question is the definition of syncrophinisity, or something like that."

"That wasn't my answer, and there's no such thing as whatever you just said. Let's see a little inside-man intel."

Still on open-channel comms, I said, "How are you doing in there, Kodiak?"

A sound came back as if he clicked his tongue against his teeth, so I said, "Give me three of those clicks to confirm comms."

Kodiak clicked three times, and I said, "Good. Now, it's one for yes and two for no. Are you alone?"

Two clicks.

"Is it just the driver and you?"

Two clicks.

"Okay, so there's more than one other person in there with you."

One click.

"Can you see them?"

Two clicks.

"Then, give me a count of the number of voices you hear."

Four clicks.

"That was four, right?"

One click.

As I sat, piecing together a plan, Kodiak spoke barely loud enough to hear. "It sounds like they went through a door. It's quiet in here."

Hunter and Gator dismounted and flanked the building until both doors were in sight.

Hunter said, "Nobody came through either of these doors. It's dead out here."

Skipper said, "We're launching a second drone with a good IR camera. It'll be on-site in six minutes. I'll feed the video to your tablets."

"Does anybody have a tablet?" I asked.

Disco held his up and shook it.

Skipper said, "I know this isn't the best timing, but I thought you'd want to know. Celeste ran the lists, and three more billionaires are missing."

I turned to Singer. "How many empty rooms did you find when you went knocking?"

"They were all empty, but that doesn't mean they were missing."

I wondered if I'd ever develop a system to manage the thousands of bits of information I needed to run an operation efficiently.

Skipper said, "The other three catering vans are on the move."

"Are they heading this way?" I asked.

"I'll let you know as soon as they clear the two remaining gates. You guys put one of them out of commission."

I tapped my fingertips on the seat between my knees. "I say we wait and see where the other vans go. If they come here, we hide and wait. If they don't, we make covert entry and search the building. There's more going on in there than just convenient parking for a catering van."

Heads nodded, and Skipper said, "These three are heading northeast. They're not coming to you."

I said, "Let's give it sixty seconds to make sure they're not coming here by some other route. Also, Skipper, get somebody headed this way with at least one more SUV. Two would be better."

"I'm on it," she said. "Oh, and they're definitely not coming your way. There are no roads that turn off the one they're on for two or three miles."

"In that case," I said, "we're going in. Let us know as soon as those SUVs are rolling. Make sure whoever brings them can shoot. This thing may get ugly."

"Roger."

We moved from the vehicle, and Mongo pulled his pick set from a pocket. With the skill of a locksmith, he had the side door open in seconds. We moved inside cautiously and as quietly as possible.

Clark said, "I guess that answers the parking question. They're all parked in here."

"There's four cars plus the van, but where is everybody?" Gator asked.

Hunter moved to the van and slipped inside. When he returned, Kodiak was on his heels with his pistol drawn. Singer handed him a rifle, and he holstered the sidearm.

I whispered, "Didn't you say you heard a door open and close?"

Kodiak said, "That's what it sounded like, but it closed pretty hard."

"Spread out and cross the floor quietly. It could be a basement door."

The team spread out and moved in silence across the floor of the building. We weaved our way around the parked cars until Hunter whispered, "Check this out."

I glanced over to see him tapping the lower corner of a windshield on a Mercedes sedan. Three white stars on a blue background were lined up beside the base access sticker labeled "Joint Base Lewis–McChord."

"That's General Biggs's car," I said.

Hunter shrugged. "Maybe."

How many three-star generals could there be in the Pacific Northwest?

Singer interrupted my thought. "Got something."

The whole team looked up to see him standing by a pile of debris near the rear corner of the building. We moved in on him until the shape of a horizontal hatch appeared on the floor.

Clark said, "Looks like College Boy got one right. Are we going in?"

I said, "Yes, we are, but we're doing it slowly and silently. If my gut is right, there's about ten billion dollars in net worth down there, and I don't want to answer any lawsuits from the families of dead rich guys."

Gator and Kodiak lined up to move first. Hunter and Disco backed them while Clark and I brought up the rear. Singer and Mongo staged to man the hatch. Everyone press-checked their weapons, ensuring a round was firmly seated in the chamber.

Nods all around said we were ready to roll, so I said, "Skipper, we're making entry."

Her voice came back with, "Wait, Chase. You need to hear this."

Chapter 38

Silent Thunder

I froze in place. "What is it?"

"It's a broadcast on Charter News Network. Listen for yourself."

She configured the broadcast to play through the transmitter in the op center. An electronically altered voice spoke in a calm, measured tone.

Citizens of the world, the time has come for them to pay their fair share. You know who they are. The billionaires of the world who live in the lap of luxury while the working class struggles to feed their children on wages that make them little more than indentured servants or modern-day slaves to the corporate elite.

I swallowed hard as the voice continued.

We are every man and every woman. We are the huddled masses, the laboring weary, and we have no demands of you. We want no ransom. We have no terms of surrender. We have only one desire, and that is to let the world see these elitists, these moguls, finally pay the only price we will accept. This we do to prove to the wealthy overlords of the world that they are not untouchable. Their money cannot buy them freedom from commoners and serfs like us . . . like you. We will finally hold them accountable for their greed, for their treachery, and for their refusal to share the wealth they've whipped from our flesh for hundreds of years. Tonight, the world will know and understand the power of the people for the first time, so the next generation of robber barons will think twice before treading on our backs.

"What are we listening to?" I asked.

Skipper answered immediately. "According to the news reports, this group is claiming they will execute ten of the world's wealthiest men in real time tonight. Chase, I think you're about to walk in on this broadcast."

I took a step back and motioned for the team to follow. We retreated behind the parked cars, and I took a knee. "If Skipper's right, everything we do in the next few minutes of our lives will be captured on camera and broadcast all over the world. We can't allow that."

Hunter said, "Are you telling us we're not hitting these guys because they've got cameras?"

"No, that's not what I'm saying. I'm saying the cameras are our first target. We're making a dynamic entry, but we're doing it with our chins down and our caps low over our eyes. The first two in the stack —Gator, Kodiak, that's you two—will hit the most dangerous targets, and Hunter and Disco, your targets are anything that look like cameras of any kind. Got it?"

"We got it," Hunter said. "But I'd sure like to get a peek inside that basement."

With our open-channel comms, everything any of us said raced through space and time and ended up in the ears of everyone else on the team almost instantly.

Celeste said, "The whole world just got a peek inside that room. I'm sending it to your tablets now."

Hunter scoffed. "We don't carry tablets into a close-quarters battle."

"Sorry. I'm still learning. It's coming to your phones," she said.

We took twenty seconds to study the images on the screens of our phones, and Kodiak said, "All right. That helps. We'll have control of that room two seconds after Mongo rips the door off the hinges."

"Don't get cocky," I said. "These guys aren't amateurs. Keep your heads on swivels, and don't get dead down there."

The energy of the team was almost palatable. Each of us buzzed with enough energy to power half of Oregon, and we were about to unleash that power on an unsuspecting force who believed they had the world in the palms of their hands.

Skipper said, "Chase, the drone just arrived on-site, and there's a satellite dish and antenna array on the roof of the building. Do you want me to take it out?"

"Can you do it without waking the dead?"

"Probably not."

"In that case, leave it alone for now, but keep the drone in firing position. On my command of execute, blow it to hell."

"Yes, sir."

"Everybody good?"

Heads nodded, and boots moved back to the hatch and into the assaulting stack.

I could've sworn I heard the heartbeat of every man around me that night. The calm, capable warriors under my command weren't fearless. The absence of fear is insanity. My men were brave—the possessors of the will and ability to suppress and overcome fear when the moment demands it, and we stood on the precipice of such a moment.

I locked eyes with Mongo, and he spoke a thousand words with the simple drop of his chin.

"Execute! Execute! Execute!"

The giant of a man threw open the hatch as if it were made of tin, and our stack descended the stairs like thunder rolling through a mountain gorge. An explosion echoed overhead as if God Himself were driving us forward. Without consciously counting, I felt nine rounds roar from the muzzles of the lead rifles before Hunter and Disco splintered the two cameras affixed to tripods in two corners of the space before turning their weapons on the hooded terrorists. Clark and I covered our sectors and watched as the formerly brave men on camera became terrified children begging for their lives. Their accents may have been Turkish, but their pleas were the cries of cowards—the same cries I'd heard all over the world when people who believed they were unstoppable finally met their fate.

In the seconds that unfolded in front of us, I saw the world with clarity unlike any other moments of my life. Living on the edge of survival and honor and duty gives a man the vision in those moments to see what others cannot—the tiny, almost imperceptible movements of a terrorist's wrist as his thumb depresses the trigger on a detonator, or the twist of the man's hips when he's reaching for a weapon. The tiniest details become flashing neon signs in those moments, and I wasn't alone. We all felt it. We all experienced it. And we all acted on the acuity it gave us to dominate the environment and overcome any enemy with violence of action unlike anything they'd ever experienced.

As a man by the first demolished camera sent a hand to his waistline for his holstered weapon, three rounds left my muzzle almost simultaneously, the first two puncturing his chest and the final round boring through the cartilage of his nose. He was dead before his body came to rest, and he wasn't alone. Three similarly placed rounds terminated the life of the second cameraman who'd managed to actually grip his pistol before he perished in a cacophony of echoing rifle reports.

The two men bellowing for their lives threw themselves to the floor, but that didn't make them any less of a threat on innocent lives. Kodiak landed the heel of his boot in the center of one of the beggars' foreheads, sending him tumbling backward with his arms splayed across the floor. The second of Kodiak's blows came from the butt of his M4 against the hooded man's temple, rendering him little more than a heap of unconscious flesh.

Two more rounds cut through the air across my shoulder and into the skull of a man raising a rifle from the back of the room. The shots had been Clark's; the report of his custom-made suppressor was impossible to mistake. Gator kicked the other beggar from his knees, sending the man tumbling onto his face. He planted a knee in the center of the coward's back and raised his rifle on the single remaining terrorist in the room.

The final hooded man slipped skillfully behind one of the billionaires who was tied to a straight wooden chair and extended one hand over the tycoon's left shoulder with a plastic detonation trigger under his thumb. In his other hand, he held a knife with a serrated blade that had to be a foot long. The razor's edge of the blade came to rest against the flesh of the victim's neck. With the heel of his hand buried against the collarbone of his planned victim, the terrorist dragged the chair backward until he was literally backed into a corner. No one had a shot. No one had the angle to drop the would-be killer without hitting the innocent man in his grasp.

In the instant we realized our impasse, the man spoke through the material of his hood. "Every chair is wired with enough explosive to tear a man's body apart. If you do not drop your weapons instantly, I will trigger the explosives, and I will have accomplished my mission. If anyone moves other than to drop your weapons, I'll slice this man's head from his spine. Drop your weapons. Now!"

I had the best angle to lay my rifle on the ground and fire a shot between the bound man's feet and strike the terrorist's knee. If I missed, I could tear through the flesh of an innocent man's foot, but our options were dwindling in that moment. Taking the shot just as my rifle hit the floor might be my one and only opportunity to keep the billionaires alive and end the worst day of their lives. As I knelt to lay the rifle on the concrete floor and thumb the trigger, I heard something behind me that I couldn't identify. Maybe it was a slight groan followed by a barely audible hum.

I pressed my trigger the same instant I heard the sound, and I watched a scene unfold before me that I never could've imagined. The chair collapsed, sending its occupant to the floor with Gator airborne above him, one hand wrapped around the detonator and a forearm driving the glistening blade down the front of the victim's body. Blood poured from the ears and nose of the terrorist as he melted behind the billionaire.

Nothing about the scene made sense until I turned to see Singer hanging upside down through the hatchway with Dr. Celeste Mankiller's pulsed energy weapon pressed to his shoulder.

The sniper scanned the room with his practiced eye for more targets of opportunity and then declared, "Clear!"

The team echoed the sniper's announcement, and for the first time since we plunged down the stairs, we drew a collective breath of relief and victory.

Epilogue

Since the day I inherited Bonaventure Plantation from my great uncle, Judge Bernard Henry Huntsinger, my favorite place on the planet was the enormous gazebo housing the Revolutionary War–era cannon overlooking the North River. That's where I found myself ten days after the fateful encounter in the subterranean lair of terrorists hell-bent on ending the lives of ten wealthy businessmen from around the world. They failed, but we did not. Everyone who made that victory possible was sitting around my cannon in the humid evening air of late May in the South.

Since that Oregon night that felt like so long ago, the team and I received no fewer than two dozen offers of employment as personal security for the rich and famous, from all corners of the globe, and for salaries impossible to imagine, but every one of us refused those enormous paychecks to cling to each other and the solemn vow of devotion we silently professed every day of our lives to defend, protect, and preserve the cause of freedom wherever treachery threatened to strike.

Former General Michael Biggs wasn't surrounded by his family and friends on that evening. Instead, he would spend the night, and likely the rest of his life, in a cage. A litany of charges from domestic terrorism to conspiracy to commit murder hung in the balance against the bitter old warhorse whose hatred of the wealthy drove him to conspire with foreign operatives to showcase that hatred on the world's stage by killing ten of the men he flippantly called brothers in a fraternity of boys masquerading as men. Hatred is the vilest of all sicknesses of the human heart, and Michael Biggs was its greatest sufferer.

I was first to raise a glass on that evening. "To the finest team of professionals on any battlefield anywhere on Earth. It's an honor to call you teammates, but it's a blessing from God to call you family. May we live long enough to see the day when our swords grow rusty because the world has learned to embrace the peace we fought with all our might to forge."

Cheers went up, and drinks went down.

Penny was next. "Here's to Tony Clark, the best detective since Sherlock Holmes, who found a missing corkscrew and a woman's killer. And I got the whole thing on video."

Anya Burinkova tried to smile through the pain and scars left from the brutal abduction she suffered at the hands of detestable men halfway around the world. "I propose toast to miracles and to people like Singer who show to us these miracles happen all around us every day."

Cheers went up again, but Anya pounded on the arm of her Adirondack. "I was not finished. I propose also toast to losing something I believed was part of who I am. Everyone knows Russian women are most beautiful women in all of world." She paused and winked at my wife. "Except, of course, for American women from state of Texas."

Penny raised her glass in return. "You'll always be beautiful, Anya. Scars can't take that away."

Anya drew her fingertips lightly across the skin of her face. "All of you have taught me that what is truly beautiful is caring about others more than I care about myself. This is what is true meaning of beauty. I will miss when men no longer whistle and stare at me because I am no longer same person on outside, but for me, I am also not same person on inside, either. For this, I must thank Singer, who taught me to pray and believe and accept. I love all of you, but for that, I will always love Singer most dear."

All eyes fell on the Southern Baptist sniper, and he raised his glass of sweet tea. "Here's to another wayward sheep added to the immortal flock. And here's to the people who taught me that my purpose is in service to others when I was on the selfish verge of hiding away in the same monastery where my brother's body rests beneath the oaks on the banks of the Cooper River. I was wrong when I believed I needed to be in that place to prove to myself that I was wholly devoted to God's eternal cause. All of you have made me understand that my true calling is sharing that cause with everyone I love, and that can't be done from behind the walls of any monastery."

Author's Note

Well, here we are again, having our little post-adventure chat. Chase and the team would call it an after-action review, or an AAR, but I prefer to call it a chat. As always, it's important to me that I open this author's note with a sincere expression of my gratitude for you including my work on your reading list. Of all people, writers know better than anyone how many options readers have to choose from, and to select one of my books—out of the tens of millions of published books available—is an enormous gift you continue to give me, time after time. I'll never tire of creating these stories for you, and I vow to do my best to never allow them to become cookie-cutter stories. I always want to surprise you, thrill you, and make you cry and cheer. Sometimes, I even hope you get a little chuckle out of the silliness. Ultimately, though, what I want more than anything else is for you to truly feel that my stories are always worth the handful of hours it takes to experience them. Time is the most valuable thing we'll ever have, and your decision to spend a few hours with my characters is a compliment beyond compare.

Since I mentioned silliness, let's kick this party off with a little bit of it. Dr. Celeste Mankiller's creation of the Pulsed Energy Weapon Prism Enhanced Warfighting System (PEW-PEWS) falls squarely into the silly category. A crude version of the weapon exists, but the problem of accurate targeting remains. It will likely be decades before the weapon I described in this story is available. I love Celeste, and I love her involvement in these stories. She gives me the freedom to think far outside anything resembling a box and create gadgets every door-kicker would love to have. If I have my way, Dr. Mankiller will stay with us for years to come, and if you have ideas for gadgets, please don't hesitate to email and let me know about them. Who knows? Your idea just might end up in an upcoming story.

They say size matters—or doesn't matter, depending on who's making the claim—but in fiction, I've come to believe it does matter. One of the most common comments I receive from readers is that they wish the stories were longer. My typical novel is around 75,000 words, but this one got out of control and encroached on 90,000. I don't know if that will become the new standard, but never let it be said that I didn't hear your pleas.

Let's talk about the Bulgarians, Turks, and Ontrack Global Resources. I hold no ill will toward the citizens or governments of either Turkey or Bulgaria. As far as I know, there is no likelihood of the country of Bulgaria melting down into civil war. That was entirely a figment of my imagination, and I hope I didn't hurt anybody's feelings by picking on that country. Likewise, I don't have any reason to believe the Turks are interested in kidnapping rich guys and cutting their heads off in Oregon. Somebody had to be the bad guy, and they made an easy target for me. Lieutenant General Michael Biggs is based on no one, and I don't have any particular disdain for flag officers. Chase and I didn't like the general when he showed up in the story, so I lumped him in with the Turks just to satisfy Chase.

Ontrack Global Resources aren't real. I made them up, and in the interest of full disclosure, I have no idea if companies such as that one exist. It sounds like a plausible business model, but who knows? Maybe I should give up this writing gig and start that business. On second thought, not a chance.

The Culver Cove Club is purely and completely fictional. It doesn't exist, and to my knowledge, never has existed. A few of you may have detected some similarities between the Culver Cove and the Bohemian Grove Club in California. I will confess that the Bohemian

Grove Club was the inspiration for my fictional boys' club, but I have no idea what those people do at their Midsummer Encampment. I don't have any reason to believe they dance naked around bonfires while high on whatever they stick in their arm or snort up their nose. All of that was fiction, purely for my own entertainment. The thought of world industry leaders behaving like idiots in the woods made me laugh, so it ended up in the book. I hope you got at least a little giggle out of the antics.

Now, it's time to talk about Clark. I know I said he was relegated to the sideline, but I'm a fiction writer, so believing what I tell you is a terrible plan on your part. I thought Clark was sidelined, but he certainly came off the bench for this game. I don't really know how he snuck back in, but before I knew it, he was right in the middle of the fight, and it felt good. I've always loved his character, and as many of you know, Clark Johnson is based closely on one of my dearest friends on the planet, so it's tough for me to picture him out of the action. So, for all the Clark lovers, he's apparently not as gone as I thought he was.

What was all that nonsense about the ships and the AIS and the Hellenic Coast Guard, and is that even a real thing? These stories do really well in the sea adventure category on Amazon, so keeping it a little salty justifies me being in that category. I'll never write nautical action adventure as well as the great Clive Cussler, but he'll always be one of my literary heroes, and I feel like it's a small tip of the cap to the master when I write something he might've enjoyed reading. AIS is real, and it is now a requirement on commercial vessels over a certain tonnage. And the people who know things about computers and satellites tell me it is a system fraught with vulnerability to hacking. I'm not sure what that means, but I love the word *fraught,* and I love letting Skipper dabble in her hacking hobby with Celeste's assistance. I felt a little bit bad about picking on the environmentalists, but I needed an opportunity to let Chase flip his lid and beat some people up for hurting Anya. He's got a lot of issues, and issues are so much fun for authors like me. Ultimately, what I wrote in that action sequence probably isn't possible, but it was still fun pretending.

I guess we have to talk about Anya now. When I invited her into this story, I had absolutely no idea this would turn into the ultimate book about transforming Anya from what she had once been and into something entirely new. She was almost invincible until she was abducted by the operators from Ontrack Global Resources. That was step number one in her transformation, but when I wrote that scene, I had no idea what was coming. After being abducted, she was beaten so badly that she required surgeries to repair her face, remedy the infection, and replace broken teeth. Needless to say, she had a bad day. Back aboard the ship, I had the golden opportunity to have some meaningful moments between her and Chase, and I've been waiting a long time to write those moments. I'm so glad I finally got to make it happen.

Then our old buddy, Chase, started worrying about Anya's soul and dispatched our favorite sniper to bring her into the fold. I gave this portion of the story a lot of thought. I didn't want that sequence to come off as preachy, but I felt it was a critical element in her transformation that I still didn't realize was happening. I don't pay attention to what's going on in the stories while I'm writing them. I simply write what the voices tell me, and it seems to work out. So, Singer dug in his heels and spent the required time with our favorite Russian to share the ultimate truth with her. Singer has a long history of being the moral compass for the team, but I've never given him the opportunity to win souls for the Kingdom before this book, and I'm so glad I gave him that latitude. I believe there is nothing wrong with a writer sharing his faith through his fiction, especially when it can play such an emotionally strong role within a story.

So, after the surgery, and as a result of the abuse, Anya lost the one thing she had that was truly hers. I've never let her come off as arrogant about her appearance, but she has always been fully aware that her face played an enormous role in her career. Beautiful women can often unlock doors others cannot, and as shameful as that it, it remains the truth. Anya didn't choose to be beautiful. She wasn't trained to be beautiful. It was simply a part of her that was uniquely hers. I took that away from her in this story, and I almost felt bad for doing so until she offered her toast in the Epilogue. When she acknowledged her transformation, recognized Penny as being more physically beautiful than she's previously been willing to admit, and thanked Singer for leading her into her new life, we got to see a deeper, more sincere side of the former Russian assassin than ever before. As dramatic as all of those transformations were, to me, one of the most touching moments was when Anya told Chase to go home to be with Penny, where he belonged. I don't know what's coming next with Anya, but I'm excited to find out. Now that I've finished this manuscript, I'll begin writing *The Russian's Envy*, book #6 in The Avenging Angel – Seven Deadly Sins Series. If you've not begun Anya's series yet, I would love for you to give it a try, beginning with book #1, *The Russian's Pride*. For those of you who enjoy Anya's character, I truly believe you'll have a great time with her series.

In closing, I must thank you again for spending a few hours with me, and I hope you loved every word of the story. Six years ago, when this journey began, I believed I could tell Chase's story in thirty books, but oh how wrong I was. We aren't even halfway through, and this is book #27 in the series. I hope and pray I get to live long enough to see how all of this works out in the end.

I'd like to leave you with one final, deep, meaningful thing to take away from this story. I've done the intensive research (45 seconds on Google), and I'm pretty sure I'm the only writer in the history of the English language to publish the term *sheep-flocker* in a work of fiction.

Cheers,

Cap

About the Author

Cap Daniels

Cap Daniels is a former sailing charter captain, scuba and sailing instructor, pilot, Air Force combat veteran, and civil servant of the U.S. Department of Defense. Raised far from the ocean in rural East Tennessee, his early infatuation with salt water was sparked by the fascinating, and sometimes true, sea stories told by his father, a retired Navy Chief Petty Officer. Those stories of adventure on the high seas sent Cap in search of adventure of his own, which eventually landed him on Florida's Gulf Coast where he spends as much time as possible on, in, and under the waters of the Emerald Coast.

With a headful of larger-than-life characters and their thrilling exploits, Cap pours his love of adventure and passion for the ocean onto the pages of the Chase Fulton Novels and the Avenging Angel - Seven Deadly Sins series.

Visit www.CapDaniels.com to join the mailing list to receive newsletter and release updates.

Connect with Cap Daniels:

Facebook: www.Facebook.com/WriterCapDaniels
Instagram: https://www.instagram.com/authorcapdaniels/
BookBub: https://www.bookbub.com/profile/cap-daniels

Also by Cap Daniels

The Avenging Angel – Seven Deadly Sins Series
Book One: *The Russian's Pride*
Book Two: *The Russian's Greed*
Book Three: *The Russian's Gluttony*
Book Four: *The Russian's Lust*
Book Five: *The Russian's Sloth*
Book Six: *The Russian's Envy* (2024)
Book Seven: *The Russian's Wrath* (TBA)

Stand-Alone Novels
We Were Brave
Singer – Memoir of a Christian Sniper

Novellas
The Chase Is On
I Am Gypsy

Made in the USA
Coppell, TX
12 June 2024

33442547R00184